MOON
KISSED

AMELIA HUTCHINS

Authored By: Amelia Hutchins

Cover Art Design: Eerily Designs

Copy edited by: Melissa Burg

Published by: Amelia Hutchins

Published in (United States of America)

10 9 8 7 6 5 4 3 2 1

Disclaimer

This book is **dark**. It's **sexy**, hot, and **intense**. The author is human, as you are. Is the book perfect? It's as perfect as I could make it. Are there mistakes? Probably, then again, even **New York Times top published** books have minimal errors because, like me, they have **human editors**. In this book, some words are not in the standard dictionary because I created them to set the stage for a paranormal-urban fantasy world. In this novel, words are common in paranormal books and give better descriptions of the story's action than other words found in standard dictionaries. They are intentional and not mistakes.

About the hero: chances are you may **not** fall instantly in **love** with him. That's because **I don't write men you immediately love**; you grow to love them. I don't believe in **instant love**. I write flawed, raw, caveman-like **assholes** that eventually let you see their redeeming qualities. They are **aggressive assholes**, one step above a caveman when we meet them. You may *not* even like him by the time you finish this book, but I promise you will **love** him by the end of this **series**.

About the heroine: There is a chance you might think she's a bit naïve or weak, but then again, who starts out as a badass? Badass women are a product of growth, and I will put her through **hell**, and you get to watch **her** come up **swinging** every time I knock her on her ass. That's just how I do things. How she reacts to the set of circumstances she is put through may not be how you, as the reader, or I, as the author, would respond to that same situation. Everyone reacts differently to circumstances, and how she reacts to her challenges is how I see her as a character and as a person.

I don't write love stories: I write fast-paced, knock you on your ass, *make you sit on the edge of your seat wondering what is going to happen next* in the books. If you're looking for cookie-cutter romance, this isn't for you. If you can't handle the ride, ***unbuckle your seatbelt and get out of the roller-coaster car now***. **If not, I have warned you.** If nothing outlined above bothers you, carry on and **enjoy the ride!**

FYI, this is not a romance novel. These characters are going to **kick** the shit out of each other, and **if** they end up together, well, that's **their** choice. If you are going into this blind, and you complain about abuse between two creatures that are **NOT** human, well, that's on you. I have done my job and given you a **warning**.

No babies that occur or are conceived because of this work of fiction are the author's responsibility. Blame the penis mojo that you rode like a bronco, not me.

Dedication

The world is a shit-show, and we're all stuck in it together. Remember, you're one person in a sea of assholes, and we're all swimming in the same direction. If you see someone in need of a lifeboat, don't let them drown, not when you can help them. Kindness is free, and so is being a decent human. One world, one race, one chance to be the best you can be in this lifetime. Don't be the problem, be the solution.

Other books by Amelia Hutchins and reading order for series

THE ELITE GUARDS

A Demon's Dark Embrace

Claiming the Dragon King

The Winter Court

A Demon's Plaything

More coming – To Be Announced

A GUARDIAN'S DIARY

Darkest Before Dawn

Death before Dawn

Midnight Rising – To Be Announced

PLAYING WITH MONSTERS

Playing with Monsters

Sleeping with Monsters

Becoming his Monster

Becoming her Monster Spring 2021

WICKED KNIGHTS

Oh, Holy Knight

If She's Wicked

If He's Wicked – To Be Announced

MIDNIGHT COVEN BOOKS

Forever Immortal

Immortal Hexes

Midnight Coven

Finished Serial Series

BULLETPROOF

Bulletproof

Fireproof Damsel – To Be Announced

Silverproof – To Be Announced

MOON-KISSED

Moon-Kissed

KINGDOM OF WOLVES

Alpha's Claim – Spring 2021

If you're following the series for the Fae Chronicles, Elite Guards, and Monsters, reading order is as follows.

MOON KISSED

AMELIA HUTCHINS

Prologue

250 years ago

Staring out the large window in my bedroom, peering over the kingdom, I watched as the morning sun rose. Turning back toward the room, I studied the white eyes of the seer. In her hands was the ancient tome, one that no other creature had held in a millennia.

Long black curls flowed down her shoulders in waves, invitingly. Candlelight swayed with the wind in the room from the powerful magic she created from her soul. Watching her, I folded my arms over my chest as her eyes returned to the soft violet that promised heaven and yet delivered no comfort.

"Your mate will be born soon," she announced through a husky, rasp-filled tone that spoke of seduction. "She will be born into the moon-touched clan, and once you read from the tome, she will be brought to you by the power of the book. Your mate will be fire and ice. She will be beautiful and strong. Everything you crave will come to you, but only if you read from the Book of the Dead."

"That book is known for taking away what you want," I argued, watching her full mouth curve into a sardonic grin. "It never gives you what you crave." Noting the way she tensed, I hesitated.

"Everything comes with a price," the seer stated, her shoulders slumping before she placed the book onto the table, opening it to the page in which she wanted me to read. "All magic has a cost, and all knowledge comes from that cost. You asked me to find your true mate; after losing who you had assumed was yours already, I would think you'd want to take this chance. The universe only allows us to have one mate in a lifetime. That you have another chance at finding her if she's reborn, well, few can find them twice. If you ignore what I have foreseen, then that is your choice. Considering who you are and what she will be born to be, I doubt your paths ever cross naturally. You are of the night, and she is of the light. She will be born of the same clan as her first birth. Would you give it all away to another man? Or will you pay the price to know her taste and to feel your cold, deadened heart beating again?" she pried, her pretty violet eyes watching me with a burning need.

"What is the cost?" I demanded, watching the sparkle shining within her eyes.

"I can't tell you that. A life? A thousand lives? What do you care? You're no saint, and the taint of lives lost won't bother your soul. You forced a king's hand, and he sent his daughter away where you could never find her, and she connected her life to that of another. Will you chance to lose her again? Will you risk your true mate meeting another and falling in love before you can find her?"

"No." I swallowed past the lump those words caused. Moving toward the seer, I watched her tense from my nearness. "How will I know my true mate when I see her?"

"You won't, not until it is time. Mates are tricky things, and only something unique between you will forge the bond. It could be as simple as a look or a kiss that makes you feel her within your soul. Why you would even want to find her is beyond me. Once you do, you will never feel another's touch because your heart will only beat for her."

"Your mate died, and when he did, what did you feel?"

"Nothing, which is what I prefer," she returned icily, and I smiled, nodding. "There was freedom in knowing my husband was dead. There was also a numbness that began and has yet to stop growing in my soul."

"I know that numbness well. I feel nothing, nor have I for a very long time. Three hundred years ago, they sent my mate away, far beyond my grasp. I was too young to understand what it meant back then. I taste no food or wine. I take pleasure, but it is muted at best, and I never feel satisfied. I have an endless hunger to know the feeling of my mate and to experience the true pleasure of living..." I slid my fingers over the book's pages, smoothing them out with my fingertips. "I am merely an endless night that hungers for her pleasure and to know her touch. I tire of the cold, eternal chill that aches deep into my bones. I wish to know the warmth of my mate and to feel it shining upon my face."

"Then read from the book and find her. Fuck the consequences," she laughed coldly. "Read from it, and I will tell you how to find your mate."

I focused on the text inked across the parchment, whispering the words. I watched as the glowing letters left the pages and danced onto my fingertips that still touched the ancient tomes. More words slipped out, pulled from my throat until it forced me to finish reading all that was on the parchment. The moment the last syllable danced from my tongue, the tome closed, slamming shut.

Spinning toward the seer, I watched her smile go colder, evil. Her eyes turned to white, and her lips moved strangely, as if someone was controlling her. "Where the mountain touches the sunlight, and the night reached between, claim your young mate when the sickness is finally seen. She will enter your life as a warrior, with fire untold and fury in her bones. Your moon-touched mate will be born in two hundred years. When the sickness begins to consume her clan, and the warriors pass through the mountain in search of a cure, retrace their footsteps, for she will follow them in search of her destiny."

The seer grinned at me, and a familiar expression took hold of her face, twisting her features into an evil I have searched to destroy. "One kingdom has become two. The Kingdom of Light ruled by the moon, and the Kingdom of Night ruled by you. Reading from the Book of Death has broken free a plague of darkness that will spread through both kingdoms, killing and consuming all that it touches."

"Did you honestly think I wouldn't figure out who

you worked for before considering your lies, Seer?" I exhaled, watching her features shift and eyes return to violet once more. "Tell your mistress I am still hunting her. Once I find her and the Book of Life, I will end her once and for all. She can bathe the world in darkness, but her time is near for what she did to my father in her rage. Tell my mother that I am coming for her head and that nothing will stop me from taking it this time."

"She hears all we speak and isn't afraid of a child cursed by his own hand. You have brought this upon yourself. I suggest you find the one you thought worthy of cursing this land, bathing it in eternal night just for a taste. You have your mother's hair and her face, but your soul is as dark as the one we took from your father before sending him to his grave."

"How do I reverse the curse?" I asked carefully, tone filled with ridicule.

"To end this eternal night, and the plague of darkness, you must claim your mate and give birth to a new life. If you cannot produce a child, everything will have been for nothing, and darkness will consume both kingdoms. As there was a cost to read from the Book of Death, the same is true for the Book of Life. To counteract the curse, your mate must read from the Book of Life, the price for which will be life. Once the life price is paid, the world will be freed, and eternal night and the plague of darkness will recede."

I laughed coldly, shaking my head at the plan my mother had put into place. "In other words, my mate has to give me a child, and then her life will be sacrificed to the book in which she reads?"

"The sacrifice of life is the only way to end the curse

that you just placed upon the land. I warned you that there was a cost," she hissed, and I smiled cruelly.

"Kindest regards, mother," I said while holding the seer's stare.

My sword swung before she could respond, sending the seer's head sailing against the wall before bouncing across the stone floor. The male behind the tapestry in my room's hidden alcove stepped out, turning to see the moon rise in the middle of the morning.

Moving to where he stood, I pushed my bloodied blade into the sheath on my hip. Outside, the sun had begun to vanish, and in its place, night slowly spread over the land. I swallowed down unease, dropping my stare to the people in the street watching the shroud of midnight settling on the kingdom. I turned, staring at my best friend, who frowned.

"What the hell just happened?" he asked in confusion, his brows drawing together to crease his forehead.

I glared at the people rushing into their cottages, hiding from the night and the plague of darkness, creeping over the mountains toward the castle. I'd done this. I'd craved the ability to touch, taste, and indulge in everything that I'd missed out on when I'd lost my mate.

I'd pay the price. The first thing I had to do was locate where the Sacred Library was hidden and destroy the Book of Life. Afterward, I'd figure out another way that didn't include my mate reading from a book that would end her life.

"The endless night has begun." I smiled, staring out over the darkening skies. "Our kingdom will survive it, but others won't. It's a gift from my mother. It's what she craved when she killed my father and ensured that I would never have my mate. My mother thinks she can prevent me from living a life with my true mate as she unleashes her plague and the creatures that live within her darkness. She has underestimated my determination to get what I want."

Chapter One

Present Day, Alexandria

Carefully, I studied the quiet town below. My lips curled into an uneasy frown as I watched the spread of darkness. Torches burned brightly, yet no sign of life had appeared. We'd been on the cliff for over an hour, standing silently while watching the town for any proof of life. No sounds of merriment came from the usually jovial tavern in the middle of the tiny village, frequented by travelers making their way through the two kingdoms. We'd been in this town a hundred times before and never had the darkness spread through the passes to bathe it in its murderous grasp.

My eyes zeroed in on something that blew across the street, and my heart sank deep into my stomach, tears swimming in my eyes. What I thought to be paper was the husks of the inhabitants of the village. When darkness consumed the light of the living, it spat out a withered husk that looked like leather. Swallowing past the bile as several husks were strewn across the path leading through town, I exhaled.

My team of moon-touched warriors was tasked with retracing the steps of another group who hadn't checked in or returned in months. My brother, Landon, had been among the party of warriors who had gone to investigate the clues regarding the Sacred Library's whereabouts. If they discovered it, they'd failed to send word back or to return to the Kingdom of Light.

The Sacred Library was lost when the darkness had first appeared in the world, consuming everything it touched. Soon after, creatures started evolving and receiving powers. The darker the world got, the stronger the Moon Clan's powers grew, and we began to age into immortality. But so, too, did the Kingdom of Night and the monsters that crawled out from the shadows of the spreading darkness, feasting on those who held inner light.

The Temple of the Moon Goddess had glowed with energy, beckoning those who held her powers into it, and a new era had begun, forming the Order of the Moon. The Order trained and employed an elite group of warriors with powers fed to them by the moon herself.

Each warrior with me had been plucked from their homes at a young age and trained for battle. Most were happy to be chosen, considering the power they held was a blessing. To be selected and taken from your home, guaranteed your family's protection from the Kingdom of Night and the plague of darkness. Others, like us, found it a curse to be taken from their families and sent off to fight a battle that we'd neither wanted nor craved.

There wasn't a choice if the moon called you, and no

one fought to end the selection process. Most of us were chosen so young that we didn't remember our homeland or the families we'd left behind. I'd had Landon, but we were brother and sister; both called to serve the moon. Our family was also one that had always serviced. I'd grown up inside the temple and had begun training before I could fully form sentences.

Lately, the Order was keeping secrets, and with the moon sickness passing through the lands, it was growing harder to trust them. The sickness only seemed to affect the moon-touched creatures. It was spreading like wildfire through the Order, so months ago, they'd sent out a large, handpicked group of warriors to search for the Sacred Library. No one knew if it had survived the plague of darkness or had been consumed by it like everything else.

"It doesn't look like anyone is alive down there," Amo stated through the mask she wore, her hair covered by the heavy cloak. Our cloaks concealed our identities and protected against the long winter that had started a decade ago on the Badlands border.

"Someone's alive down there," I announced, countering her statement. "The torches burn for only a few hours before depleting the oil. Someone lit them recently."

A loud squeal cut through the air, piercing the night. Turning, I saw Amo hold out her gloved wrist for Scout, the owl she'd trained from an owlet, to land. He was a beautiful, white snow owl with large wings that flapped, creating a soft wind around us as it settled on her arm. Amo clucked her tongue and held out her other hand as Scout dropped the husk into her hand. Passing his bounty off to me, Amo withdrew his treat before allowing him to crawl onto her shoulder to devour the morsel of meat.

My heart clenched as I brought the husk to my nose, recoiling from the scent before peering out over the town. Amo's throat bobbed, and she turned, locking her gaze with mine. Her head shook slowly before she tried for words, failing. I handed her back the husk to confirm what I'd smelled on the victim's dried flesh.

"Days or maybe a week since they lived," Amo said vehemently, her grief turning to rage. "You won't find anything living down there. Not anyone from the town, at least. Whoever is down there, they're either immune to the darkness or one of our people pillaging through the dead's coffers."

"We're going through the village either way." My spine tingled as if eyes were on us, watching. Unease flitted through me, yet I ignored it. "We can't spare the time to go around the mountains, not and make it to the next town in time to meet up with the others. We need to know what they found. Once we enter the village, if we encounter anyone, we will dismount and sneak around anything present since the horses won't be able to move quicker than our blades. Plan for an ambush; hope it isn't one," I stated, moving back to mount my horse, Chivalry.

The ride down the cliffside was slow and treacherously steep. We didn't dare enter through the main entrance into the town, knowing whoever was there, watched it for travelers. Under cover of darkness and the cloaks we wore, no one would be able to discern who or what we were. The sliver of the moon offered little magic to fuel our power, which meant if we faced off against an ambush, our skills and training would be used instead of the moon's magic.

Inside the village, we moved silently along the sides of the houses. After a few nerve-racking moments, we turned onto the main street, and a husk blew across our path. I swallowed down the bile that burned the back of my throat again. No sound met our ears as we paused, looking through the shadows with our enhanced vision to ferret out any hidden enemies.

No one spoke as we started forward. The horses' hooves' over the cobblestone was the only noise heard in a once-bustling village filled with life. The shop windows were covered in dust, a telltale sign the inhabitants hadn't been alive in more than a week. No stench of death or rotten bodies met my nose. Nor did any coppery tang of blood fill the air, which was a telling sign of a battle. Nothingness was here, which caused my throat to tighten from the loss of life within the village.

The touch of darkness was absolute death to those not immune to its murderous grasp. It consumed everything but skin, leaving only a leathery scrap of flesh behind. Books sat abandoned on a bench where a small leather husk remained stuck beneath it, as if the victim had been holding them when caught by the icy claws and sucked dry.

A door opened ahead of us, and the horses stopped. Slowly, they stepped back with a click of our tongues against our teeth. The subtle scent of male wafted heavily in the air, tingling in my nose, and I sat still without breathing.

"We're not alone." I swallowed, climbing down from my horse while the others silently followed my lead. "Chivalry, stay out of the way," I ordered, barely above a whispered breath.

Nervousness filled the group at the sound of us drawing our weapons. The tension mounted with the gentle clang of metal filling the darkness while we pulled down our facemask and prepared to fight.

Apprehension took hold, sending a shiver of restlessness rushing down my spine. I nodded toward a large home, noting the door was still open and no lights burned from inside. The door shifted, and I paused, nodding twice before jerking my chin to the right. It was the signal that we would move toward it as one unit and clear the home out together.

The others followed my lead, creating an arch that spread out like wings behind me. My silver cloak ruffled in the breeze, sending an icy wave of wind up my back. The short blades I held ignited with blue moon scripture, pulsing with magic. It was the only indication of who we were until the moon raised high in its precipice. Considering it was a new moon, it wouldn't offer us much light to ward against the darkness, nor would it provide us any power.

At the door, we all paused, then I rushed in first. Barely avoiding the red rune-covered sword that swung at me, I lifted my blades, scissoring them toward the warrior. If he were untrained, it would have easily unhanded him of his weapon. Unfortunately, it hadn't. I spun as my team slipped behind me into the house. They took defensive positions at my back, guarding it as more hooded figures engaged against us.

I watched the sparks my blades created while trying to hold the sword between them, failing. A foot lifted, and I jumped back, moving outside, barely avoiding the boot from hitting my stomach and knocking me down. Dancing around and onto the porch, I ducked as the sword sang past me, slamming into the wood baluster.

I lifted my foot, slamming it into the *very* male appendage that was every man's weakness. The grunt that expelled from his lungs was satisfactory, but it hadn't slowed the warrior down. I shot backward again as he swung angrily. Lowering my body, I sprang into the air, flipping over the steps when the sword swerved toward me again. It sang through the air, driven by the anger of the male wielding it.

The man leaped from the porch, following me with his swords cutting through the air as the loud sounds of metal clashing continued inside the house. The combatant slammed his sword into my blade, causing my hand to burn with the pain from the hard blow driven by formidable strength. I swung my second one, narrowly missing cutting through the man's middle, but he bent his body back at the last moment, and my blade caught air instead of flesh. His foot slammed into my stomach, and I gasped, moving deftly with agility learned from training.

His sword sailed toward me, crashing loudly against one of my blades, sending the weapon flying out of my grip. I lifted the second blade in time to deflect his return swing, falling backward as his leg swept against mine, unseating my feet.

I rolled the moment I reached the ground, dodging the sword he sent toward me. I growled as my cloak stuck on something, tearing at it until I freed it. Jumping to my feet, I barely deflected more powerful blows until I went on the offense, parrying his firm, punishing strikes until I spun, swinging up to dislodge his blade.

The moment I'd disarmed him, he rushed forward without warning, taking us both to the ground. The crash onto the hard surface made my teeth chatter as pain rocked through my spine, and my weapon went sailing across the cobblestone. With his heavy weight holding me down, I thrust my hips up, trying to unseat him. Grabbing my arms, he held them above my head while I continued to buck wildly.

I couldn't see into the darkness of the cloak he wore. I couldn't make out his features or judge his species. Growling in rage, I intensified the bucking of my body against him until my knee slipped between his thighs, ousting him from my waist, rolling us into the opposite position.

I slipped my hand to my boot, intending to draw the blade within, until the moon shone down, forcing us to pause as it appeared with a shot of power its light held. My eyes lowered to the creature, finding ice-blue eyes staring up at my white hair and moonlit eyes. My lips parted, and he lowered his gaze to them, narrowing his eyes while he took in my delicate features.

I should have been using his surprise against him, but I couldn't look away, held captive by the masculine face that was sharp edges and lines that looked at me hungrily. It probably wasn't the best time to appease my curiosity.

The warrior's lips curled into a grin, and he rolled us without warning, using the moon's sudden appearance to catch me off guard. He lifted his free hand to his head, pushing back his cloak to reveal midnight-colored hair and silver flecks of moonshine dancing within his eyes.

He studied my face and then turned toward the fighting still occurring in the house where the moonlight hadn't reached. His lips parted, but he paused at the sickening snarl of dark creatures exploded all around us.

The warrior turned, whistling loudly at the sound of creatures from the plague of darkness entering the town. I swallowed, taking in his high cheekbones and full mouth. He wasn't like the men of the Moon Clan, or delicate as most of them appeared. His eyes slid back to me, finding me watching him silently.

"Who are you?" he demanded, and I resumed struggling to get away from him before the dark creatures reached us and ripped apart our bodies. "I asked you a question. I expect it to be answered, little girl."

"Get off me, you ogre-ass tramp," I snarled, working my legs up between us. He lifted his body a smidgen, staring down at my knees that were rising between his.

When they were high enough, his eyes lifted with confusion as the smile slid across my lips. I parted his legs, using my leg muscles and gravity to unseat him, sending his body slamming down against the cobblestone street. I rolled away, grabbing my blade as he did the same.

"Do you want to die here?" he snapped.

"Better to die in battle than beneath some dark prick who was weak enough to sell his soul to the demons walking within the darkness," I hissed, bending down to retrieve the other blade while keeping him in front of me.

He watched me with a wicked look burning in his eyes. My cloak had fallen off, sliding from my shoulders to reveal the leather pants that curved around my muscular legs. The top I wore covered my chest, wrapping around my breasts, crisscrossing over my shoulders to wrap around my waist. It was lightweight and made to protect vital organs while not weighing me down.

The warrior didn't move or strike out again, choosing to watch me instead. I frowned, going into a defensive pose while the sound of swords within the cottage went silent. My attention flicked toward it, and a line of worry creased my forehead. I started forward, and he bowed his head, cold wintery eyes watching me step toward him.

Before I'd reached him, he vanished, and I paused, peering around the empty street. Swallowing past the nervousness, I moved toward the silent house. Steel sang through the air, and I barely brought mine up in time to deflect a punishing blow. He was fast, and the spicy masculine scent he radiated was playing hell on the woman within me. I paused and took note, even though he was trying to kill me. Why was my magic not shielding me from his scent and masculinity? I should have been immune to the lure of men.

"You're out-skilled, little girl," he growled, his voice low, raspy, and surprisingly sexy.

Had he just told me I was out-skilled? I laughed, swinging my twin blades hard and fast until sparks filled the street. I swayed toward him, moving in quick precision, fighting to disarm him. The warrior perceived every move, easily deflecting every blow with his much larger weapon and strength.

"You're tiring," he growled.

I swung both blades, scissoring his before twisting my body in the air to use my full weight to take the sword by force. I landed, swinging my leg low, which took his legs out from beneath him before lifting my blades into the air. I intended to pierce them through his shoulders, but Amo's groan sounded, and my eyes rose to see a sword held against her throat.

"Enough," the male demanded, thrusting his leg out to send my body to the ground, hard.

I gasped for air, sitting up only for him to slam down against me, holding me to the ground as frost-colored eyes searched mine. He was ruggedly handsome, with clean teeth that caused my eyes to lower to his full, luscious mouth. Silently, we took each other in until he pushed his elbow against my throat and grabbed the rainbow-colored tendrils of my hair, bringing it up against his nose. Was he fucking sniffing me? Creep.

"I'm going to stand up, and you're going to stand with me. If you fight, your team dies. Do you understand me?" His eyes held mine prisoner in their chilly depths. When my only reply was to nod, he chuckled coldly, "I want words, Little Bird."

"I understand but know this; if you hurt my team, I will slaughter you and your men, and I'll wear your fucking face with pride, asshole. Now, get your ogre-ass off of me."

He didn't release me, choosing to glare down at me until I became highly aware that he was aroused from fighting me. This man wasn't just good-looking; he was gorgeously dark and delicious in all the right ways. High, sharp cheekbones were visible, with a five o'clock shadow that adorned his strong jawline. His body was covered in thick muscles, and one pressed hard against my stomach.

Gradually, he backed up, still staring down at me with curiosity burning in his eyes. He grabbed my hand, yanking me to my feet with a quick jerk. Men moved in around us, collecting my weapons while he towered over me.

"You're now the prisoner of the Night King," he announced.

My blood turned to ice in my veins. Lowering my attention to the armor he wore, I noted the colors of midnight-blue and black that covered it. On his chest, clasping the cloak onto his back, were silver chains and a coat of arms with dual swords and the moon set between them, pierced by both blades.

Slowly, my eyes drifted back up to lock on his with loathing. Their kingdom was filled with people rumored to have made deals with demons to be immune to the plague of darkness that slowly reached for more land each day. They also raided our lands, stealing food and women from the villages to fill their bellies and warm their beds.

"What the hell would your king want from us?" I asked coldly, tightening my hands into fists at my side.

"That's between you and him. I'm just here to bring you to the Kingdom of Night."

"No," I stated, folding my arms over my chest, digging in my heels. "You're not taking me to your king, asshole."

"Oh, but I am. Either gagged, bound, unwillingly or willingly, you're coming with me, Alexandria of the Moon Clan," he warned.

Chapter Two

Glaring at the obstinate male, I studied how he issued orders to his men, fully in control. The house they'd hid in wait for us was emptied and cleared out on the main floor. His men escorted me inside while Amo and the girls watched, clucking their tongues. The meaning made a smile spread on my lips, and I nodded softly, which didn't go unnoticed by the asshole who demanded I march forward.

Inside was clean, and while destroyed from the sword fight that had gone down, I didn't smell the decay of rotten food or dead inhabitants. We moved up a staircase before he paused in front of a door and grunted to get my attention, holding his arm out toward the entrance. Narrowing my eyes on him, I slid my gaze to the soft glow within the room.

Scowling, I made a mental note that he held some magic if he'd lit the candles without having to achieve it manually. I stepped into the room, and my spine stiffened.

On the bed were the hallowed husks of what looked like a family. Hot breath fanned my shoulder, and I moved forward cautiously, continuing to stare at the victims.

"Bloody hell," he groaned, pushing his fingers through his hair, discovering what held my attention. He moved toward the bed, grabbing a blanket which he folded around them. He placed the family's remains outside the door before reentering with a dark look burning in his stare. "Sit down."

"No," I argued, even though I was exhausted and my body ached everywhere. I didn't take orders; I gave them.

He turned, lifting a dark brow, causing his eyes to sparkle with a silent threat. The warrior groaned, moving toward me slowly. He picked me up over his shoulder and discarded me in a large, winged back chair that sat before a cold, empty mantel. His lips moved as he sat in the seat opposite of me, and a fire magically started within the fireplace, crackling to life.

I watched him remove the armor from his legs and arms, and then his heavy boots. He then stood, doing away with the chest plate that had kept my blade from finding a home in his stomach. It hadn't even looked like armor during battle, causing me to aim for his heart, yet what I'd thought were merely clothes was armor. Dick.

He didn't stop there. He lifted his shirt off over his head before peering around the empty room. I took in the broad, muscular physique of his back. He was all smooth, powerful, and toned muscle that was just enough and wasn't too much like some men had. The toned muscles of his back flexed as he reached for two glasses. He picked up a bottle of whiskey that sat beside the bed, turning to peek at my curious eyes. Once he'd balanced all three, he smiled darkly at me.

Returning to the chairs, he placed the glasses on the small side table, pouring them to the rim before offering me one. I studied his outstretched hand like it was poison, and he inclined his head, cocking it to the side while he waited for me to accept the drink, with a challenge dancing in his eyes.

I grabbed it, sitting back quickly before holding it to my nose, watching him like a viper. Once I was assured he hadn't poisoned it, I took a swig and swished it around in my mouth before swallowing, enjoying the slight burn as it went down.

Looking toward the fire, I fought the need to run my eyes down the hard, chiseled body he'd bared. His muscles were well-defined and curved in sharp, contoured lines that my eyes wanted to caress leisurely. His body was sleek, powerful, and covered in midnight-colored tattoos wrapping around his hips and moved up to his shoulders, disappearing behind them.

There was a preternatural grace to his movements and body that drew my stare back to it. When I lifted my gaze to his, I found him studying me as I had done to him. His eyes glittered brightly, sparkling with amusement, most likely from the blush filling my cheeks from imagining that toned, sleek body against mine, moving in sinful ways. Swallowing uncomfortably at my train of thought and the direction my libido walked me into, I blanched. I was eye-fucking the ogre-fart who had just outwitted me.

My gaze averted to the fire, observing him out of the corner of my eye as his jaw clenched. He continued to study my moonlit profile, painted colorful by the moon's shining light.

Without the moon, I would appear normal and plain. My rainbow-colored hair would turn platinum, while my sparkling eyes would return to a deep azure blue that looked bright because of my skin's paleness, and had the moon been full, it would have revealed more of my true nature. Unlike his bronzed flesh, mine was much paler and lacking pigment. He should have been anything but tanned with the lack of sunshine in their kingdom.

"You were looking for someone. Who was it?" His question caused my teeth to grind together before my stare slowly slid back to his. "I asked a question, Little Bird. I expect an answer."

"Suck a dick, asshole," I chuckled, lowering the hand that held the drink.

Without warning, I tossed the whiskey into his face and rushed toward the door. I didn't make it there, not even close. His body slammed into mine, taking me to the floor hard and punishingly.

He weighed more than my horse did. Using my leg, I rolled him over hard but didn't stay on top for long. His body lifted before rolling, holding me beneath him, trapping me with his weight. He stretched my body, forcing my arms over my head with one hand, the other pushed against my throat. It was a dominant move, exerting control that I needed to fight.

My hips bucked his body, and my eyes rose to lock with his. The look burning in his gaze was savage, hungry, and carnal lust all mixed into one cup of *oh hell no*. Swallowing hard, I shivered beneath the hand pressing against my larynx threateningly. His mouth tightened, and his eyes turned hard as if he didn't like the fact I had stilled. Had he wanted more fight? I wasn't done struggling to escape, but his touch had given me pause.

The sound that left his throat was strangled, almost feral. I trembled from need, flabbergasted that beneath his body, mine responded. Bodies were stupid and pathetic like that.

He noticed, and those light blue eyes lowered to my mouth as he smiled cruelly, holding tighter onto my wrist. The hand on my throat remained the same, there to prevent me from fighting him. It was a silent threat of violence that if I so much as moved a muscle, he'd make good on it. How fucked up was it that I wanted to see if he would?

I parted my lips, and he lowered that icy stare to them, dropping his head as if he intended to claim them. I wetted my lips, but his mouth never brushed against mine. Instead, his nose rubbed the soft column of my throat, and I bucked against his touch. Panic thundered through me at the proximity of his mouth to the artery, feeding blood to my brain.

"Hold still, woman," he demanded, inhaling my scent before he lifted back. The asshole watched me struggling beneath him until something very male and dominant pushed against my apex. "I'd hold still if I were you. Unless your thrusting body is an invitation to soothe the baser needs of your cunt," he rasped out abrasively, his voice wafting over my skin.

"Get the fuck off of me!" I demanded through the panic invading me, burning with resentment that I was considering doing just that. His smile curved into a wolfish grin that promised to draw blood. "You ogre motherfucker, get off of me now!"

"No," he growled, watching me jerking beneath him. "You're rarely out of control of what's happening to you, aren't you? You like control, and you have none at this moment, and it burns like acid through your veins, doesn't it?"

"I'm going to eat your fucking face!" I slammed my head into his, gasping in pain as he released me to grab his nose that was pouring blood everywhere.

I was up in an instant, rushing from the bedroom into the empty hallway. I looked toward the staircase, hearing men's voices below. Hurrying in the opposite direction, I inched toward the darkness. I began trying doorknobs until finally finding one unlocked, and I slid into the room, softly pulling the door closed behind me.

I lifted my hand to my lips, finding them bloodied from where his nose had connected with them. I stepped back, spinning in the darkness, and screamed as I was picked up and slammed against the wall. My head bounced off the plaster and fell forward to slam into his chest. Baby blue eyes sparkled with exhilaration until I pushed against him. Not with strength, but with the magic of the moon that entered the room at that exact moment, and I forced myself into his mind.

I was no longer in the same room. I was within him, seeing from his eyes, witnessing something from his past. My eyes slid around this new room filled with darkness where he was naked, his body glistening with the silver moonlight that lit the woman's face that he was pleasuring. I watched her beautiful features soften as her lips parted, his name escaping in a whisper while he pounded against the flesh in which she'd let him sate his unending hunger.

"Torrin," she uttered in lust, her voice a melody he ached to hear.

"Shut the fuck up and come for me," he demanded, unable to get deep enough or feel enough. "I need to feel your pain," he admitted, needing her *pain to find* his *pleasure.*

The hunger was eternal, and not even she could sate the need he felt. Torrin pushed her legs up further, and I watched her eyes light with pain at the sheer size of his cock. His mouth lowered, claiming her lips to devour the noises escaping her lungs.

Pain.

Torment.

Terror.

Torrin was the monster who delivered her pain and pleasure. He enjoyed the look of terror that flashed through her pretty eyes while his body thrust and jackhammered into hers without mercy. Tears slid from her eyes, and Torrin moved faster, harder, pushing his hand down on her throat while she gasped for air. I felt his need to taste her pain. Worse than that, I felt his need to give her pain. He wanted to leave her covered in marks on her beautiful skin that would welt, standing as a reminder that she'd been his.

Torrin gave her pain when he sought pleasure. He didn't relent, couldn't. I watched him fuck as a beast possessed. The need to seek the hunger's edge driving him to madness as her moans turned to whimpers and then cries of pain instead of the pleasure he'd wanted to give her. Unsatisfied, Torrin pumped his hips a few more times and started moving slower, easing the pain to bring her pleasure.

Bodies could break.

Minds could close down.

I could feel what Torrin was feeling and glimpsed his inner turmoil through brief flashes of his memories. He stopped seeking bedmates when the need to fuck became primal, and he hurt those who thought to take pleasure with him. He started allowing another male to feed them pleasure while Torrin gave them pain. That way, they never knew Torrin was delivering pain as he sated his hunger on their bodies.

He made them imagine it was an incredible pleasure they felt, and it worked. He found release with them. Lately, though, it too had become numb and muted over the last fifty years. He turned, staring out the window where the darkness filled the kingdom, before looking down at the woman, who stared like an entangled animal snared in a trap.

Rolling off of her, Torrin moved toward the table, dick covered in her juices and still fucking hard enough to wield as a blade. My body shuddered, listening to her retrieving her things and rushing from the room in fear.

Exhaling, he placed his hands onto the ancient wooden table in the bedroom and poured over maps marked with locations, showing information regarding the library.

"Get the fuck out of my head, bitch!" Torrin snarled

angrily.

He ejected me from his memories and grabbed my throat as a strangled cry expelled from my lips. Torrin slammed my head against the wall, and darkness washed over me. My body slumped into powerful arms that caught and lifted me.

Chapter Three

The sound of flames crackling against wood woke me from a pain-filled sleep. I whimpered, trying to place my hands onto my head, only to find them tied to the arms of the chair. My eyes glared down at my naked thighs, slowly moving to the rope wrapped around my knees, wrist, and leading up to my throat. I gasped, leaning forward, and my legs parted. I placed my head down, studying the way my body moved.

Frowning, I glared at the ropes, noting the thick knots that wouldn't allow me to escape. I moved my hands, and my knees rose higher while something behind me squeaked as if I were on a pulley system. My brows furrowed as my attention swung to where I sensed Torrin's presence.

Torrin, Head of the Guard, the dark warlord of the army that served King Aragon, reclined on the bed, silently observing me while I took in how helpless I was. I swallowed past the pain in my head, staring at the sleek, toned muscles on display.

His arms were sprawled behind his head, folded, while an impassive look held my stare. He was all toned muscles and dark tattoos that drew the eye to them, keeping them prisoner while I tried to discern what the inked text said or meant.

"What kind of shit is this?" I whispered past the dryness in my mouth. How long had I slept? Groggy from pain and from endless days of riding to reach this village, I dropped my head back. Torrin pulled on the rope, forcing my legs open, leaving me in a sinful position as I snapped my head upright, glaring at him murderously. "I'm going to enjoy cutting you up into tiny pieces and eating you."

"You talk too much about murdering people for something so weak," he grunted, moving to sit up, which caused his muscles to ripple and bunch tightly at his abdomen. My eyes slid over the masculine form, drinking in the sight of the warlord who had seen more wars than I could count.

I'd heard of Torrin, of his mercilessness in battle and the coldness he exuded toward his enemies. If this asshole had wanted me dead, I'd be dead already, and we both knew it. He was keeping me alive for something more than dragging me to his king's feet and dropping me there.

"How did you get into my head?" he asked, standing up to move closer to the chair. I slowly adjusted my eyes, yet I could still not take him in without becoming a puppet as he neared where I sat.

I'd been knocked out when the moon-sight activated,

which meant for the next few hours, my eyesight would be utter shit up close. I repeatedly blinked, trying to force it to revert to my heightened sight, but failed. I closed my eyes tight because the head pain would worsen from seeing triple of everything if I didn't.

Moon-sight was the ability to see within the darkness, fed to us by the moon. If the moon were only a mere sliver, we wouldn't be able to see into the darkness. Tonight, though, it was a crescent moon, allowing me to use it's light because it wasn't a full moon. Firelight didn't affect me, but being trapped in a room with lanterns lit forced my vision to swim after being in the dark for so long. Plus, the pain was piercing my skull.

Something pushed against my lips, and I groaned, turning my head, which, of course, opened my thighs more. My eyes opened, narrowing as one hand gripped my jaw tight, and the other pushed a finger against my lips.

"Suck," he ordered.

The scent of moonflower dust hit my senses, and I opened my lips, moving my tongue over his finger, covered in the substance.

Torrin hissed the moment my lips closed around it, licking every speck from his finger until my teeth skimmed the offending intrusive appendage. I licked more until I was certain I'd consumed all the dust, slowly dancing my tongue around the finger he'd pushed in between my lips. Biting down, I enjoyed the hiss of pain that escaped him. His hand against my jaw tightened, applying pressure until my mouth opened to release the bleeding finger.

I opened my eyes to find him studying my lips while my tongue darted out, dragging over them to claim the dust and blood left behind. To the Moon Clan, moonflower dust was addictive and caused our bodies to heat and burn with need. It was an aphrodisiac but also a cure that remedied moon-sight sickness, among other things.

"I want to know how the fuck you got into my head and could see my memories," Torrin demanded and then snorted when I just continued staring at him. His hand lowered, and his fingers pinched the muscle of my thighs that connected my sex to my leg.

I gasped, crying out as he watched me through impassive eyes that studied my reaction. I closed my lips and stared at him in an open challenge. His other hand lifted to pinch the other side as knuckles skimmed over my sex, and I trembled violently, which caused his eyes to drop to where my body clenched with need.

It wasn't something that I'd meant to do. My response to his touch had been a knee-jerk reaction that had made my entire body clamp down with desire. Torrin's eyes narrowed to angry slits, and he stood abruptly, moving toward the chair across from me. He ran his thumb over his bottom lip before he grunted and steepled his hands in front of his mouth.

"What the fuck does your king want with the Sacred Library?" I demanded, uncaring that I wasn't in a prime position to interrogate him, but, hey, obviously I had to try. Right?

"How the fuck did you get into my head, little girl?" he countered.

"I'm not little. You're an ogre, Torrin." Those frost-colored eyes lifted to lock with mine, holding them prisoner as a sinfully dark smirk played on his lips.

"Did you enjoy watching me fuck her?" he countered huskily.

I swallowed hard, dropping my eyes to the monstrous cock that had been pounding into the woman, who hadn't been tiny by any means. She'd been much larger than me, and she'd had actual tears of pain escaping her eyes. He'd craved violence, which should have horrified me, yet it hadn't in the least bit.

Curiously, he hadn't finished with her while she'd come twice in the matter of moments I'd watched her through his memories. That, and the map, had been worth the pain I endured to reach inside the mind of someone and see what or who they were. Normally, they never knew I was inside their minds, but Torrin felt me there immediately. It was disturbing and a little unflattering how quickly he'd sensed me searching his memories.

We were at an impasse. His eyes searched my face while I felt the telltale sign of a blush, heating my pale cheeks. Torrin's lips curved into a knowing smirk that I wanted to slap from his face. *Violently.*

"You undressed me," I stated, not bothering to frame it as a question. It was a fact.

"You got blood on your—whatever the hell it is you women wear. It's being washed since we're about to travel through the passes, and there are starving creatures within the darkness. I figured it was easier to have it cleaned than bring you to my king in torn up pieces. Not that I'd be opposed since you'd be much easier to deal with."

"I won't help your king, so you might as well walk away now."

"Oh, but I think you will. You see, your people are suffering from moon sickness, and you're after the same thing we are. You want to stop your people from dying, and we want to find the library that holds the answers you seek."

"I'd rather suck you off than help your king find the Sacred Library," I admitted, watching his eyes sparkle with intrigue, lowering to my mouth. "What could Aragon possibly want inside that library, anyway?"

"That's not something I'd ever tell you," he growled, rubbing his eyes.

I injected myself into his mind, closing mine off to him. Instead of gaining access to his thoughts, I was met with a vision of him peering down at me. My legs were up around his shoulders, and he was devouring my mouth as I whimpered, crying out for him to thrust harder, faster, and deeper. He lifted, showing me how he looked within my body, and I ejected my mind from him, gasping as pain lanced through my head and blood dripped from my nose.

Wintery eyes sparkled with amusement. I continued struggling to regain control of my breathing that was ragged and stiff, unable to get enough air into my lungs. Nausea swirled through me, and I blinked past the pain that caused my eyes to water. He'd fucking blocked me from his thoughts, showing a vision of *us* together. I trembled at how his cock had looked within my poor vagina.

A knock at the door sounded, and Torrin stood, stretching his arms before he walked to the door and accepted the clothing. He walked back into the room and dropped them beside where I sat. His eyes locked with mine, and he smiled wolfishly, leaning down and holding his mouth a hairsbreadth away from mine.

His hot breath fanned my lips, forcing my eyes to close. I waited for them to skim across mine. Dark, deep laughter escaped his throat as his hand slid through my hair, gripping it firmly while he tugged on it, stealing a moan from my lips.

"You try to get into my head again, and I'll use my magic on you. Mine makes your nightmares into reality and holds you there in my mind until I allow you to escape. I can do whatever I want in your dreams, and when you awake, you'll still feel me there. Now, be a good girl and get some rest. We have a long trip ahead of us."

"You expect me to sleep like this?" I asked, watching his lips curl into a smile.

"You should try because you look exhausted. You just fought off a horde of dark creatures less than three days ago, Alexandria. I know because I've watched you from the shadows. You were led here because I wanted you to be. Your brother wasn't ever in this village. He never reached this far before the sickness set in," Torrin stated, exhaling as he lifted the glass and polished off the whiskey.

"How do you know that?" I asked softly, hiding the pain his words caused me. My chest tightened, and I swallowed hard past the uneasiness that fought to swallow me whole.

"Goodnight, Alexa." He smiled tightly, ignoring my question as he returned to the bed, lying down.

My eyes swam with unshed tears, pricking my pride while my chest constricted with pain. Landon had shown signs of the moon sickness before he left. Or at least, the first sign of it. I turned my eyes to the fire, watching the flames dance as the use of my nickname clicked.

"How did you know that?" I asked, turning to look at him. "How did you know that was my nickname?" It wasn't, not really. I was Lexia to everyone but Landon, who preferred to use the name my mother had called me before she'd died from a raid by Aragon's people.

"Your brother told me, right before he ended up in chains."

"You have him!" I growled.

"I don't, but he is being held somewhere to prevent him from succumbing to the moon madness. Or, more to the point, he's someplace that he can't hurt anyone else as he suffers from the sickness. I'm certain he's past the beginning stages by now. You already knew that, though," he stated impassively. "If you hadn't known he was sick, you wouldn't have broken protocol and come out searching for him without the backing of your Order."

"They sent me to find him," I hissed.

"No, Alexandria. They sent you to find the library because they had already written him off as dead. Landon and his entire team were infected, and yet the Order still sent them. Why?" he asked, smiling coldly as I narrowed my eyes to angry slits. "Because the Order didn't want them to expire where the others would see it happening and lose faith in the Order of the Moon," he said softly, turning onto his side, which bunched the muscles of his abdomen. "Now I have your attention, don't I?"

I swallowed, closing my eyes before turning back to the crackling fire. If Torrin knew where Landon was, he knew that I'd come for him. The thing was, if the king got inside the Sacred Library, he could destroy the entire world. It held the first spells of our race and the history of the world. What would he possibly want from within it?

If I helped him to locate the library, would I be damning everyone to something worse than the plague of darkness? It was said that someone in Aragon's line had read from one of the books, unleashing the frozen darkness onto the world. What if I helped him, and I lost myself to save Landon and the others in doing so? I'd seen my death once in a soothsayer's dream, bathed in shadows that made it near impossible to know who it was that had murdered me, yet I'd felt the truth of it to my core.

"Sleep, because we leave at dawn."

"There is no dawn anymore. Only darkness resides within these mountains," I whispered icily, not bothering to tear my eyes from the fire. "Your king wants one of the books, the Book of Life or Death? Which one is it that Aragon craves to read?"

"If I told you, would you shut up and go to sleep?" he asked, and I turned to see Torrin close his eyes.

"Yes," I whispered before sucking my bottom lip between my teeth.

"Liar. You suck your bottom lip when you lie, Alexa.

Go to sleep, or I'll gag you so I can."

"Right…" He slipped off the bed and grabbed the curtain to rip a large section of it off before moving toward me. He smiled coldly as he lowered to a crouch in front of me.

"I warned you." Standing, he leaned over me, securing the cloth around my mouth. I growled, but the fabric muffled the noise. Torrin patted my head, lowering his lips to my ear. "Sweet dreams, pray that I am not within them, Little One. I find I rather enjoyed the sounds you made when you entered my mind. Keep me awake tonight, and I'll make certain you don't sleep for days while we travel through the Badlands."

Chapter Four

The mountain passes were covered in thick snow, making the large party move slower through the slippery trail. We'd been on the path since dawn, or what would have been dawn if the entire mountain wasn't bathed in the darkness. There had been no sign of animals or people since we'd traveled past the first village.

The girls on my team paired up and rode with Torrin's men. None of us were allowed to ride on our own mounts this morning, and none of us spoke, ignoring the men and their comments to one another as unease filled us. Until we knew what their actual intentions were with us, it was best to remain silent and listen.

Repositioning my body, I stiffened against the masculine form behind me. If Torrin noticed, he ignored it. It was mortifying to be forced to ride with the pompous cave dweller, and it had pissed Chivalry off to no end that I wasn't to allow to ride him.

I hissed as Chivalry nipped my leg once more. Leaning forward, I patted his head even though the arm around my midsection tightened. Torrin grunted while he watched me, comforting my horse. Chivalry chose that moment to toss his head back and neigh loudly, complaining.

"I know, Chivalry. The stupid warlord is making me ride with him. Don't be cross at me. You're still the best boy ever, and the only boy for me," I cooed, reassuring my horse that I wasn't willingly choosing to ride with the brainless warrior instead of him.

Another grunt sounded, and then the warhorse I was on reared back on its hind legs, sending me flush against Torrin's heat. I peered around the trail while he got the stallion back under control, slowing it to an easy walk.

The surrounding woods were silent, which wasn't normal. Usually, the creatures immune to the darkness would be prowling, hunting, or scurrying around. They weren't today, which meant either they were afraid of the group passing through, or something worse was within the forest that had only months ago been teeming with life.

A scraping noise started to the right of the path, and we paused to search the woods. The hair on my nape rose, and a shiver of unease settled within me. The warlord's arm tightened around me as if he was expecting to have to move quickly.

"Hold still," he gritted as I adjusted, settling closer until I'd felt his body molding against mine.

"Something is coming," I warned at the same moment something dropped from the sky, snatching one rider at the front of the line from his horse.

"Into the woods!" Torrin ordered, and before I could argue that we may not want to enter the woods where we could be separated from the others, he moved toward them.

"They may want us to go into the forest!" I screeched as all of my warning bells were triggered, screaming that we were purposefully being split from the others.

"Hold on and shut up, woman," he growled, pulling Chivalry with us.

Inside the woods, darkness reigned. Still, no sound met our ears. Not until something whizzed past us, zigzagging through the woods. One minute we were on the horse, and the next, Torrin had dismounted fluidly with me in front of him, forcing me behind him with the cloak still covering me.

"I need weapons," I growled. Hearing Torrin's grunt of disagreement, I bristled.

"No, you don't. Shut up and stand there."

My head snapped to the right as a shadow moved within the darkness. Turning, I placed my back toward the obtuse warlord and faced the road where a horse laid unmoving. The ominous sounds continued, growing louder until a sinister form met my wide, horrified stare.

Standing in front of me was a faceless body hovering over the ground. Bloody clothes hung over its form, the stench pungent and obnoxious until it was sickening. Beneath the bloodied clothes it had stolen from its victims was grotesquely disfigured, graying, rotten flesh. My eyes burned from the reeking stench, and my stomach roiled with bile pushing up against my throat.

"Reapers," I whispered, barely audible enough to be heard by Torrin.

Reapers were scavengers of the Darklands—a place filled with death and despair. No light touched them and hadn't for a very long time. The plague of darkness created monsters like reapers and other creatures that devoured those who still held light within them. They fed on corpses and victims left behind by the stronger beings that hunted the living down, sucking their marrow from their bones like juice from a fruit. Reapers came in behind those creatures, feasting on the remains of what was left, stealing their clothes to hide the skeletal, emaciated form that comprised their bodies.

The reaper shot forward, and I was shoved to the ground by Torrin's large hand, barely avoiding the blade that moved, swinging wide to cleave the monster into two parts. I was yanked from the ground as Torrin made a loud clicking sound with his teeth, forcing everyone back to the road.

"I told you they were trying to separate us," I snapped, but he ignored me.

The moment we reached the road, more reapers slithered out of the woods to surround us. I could hear the others making their way toward us, still riding their mounts. I dropped my cloak, pulling my power from deep within me to ignite like a flame within the darkness.

My skin glowed iridescently, illuminating the dark road. My hair floated, glowing white within the darkness, remaining platinum without the power of the moon to highlight my vibrant colors. My skin pulsed, swirling delicate, silver markings that covered my flesh as I lifted the shirt over my head. I exposed more light before I sent it shooting toward the reapers, which jerked back as if they'd been physically struck.

I felt my team sliding in around me, shedding their clothes to reveal light much weaker than my own. Light terrified the creatures of darkness, or at least ours did. It drove them back into the shadows, forcing them to abandon their hunt of living beings. The reaper's behavior was off, growing bolder with the new area to hunt inside.

My eyes filled with light, and my lips parted to whisper the words of a spell that danced on my tongue, forcing the beings to remain in place while the light pulsed through them. The reapers imploded one by one, folding into themselves until the sounds of their bones popping and cracking with their final death filled the clearing.

When it was over, my body sagged, and strong arms caught me, lifting me. I glanced into Torrin's angry stare and then lifted my eyes to the sky, seeing something move directly above us. Slowly doing a double blink, I watched a body fall toward us from the sky.

"Move," I whispered weakly, and Torrin sidestepped seconds before the body would have landed on us. I shivered and pressed my head closer to his shoulder, uncaring if I looked weak.

I knew how the body on the ground looked. It was a corpse, sucked dry of moisture and marrow, with nothing but skeletal remains left. It was in the beginning stages of becoming a reaper. Swallowing bile, I gagged at the putrescent odor and cadaverous, decomposing organs.

No one spoke as we backed away from the body of the fallen warrior. The loud screech that had ripped through the darkness, moments before he'd been plucked from his horse, sounded again. I was dropped to the ground as Torrin withdrew his sword in a lightning-fast move, slicing through the air like a whirlwind as the red runes on the hilt glowed, causing the blade to pick up speed.

Torrin wasn't just skilled; he was freakishly fast, each swipe aimed with precision. Pieces of the creature dropped from the sky without it ever touching the ground whole. He had sliced it into tiny parts, cutting it in midair until chunks pelted the ground.

I didn't move, didn't gag at the blood now covering me from head to toe from Torrin, slaughtering the monster adeptly and skillfully.

Torrin turned, staring down at me with a look of annoyance while I studied the sword he had used. He cleaned the blade before pushing it into the scabbard, crouching down to pluck a sizeable chunk of rotten meat from my chest before cocking his head to the side, surveying my pale, glowing face.

"You fucking stink," he announced.

"You just cut up whatever the hell that was *on* me. Did you expect me to smell like moonflowers?" I grunted, pushing up into a sitting position.

"I would have preferred it if you'd have tried to dodge at least some of the dead flesh falling from the sky."

"I did, the entire…" Hissing started behind us, and Torrin exhaled, drawing his blade as the warrior turned reaper stood, spewing poisonous spittle at us.

Torrin stepped in front of me, barring the poisonous saliva from reaching me. He grunted, slowly lifting his blade. He spun and ended the reaper's life before it had even begun with the first feeding. Torrin reached down to rip off the patch that adorned the uniform's shoulder, pushing it into a pocket.

"Let's move," he ordered. "There's a town a few miles away from here. We'll find lodging for the night and tend to the wounded there."

I stood, picking chunks of the creature off my skin. I started toward Chivalry, but a hand gripped my wrist, pulling me backward. Turning, I stared into frost-colored eyes that warned me not to push the issue of riding my horse again.

"I stink," I whispered through chattering teeth.

"You're also freezing because you did a strip show in the middle of the fucking mountains. The temperature is dropping, and you're almost naked." Torrin pulled off his cloak to wrap it around my body. "On the road, further down, is Alexandria's cloak; retrieve it and let's move out," he ordered, sitting me on his horse as if I weighed no more than a feather. "Over there." He pointed to a warrior who slipped into the woods, then returned with my soiled cloak.

I pulled Torrin's earthy scented cloak around me and held it up to my nose. Silently, I inhaled the smell of citrus, masculinity, and sandalwood. He narrowed his eyes on me while I watched him, frowning as I found the combination enticing. His icy stare held mine, not looking away until I lowered it and scooted forward, giving Torrin room to mount behind me.

"You can bathe at the inn," he stated, and I shuddered at the putrid scent of my skin. "You will bathe because you fucking reek."

"Do you intend to watch me take a bath?" I frowned at his dark laughter that vibrated over my flesh, sending a shiver rushing down my spine to wrap around my ovaries.

"I may since you're sharing a room with me again, Alexandria," he said in a raspy tone that grated on my nerves.

"Will you do something for me while I bathe?" I whispered, feeling his nose pressing against my ear, uncaring that I reeked of death.

"What's that?" he asked, tightening his arm around me.

"Hold your fucking breath until I'm done?"

Torrin kicked the horse forward without warning, forcing me to yelp in surprise. The arm that held me released, forcing me to grab for the saddle or chance falling. I growled, pushing my ass back to grasp the pommel, making my backside connect with something masculine. I turned, glaring over my shoulder with a withering look that died a short death at finding glowing winter-colored eyes smiling at my discomfort. It was going to be a long ride to the village.

Chapter Five

We entered the inn with only a portion of the war party Torrin had brought with him to capture us. The inn was also the tavern, and instead of moving toward the stairs, I was directed behind it by Torrin, who pointed to a bucket of sudsy water.

"Wash up because I intend to eat before we retire for the night," he ordered, turning his back on me.

I slipped off the cloak, studying the dark-eyed creatures that watched my every move. We'd stepped into the Darklands, where only those who could live through the poisonous shadows remained. Unlike the other side of the mountain where we'd been, the king and his people were immune.

Kneeling, I grabbed a scrap of cloth from the pail and slowly began wiping myself clean. I studied the layout, learning each path out of the town. More creatures started coming out of the small homes, staring at me with something akin to curiosity.

Long ago, the Night King had removed those with the moon-sight from his lands. No one was certain why he'd banished the moon-touched people. But then he held no love for his people, or so the rumors said, and he loathed our kind.

The people of the Darklands had adapted, growing immune to the darkness that had swallowed his land entirely, unlike those who weren't immune to the darkness like the moon-touched people. The darkness didn't consume those from the Darklands, which had spiked our interest in discovering why they were immune, while others were devoured. King Aragon had intervened, sending his troops to guard their borders against us entering.

I used the cloth to wash my chest and neck, turning my attention back to Torrin, who had spun and now watched me with attentiveness burning in his wintery gaze. Those heated eyes slid to mine before they lifted, glaring at the people who were openly gawking at me.

"It's been a while since they've seen your kind here," he stated softly, baring his teeth when one man got too close for his liking.

"Your king banished my kind," I muttered, dropping the cloth back into the bucket while Torrin grabbed the cloak. I frowned as he stepped forward, draping it over my shoulders. His knuckles brushed my collarbone, and I shivered, watching his eyes gradually lift to hold mine.

"So he did, but with good reason. Your kind wanted to dissect our people," he growled, tightening the cloak with his clasp. "If you make a scene in here, I'll make tonight really uncomfortable for you."

"Do you intend to tie me up again?" I asked, holding his heated stare with one of my own.

Torrin wasn't beautiful. He held the look of strength and masculine beauty around him. His eyes whispered of a dark soul, one that knew pain viscerally. It called to mine, and that created a curiosity that bothered me.

His armor hugged a body that was hard lines of strength and muscle that rippled with power so much it exuded from him. Soft-looking, feather-like black hair dusted his shoulders, loosened from the tie that held most of it back. He was taller than me by a good foot and wore his height with easy self-assurance.

The five o'clock shadow on his face looked right on him, exposing full, lush lips that promised pleasure. His teeth were clean, even, and white, unlike most men who held some yellowing from uncleanliness. This morning when he'd awoken, Torrin's disheveled appearance had made my body heat with a need I didn't want or understand.

He had a dominant personality and an arrogant air to him. His mannerism was confident, yet I wasn't sure if he looked at me with disdain or hunger burning in his eyes. He was hard to get a read on, which I could usually discern in the first few minutes of assessing someone. I couldn't get much from him, though, as if he was some persona that didn't match up.

Torrin and I entered the tavern, and he paused to look around. There was a large crowd gathered around the long table where the rest of our group sat for dinner. Torrin grabbed my hand, intertwining his fingers through mine, then stared down at our hands, where tingling started from his touch.

A dazed expression dominated his features, and then wintery eyes lifted to mine, narrowing to curious slits. His voice was low, echoing in my ears, while the others boomed around the behemoth room in which we stood. Torrin yanked me forward, and I released the breath I'd been holding.

"What?" I whispered, chewing my lip nervously while he searched my face.

"Stay close, woman," he snapped, pushing his elbow through the crowd of onlookers to reach the table. Once there, he pulled out a chair, and I lifted my brow, silently sliding into it with uncomfortable warmth filling my cheeks.

Pheasant and other meats were piled in heaping amounts on plates that sat in the middle of the table. It didn't take a genius to figure out that the tavern would turn a massive profit tonight because of who had walked through the doors. Amo elbowed my ribs, forcing me to turn to look at her. Arms wrapped around me, and I chuckled.

"Are you okay?" she whispered.

"I am. Are you guys?" I asked, pulling back as something poked into my side.

Turning, I glared at Torrin, who watched me through darkening eyes. I righted in the chair, my mouth watering at the thought of actual food I hadn't needed to hunt, kill, or skin. The men watched us, slowly noting that we sat silently waiting.

"Eat. You're too damn skinny," Torrin grunted, and I gave him serious side-eye from the comment.

"I am not skinny," I grumbled crossly.

It offended me that he thought I was thin when, in fact, I was all muscle. I trained for battle and had since before I could even hold a blade. I'd spent my childhood learning strategy, war tactics, and how to maneuver an entire army onto a battlefield before the enemy ever sensed we were within fifty miles of them.

"Eat, because I intend to sleep so we can slip out in the morning," he muttered, lifting a goblet of ale to his lips. Something grabbed my shoulder, and Torrin moved swiftly, yanking the man up by his robes. "Do not touch her," Torrin seethed, his eyes flashing a warning.

"She's beautiful," the man hissed, and I turned, staring into black, sightless eyes with dark, pulsing veins, spider-webbing down his face. Even dangling from Torrin's hold, he reached for me, forcing me to scoot back.

"Isn't she, though?" Torrin grunted, sending the man sprawling onto the floor. "She's under King Aragon's protection, and your unwanted attention is preventing his guest from eating her meal. Now, stop gawking and go back to whatever it was you were doing before she and her team got here," he ordered, and I watched the crowd immediately disburse. "Eat, Alexandria."

I shook off the weirdness of the man's touch and lifted the ale, downing it in one drink. I turned, looking at my girls, who were wide-eyed and looked as confused as I felt. Torrin began dishing up my plate while I polished off another glass of ale, and a woman rushed forward to refill it.

Her eyes never left mine, holding them as the ale sloshed over the rim of the goblet. Her mouth lowered, and before I could prevent it, her lips touched mine, and she moaned loudly. My eyes grew large and rounded, and then her tongue slipped into my mouth, searching for mine. I pulled backward, but she dropped the pitcher of ale, pushing talons into my arms while she sucked my face, literally. Gone was her tongue, and in its place were thousands of tiny suction prongs that I felt were draining me.

Something warm splattered over my face as her mouth went lax against mine. I pulled back, staring at the top of her head where a sword had pushed through her skull. I backed up onto Amo's lap, and her arms wrapped around me, holding tightly.

"So, that happened," she offered, both of us watching as Torrin withdrew his sword, shoving the body aside before he sheathed the blade and lifted his ale.

"Eat," he stated, and I didn't move. "We're about to be in an area with little to no food available to hunt. I suggest you enjoy your meal and the ale tonight," he growled, shoveling food into his mouth, staring at me.

Crawling off of Amo's lap, I grabbed the fork, tasting the meat and frowning. It was deliciously roasted to a texture that melted in my mouth. I moaned around the fork and heard a deep growl. I turned with the utensil still in my mouth to find a new male studying me with interest burning in the azure-colored stare.

"New pet, Torrin?" the man asked, walking around the table to sit opposite of me. "She's rather—delicate for your appetite. Hello, beautiful. I'm Zane. You are?"

"Alexandria," Torrin answered, glaring at me before his attention moved to my plate and back to the male watching us through sparkling eyes.

"Beautiful name for a beautiful girl," Zane snickered wickedly, leaning both his elbows on the table before sliding his attention around it slowly. "Aragon allowed an entire assassin squad of moon-touched pussy within the Darklands? He has lost his fucking mind, hasn't he?"

"Did you need something, or did you just come in to drive me bug-fuck crazy, Zane?" Torrin sneered, pushing his plate away before peering at the male through cold eyes.

"Are you fucking him, sweetheart?" Zane asked, his eyes leveling me with a dark stare of curiosity that sent discomfort flowing through me.

Zane was beautiful, with a heart-shaped face framed by dark, cropped hair. His eyes sparkled with amusement, and his mouth curved into a beguiling smile that made my heart ratchet up a beat. His voice was smooth. It was like dark magic bathed over sinful wickedness that made something within me feel uneasy in his presence.

"I don't see what me riding his glorious cock has to do with you, sir," I whispered demurely, kicking into the character of a naïve beauty that made men underestimate me.

"Oh, gods, you're absolutely precious," Zane chuckled. Leaning closer, he smiled hungrily. "Has Torrin marred that beautiful flesh yet? He enjoys punishing his bedmates, beating them until they beg to be freed from his touch. It's why he and King Aragon share their women often."

"Who doesn't like pain with their pleasure?" I asked in a sultry tone, feeling the heat of Torrin's stare charring my flesh. I turned my hooded gaze toward him, licking my lips. "Isn't that right, big boy? You do enjoy marring my flesh and making me ache so wickedly. I especially enjoy when you let that dark side out, and you push my legs up, so you're buried so deeply into my womb I weep when I come for you."

Torrin's eyes burned while he watched me. I swallowed past the lump that grew in my throat from holding his heated stare. I'd intended simply to mess with him, playing a part for the asshole who was too pretty to be my type. However, I hadn't expected heat in Torrin's gaze to burn me so fucking hot that my insides melted and my body grew aroused from the stare alone.

"I especially love it when you come for me, Lexia. Your noises for me are fucking delicious when I stretch that pussy with my cock, and you beg me to fuck you harder," Torrin growled. His raspy voice rolled over me like sex and silk, grating against my nipples, which pebbled from the sound of his voice alone. A throbbing started in my belly, and my mouth went dry with need while Torrin dared me to act on the urges rushing through me. "And your skin reddens so beautifully when I mark you, doesn't it, gorgeous?" Well, fuck. That went sideways fast.

I swallowed hard, unable to tear my eyes from his while he searched them for permission. My core clenched hungrily with desire, tightening as heat pooled between my thighs with readiness for him to play with me. My tongue jutted out from between my lips, wetting them, which caused his hungry stare to lower, slowly noting the path it took until it vanished back into my mouth.

"Uh, you broke your vow of celibacy, Lexia?" Amo asked, her hand touching my shoulder, dispelling whatever was happening between Torrin and me.

"What?" I asked, shaken on how I'd reacted to Torrin.

"Your vow of celibacy you took when we lost the others?" she questioned, her hand tightening on my shoulder. "I'm all for you feeding that starving kitty. Lord knows she needs the cream. Feed that hungry pussy as much cream as you want her to take."

I slid my stare back to Torrin's, finding him watching me with dark interest. I shuddered involuntarily, imagining his body against mine. Sweat beaded on my neck, and I couldn't look away from the promise of pleasure in his pale eyes. His tongue snaked out, slowly running over his bottom lip before sliding back into his mouth. The entire table was silent while we intensely studied one another.

"She's very ravenous," I whispered thickly, unable to look away from the fiery heat burning in Torrin's frozen stare.

"Is she?" he asked, leaning closer until his hand touched my thigh, and I parted my lips on a sigh of need.

"Anyway," Zane snorted. "I was summoned to join you for the duration of the trip home. It seems our king needs me."

Neither one of us was willing to look away from the other. Something wicked was happening between us. I hadn't ever felt desire like I felt it at this moment. My body was on fire, and worse, there was a pulse between my thighs I'd never experienced in my lifetime. I swallowed hard, dropping my gaze to break the spell Torrin held over me.

I reached for the pitcher of ale and lifted it to my lips, chugging from it without using the goblet. I polished it off, silently setting it back down. I grabbed my fork, filling my mouth with food. Amo chuckled, tapping my shoulder.

"It's okay, just breathe through it, girlfriend," she whispered, leaning closer to my ear. "That's called lust, Lexia. It's a normal reaction when wanting to fuck someone. I know you haven't experienced it before, but that's what the rest of us feel. If I were you, I'd ride that dick tonight because maybe you'll finally come on a cock instead of having to self-soothe that poor kitty cat after he's left the room."

I choked on the food in my throat, coughing until Torrin slapped me on the back, peppering Zane with the meat that had gone down the wrong pipe. Zane glanced down at his shirt, dusting the food off, hiking one brow higher than the other. It caused Torrin to chuckle at the face filled with horror as Zane took in his shirt.

"You shouldn't have?" Zane snorted, slowly moving his gaze to Amo, who drug herself down his body. "Yummy."

"Zane," Torrin said to the male beside Amo, "I'll be sharing a room with Lexia tonight. Pair the other women with a male in each room, so they remain guarded." Torrin pushed away from the table and held out his hand out for mine. "It's late, and you stink of reaper blood, woman."

I stood as he pulled the chair out for me, swallowing past the tightening in my throat as my stomach turned with nervousness. I slid my stare to Amo and Tabitha, finding both women eyeing men with interest burning in their gazes. Torrin moved his eyes to where mine had landed, and he smirked.

"Be gentle with the ladies, men. They'll be riding hard through the Badlands in the morning," he grunted. "After you, Lexia," Torrin stated, sliding his eyes to my breasts, which were hard pebbles visible through my top.

Chapter Six

Moving slowly up the stairs, I entered the room carefully with mistrust while lost in the way my body had responded to a single look. No man had ever made feel heat rushing through me until now. I'd never experienced the butterflies or lust that the others spoke about after landing a male for the night. My experiences had been pleasurable, and yet I had never felt fully satisfied afterward. It was always as if something was missing, which Amo had pointed out not so gently—were orgasms.

Inside the bedroom, the lanterns burned brightly, and a fire crackled within the large fireplace. The room's warmth was inviting until it became apparent that only one bed sat within the room. My heart fluttered like bird wings had replaced it the longer I stared at the enormous four-poster bed with vibrant red drapes wrapped around it.

"Bathe," Torrin ordered from behind me, causing me to yelp and turn toward him.

His eyes studied me before he spun, closing the door that thudded like a nail in my coffin. He moved deeper into the room, removing his heavy armor. He stopped beside a chair and slowly slid his sparkling, wintery gaze to where I still stood, wordlessly watching him.

"You fucking stink. Bathe, Lexia," Torrin growled, and I nodded slowly in agreement. I stank, but I wasn't too keen on being nude around this male, either.

I wasn't shy about being naked around people by any means. I'd grown up in a group setting where men and women bathed together all the time. We were taught to embrace who and what we were, and sexuality wasn't something we thought of when we were naked. Yet the idea of getting naked with him was causing my brain to hiccup. My heart was thundering against my chest wall, while wings were fluttering in my belly.

The shit happening within me was making me off-kilter. I wasn't sure why it was happening, and I didn't like it. I knew Torrin had magic since I'd grown up on tales of who this man was and what he did to entire armies in battles. Shit, there were legends about his expertise on and off the battlefield.

I'd entered taverns and listened to the working women who gushed over Torrin. They'd shared their experiences in his arms and how hard and vigorous he went against their bodies. Rumors were that he was like a crazed warrior lost in the bloodlust declaring war on the female anatomy. I'd scoffed and made fun of those women for being amazed at the male behind closed doors.

Now, I was the woman with him behind the closed doors.

I walked to the bathtub, slowly undressing while I faced away from him. Sliding into the water, I noted how large the tub was. It was much larger than the ones I typically bathed in, and the room itself was elegant, considering it was within a tavern that doubled as an inn.

I stared into the dancing flames while I washed my body, pouring water over my head to work the soap into my hair, noting the room's silence. A prickling sensation settled on my neck, and I swallowed past the knowledge that Torrin was watching me bathe. Slipping beneath the water, I rinsed my hair out before I turned, staring up into frost-colored eyes.

Torrin stood naked, his wealth of muscles on display with his overly large cock hanging between his legs. Swallowing, I backed up in the tub, covering my breasts with my arms while he climbed in, tossing a glass bottle toward me, forcing me to uncover my body to catch the tonic.

"I need you to put that on my chest and back," he demanded. "After all, I got them from protecting your pretty skin from the poisonous droplets."

I nodded slowly, trying to get as small as I could manage. Climbing into the tub, Torrin spread his legs, forcing me to slide between them. He hung his large arms over the sides of the tub and rested his head against the back, staring up at the ceiling, making me look to see what had captured his attention above us. My eyes dropped back to Torrin, finding him studying my face intently.

"How long have you been celibate?"

My emotions slammed shut, and I snorted, shaking

my head. "Let's not do that. Let's not pretend either of us cares about the other. You don't care about me being celibate any more than I care about whatever is happening between you and the man downstairs. I'm your hostage, not your fucking girlfriend."

His eyes narrowed, and the tic in his jaw came to life. I exhaled, creeping forward. I'd slammed home the point that we weren't friends, and that should have stopped the fluttering in my belly as I moved closer to the warlord who put that quivering need there.

Torrin's chest was peppered in burns from the reaper's blood that had scorched through his suit of armor. I opened the bottle of tonic, settling between his legs, uncaring that I was entirely on display or that his massive cock was about to be very close to my naked sex. His eyes lowered to my breasts, and I admittedly wondered if he had found them as lackluster as the last male who had seen them.

My body was covered in scars and markings that I'd earned. I wasn't curved like Amo's body that made men go insane for a chance to be with her for a night. I had small breasts with rose-colored nipples that wouldn't even fill his large hands. My hips were narrow, and I was slender in build with a round ass that was bubble-shaped. My skin was lighter than most moon-touched, which caused me to glow brighter. My eyes were slanted and a deep azure color, but the moon's power added rainbow-colors to their depths, which was like my hair. I had a delicate nose that looked more like a button shape than anything else. My lips were full, lush, and one thing that added sensuality to me since everything else lacked enticement.

I lifted my body, settling onto Torrin's lap, and he tensed beneath me. Wrapping my legs around his waist, I somehow managed to keep my face impersonal. I felt him growing hard against my junction and frowned. Leaning over, I placed the tonic cap on the small table, bringing my breasts against his chest, and my nipples hardened at the touch.

His eyes watched me closely, noting every single move I made as I set the bottle down beside the cap and began working the mixture of sage and oils into his chest muscles. I felt a jolt of lightning when they connected with his chest. His body heated beneath my touch, slowly tensing and becoming firmer as I worked the tonic into the wounds as his muscles flinched beneath my fingers' slow perusal of his physique.

My eyes lifted to hold his as I gradually worked my fingertips against the sinewy, hard muscles of his marred abdomen. His tattoos were a work of art, of birds flying toward dark clouds that stretched over bronzed flesh. I chewed my lip, working the oil in deeper, forcing myself to slow my movements. I knew from experience that reaper burns felt like fire kissing flesh. I rubbed my hands over his chest, slowly running them over the ripped coils of his abdomen.

Our breathing was ragged and heavy, and no matter how much I denied it, I felt an attraction to Torrin. I had no intention of acting on it, but there was something undeniably appealing about him that both pissed me off and confused me.

I started to back away, but his hands snaked out, gripping my hips to hold me in place. I tensed from the strength of his hold, and our eyes met and locked in silence, speaking.

His eyes promised me pleasure—and pain.

Mine begged for him to give it to me, knowing that in pain, there would be pleasure.

It was as if we were two storms preparing to let loose against one another, to leave havoc in our wake.

I wanted Torrin, and he wasn't opposed to giving me everything I needed. Strange bedfellows, considering we were enemies. But I wasn't looking for something soft and sweet, and neither was this man.

Dark lust tended to collide. It searched likeness out and matched it at the strangest times. Monsters connected with other monsters, their ability to see beneath the surface a skill learned and honed in the shadows.

I slid my hands down my sides, rising in the silence that had wrapped around us. I leaned over, hovering my lips a hairsbreadth away from his, my entire body shuddering with need, violently wanting what he could offer me. His thumbs ran over my nipples, and I swallowed hard, brushing my mouth against his, then I yanked back. I stared at Torrin as the moonlight pooled inside the window, shocking us both out of the trance in which we'd been held.

Torrin lifted from the tub, and his cock skimmed over my mouth, and I yelped as if it had burned me as he smiled, but it was all teeth. I moved from the tub, grabbing the drying cloth before heading toward the fire.

Gazing down into the dancing blue and red flames, I prayed for comfort and perseverance to keep my vow for another two weeks until the full moon rose high in the sky. That was the vow I'd made to pay, to sacrifice one year of pleasure for each life lost under my watch. Bad leadership and one night of sex had led to four lives lost, and that was on me.

Torrin's hands touched my shoulders, and I exhaled, turning to look up into icy eyes. I started to speak, but he shoved the tonic into my hand and sat down in the chair by the fire, studying my face.

"Warriors take vows of celibacy to punish themselves. So what did you do that ended with you being celibate?" he asked, his eyes raking over the flesh that the drying cloth didn't conceal. "You can either answer my question, or you can ride my mouth to keep it occupied."

I glared at him before sliding behind the chair, staring at the marks from battles that had ravished his back. It didn't take away from his masculinity or the lust that ripped through me at the sight of sharp contours shaping wide shoulder blades that tapered down to the sexiest ass I'd ever seen.

"I made a bad call four years ago. I sent a group off with some men during the full moon without realizing they were incubus demons. Each full moon calls to us, beckoning us to breed new life. It called to me that day, and my need for pleasure overrode my ability to lead my team. I tried to step down as leader, but I'd been raised to take the role since before I even knew how to speak words. That moon call ended up with four of my sisters raped and tortured to death. The Moon Clan refused to allow me to step down and become anything else. They didn't punish me, and they should have. I failed my team, and in doing so, the cost was their lives, not mine.

I sentenced myself to four years of celibacy." My hand slid over the wounds on Torrin's back, hearing his sharp intake of breath that hitched in his chest. "I have two weeks left."

"The call of the moon is undeniable, Lexia. That would leave you in intense pain. From what I understand, the ache is unimaginable and violent if ignored."

"I find pleasure in pain," I stated, unembarrassed and as if it weren't strange.

I felt his entire body jolt from my words. He turned, gazing over his shoulder at me. His eyes looked at me in a new light that sent heat pooling in my belly as everything within me sang with need.

My eyes flicked to the moon, then slowly settling back on him, and I frowned. I knew that once the moon was full, I'd be called to answer its song. I could already feel my body syncing with it, and worse, the need was already festering within me.

"You can fuck but not find fulfillment in the act?" he asked.

"I don't reach orgasm easily." I swallowed hard past the heat burning in his gaze at my confession, as if he'd found something unique and challenging. "I've never found fulfillment with lovers, not even when the moon was full, and they released within my body. So not completing my need to orgasm is my punishment. I've not had a single orgasm in four years, not even by my hand."

"Moon-mates are rare, and you'd need one for his release to bring you to a full orgasm," He watched my face, turning impassive.

"That isn't what I meant. I have no mate, nor do I wish for one. Answering the moon's call is inevitable, but fucking and searching for the one true love we are promised isn't my singular purpose. Mating is for the weaker of our species that cannot fight. I drink a tonic to prevent pregnancy the night after I am called, or I did when I was free to find release. We don't all get called every time. Our bodies have to align with the full moon to be called, so not every full moon has been painful for me."

"You said you find pleasure in pain," he rasped, and I paused, running my fingers over his hard muscles, then backing up, moving away from him.

"I meant that I'm okay with the pain I endure during my celibacy." I exhaled, blinking at the sultry tone that escaped from my tongue like warm honey over bread. I chewed my lip, spinning to escape Torrin and the intensity of his stare.

I went to the bed where he'd placed the bags as my mind replayed the one time I'd enjoyed being with a man. He'd been violent with need. I'd felt wrong, disturbed after we'd been together. It was the closest I'd come to finding release with another person. Nausea swirled through me as memories of his rough treatment sent heat rushing to my cheeks. I'd enjoyed the control he'd held over my body. His biting hands and roughness had more than just excited me. It had unraveled a raw need within me that I'd chased ever since.

His hands slid up my spine, and fingers threaded through my hair. Torrin jerked me around to face him as pale, wintery eyes burned with fiery ice, causing the air to get stuck in my lungs. Torrin forced me to walk back toward the bed, his body trembling as hard as mine. He lowered me onto the mattress and stared into my eyes, watching the tremor of need rushing through me.

Torrin didn't release my hair, tightening his hold on it while he watched the excitement flooding my eyes. He lifted his other hand, pressing it against my throat before his mouth lowered, claiming mine in a soul-crushing kiss that, while gentle, held command for me to submit to him. His tongue speared against mine, tangling with it in a slow, hungry urgency that strung my body taut with need. When he pulled back, every fucking thing about him stirred my senses.

His eyes.

His lips.

His body.

He radiated dominance and absolute control.

"Are you wet?"

I didn't answer. I couldn't.

My tongue was heavy with lust, and everything inside of me was firing up all at once. My eyes searched his, seeking the answer in them like they would know my body's current state better than I would.

The hand fisting my hair tightened until my scalp screamed in pain. He exuded pheromones that alone made me need to combust, shattering into a million pieces. His eyes slid a cutting a path down my body, leaving a blistering trail in their wake. He lifted his hand from my throat, and before I could argue, his fingers slid against my pussy. I opened my mouth to argue his course, but they pushed into my core, stretching me deliciously full to take the answer he sought.

I moaned, releasing a ragged gasp as my body clenched hungrily around him. It quaked from the burn he created while he deliberately worked his fingers deeper into my needy flesh. Torrin spread me wide and watched as I panted for air. He held my gaze and prevented me from looking away from his heated stare. My muscles clenched hungrily against him, causing his eyes to grow hooded with need. Gradually he withdrew his fingers but thrust them in further as I moaned, crying out at the multitude of sensations he created.

Torrin removed his hand from my body and lifted his fingers to his mouth, holding my stare while pushing them between his lips to suck them clean, one by one, making obscene sounds of pleasure as he tasted me.

What. The. *Fuck*. Was. *Happening?*

"When I ask you a question, I expect a fucking answer," Torrin growled, raking his ravenous gaze from mine to my aching flesh that wept from the loss of his fingers as he slowly slid them back inside. "The answer to my question is: Yes, Torrin, I'm so fucking wet for you."

I blinked and shook my head. Arousal coated my sex, unhidden from the heady stare that took in the mess he'd created. I swallowed down the urge to beg him to fuck me. I hadn't ever felt anything so primal or urgent in my life than I was feeling right now.

Torrin watched me through knowing eyes, and the cockiness of his smile pissed me off. He knew I was fighting against duty and need. Fighting a war within my mind to keep a vow I took or give in to the overwhelming need to be fucked stupid by him.

I needed his dominance. I craved it, and I fucking hated it, but I needed Torrin to claim me. I was so fucked up in the head. I glared at him, trembling with need.

He smiled wickedly, slapping his hand against my apex, and my eyes rolled back in my head. I arched my spine and parted my legs to show him what he'd done to me. Torrin clenched his teeth so hard that the sound of his back teeth grinding together caused the pulse between my thighs to throb painfully.

His dark chuckle vibrated against my breast as he lowered his head and clamped his teeth over my nipple, painfully scraping against the delicate flesh that his heated mouth seared. Holding my stare, he ran his tongue over the hardened tip, flicking against it as if it were my clit instead of my nipple.

Embarrassment rushed through me. My cheeks tinged red with mortification at how wet he'd made me. Torrin laughed ominously, lifting to stare at where arousal coated my sex. I couldn't hide my reaction to him, and that terrified me. I was always in control. I never felt helpless, ever. I had been trained to withstand anything the world could throw at me.

Dodge the darkness and live within the horrifying night? Fuck yeah, I excelled.

Slaughter hordes of monsters like they were toddlers in a day camp in line to suck a titty? Fuck yes. I excelled.

Face down death and laugh at it? Shit, yes. I had no fear of dying.

Face off against one dominant male who promised

me pain and pleasure? Nope. *Abort*. Get the fuck out!

"No," I snarled, coming up to a sitting position, and he smiling roguishly. "You have no right to kiss me!"

"I didn't ask you if I could kiss you," he snorted.

"You don't get to taste my pussy!" *Had I actually just screamed that?*

"I didn't fucking ask if I could do that either."

"I hate you!"

"Good." He smiled callously, even though his eyes were still banked with heat.

The mother-fucking dickhead *was smug*! He licked his lips, and my anger rocketed into high gear, knowing he tasted my arousal on them.

"Touch me again, and I'll fucking murder you, prick."

Torrin slammed me down against the bed without warning. He captured my arms captured above my head, and his face was in mine before I'd even finished inhaling my next breath. His lips twisted into a sardonic smile, and his eyes burned with the challenge. Pushing his erection against my belly, he watched me fight for air while he held it trapped in my lungs with the grip of his hand around my throat.

"Let's see you fucking do it, little girl. Come on, fight me." His tone was sex, anger, and silk. My body was the sin that wanted to indulge in his lust. "That's what I thought. You can hate me, Little Bird. You can blame me for your tight pussy reacting to pain and finding pleasure in it. Fuck, you can hate me all you fucking want because I fucking like it when you do. You won't threaten my life again, though. I take it personally when people threaten to end me. Do it again, and I'll make this pussy weep by spanking your perky ass that needs and begs to be painted red. Fucking try me, woman. You push me, and I'll push you back. I'm not one of the little bitches who couldn't dominate you enough to get you off. I am all man, and I fucking crave your pain. I'd be very careful when you challenge me, Lexia. Now, get your drenched pussy further onto the bed and go to sleep before I show you why it's wet and give it what it craves."

"I really don't like you."

"I really don't fucking care."

"You're a dick."

"You're a bitch," he chuckled.

I bristled beneath his heated stare, anger burning through me to tinge my ears pink. He noted it, smiling while his eyes dared me to say the wrong thing. Oh, hell, no! I turned over, starting up the bed, only to hear something cutting through the air as red-hot pain assaulted my ass. I moaned as his fingers rubbed my ass cheek. I turned to glare at Torrin with curses dancing on my tongue, but he wasn't there. I peered around the room, finding him nowhere to be seen.

What the fuck?

Chapter Seven

I awoke to something wet and hot clamped around my nipple, nibbling it playfully. My hips rocked against the fingers sliding through the arousal from the dream I'd just had. Two fingers pushed into my body, and I moaned as the tips stretched my opening. I shivered against them until dark laughter vibrated against my enlarged peak, and I blinked past the heaviness of sleep in my eyes. A thumb brushed over my swollen nub, and then my legs were spread wide. I curled my fingers through the thick, silken hair that lowered, pushing his heated breath to where I needed him the most.

Torrin's tongue slid through my sex, and a deep growl rumbled against my apex. He snapped while continuing to lap hungrily against my core, sending everything teetering toward the edge. I double-blinked slowly, lifting to watch as his tongue speared into my body, and an orgasm danced toward the precipice. Arousal glistened on his lips, coating his chin as he slowly climbed up my body.

"Tell me you don't want me, Little Bird." Torrin swallowed hard. "Tell me you don't want me deep inside this tight body."

The need and excitement coating his words made my body sing with the awareness of the male appendage resting on my belly. He rocked his hips, sliding his thick cock over my clit, which fired up all the dormant nerve endings until I whimpered huskily beneath him. My hands lifted, testing the muscles of his stomach, brushing my fingertips over the washboard abs that I wanted—no, craved to wash myself on. Was that a thing? It should have been.

Torrin inspected my face for an answer to his question. I smiled sleepily, rocking against his hardened cock. His fingers twisted my nipple, watching as my eyes grew hooded with need, and a whimpered gasp of desire exploded from my lungs with the pain he promised and offered.

"I don't want you," I whispered, reaching between us as he started to back up slowly.

I grabbed his cock, stroking the silken shaft while he hissed. Torrin released a violent shiver, his hands slowly exploring my tits. My thumb ran over the silken top, smearing his arousal over the rounded head. The woman and warrior inside me fought for who would be the victor of the battle waging within me. Torrin growled like a starving beast, staring into my soul, waging a silent confrontation with what my heart knew would win.

He hovered above me, holding his weight up with his hands pushing against the mattress, caging my body in beneath the wall of muscles. I watched his face, enjoying the tic in his cheek that hammered wildly from my touch. Torrin's heady stare made his eyes appear darker with unrestrained lust.

He didn't pull away from my touch, watching me unhurriedly rocking my hips while I held his rigid length against my clit. He was hugely endowed, much larger than I'd ever held or taken before. I couldn't close my fist around the width of his cock, which sent both excitement and fear pulsing through me. Torrin's muscles bunched tightly at his neck, clenching while I worked my hand faster, and I noted the way his shoulders braced and tightened while he studied my unguarded, dark soul.

Trembling, I lifted my mouth for his, needing to taste him. He didn't give me what I wanted. Instead, he held his mouth further away from mine, watching me chase his lips. Torrin pulled back, and I followed him up, pushing him over onto his back as he glared up at me.

"If I were you, I'd stop before you end up fucked, Lexia," he rumbled gutturally, causing a smirk to spread playfully over my lips. His voice was sex and lust, both dripping into my soul with a need to make him crawl through glass for the orgasm he craved.

"Lie back and shut up, Torrin," I ordered, watching the muscle in his jaw pulse at being given a command. In his position, I was betting no one had the balls to demand anything of this man. No one but me, and I was enjoying the darkness that entered his pretty frost-colored eyes from being ordered around.

Torrin opened his mouth to argue, but my head dropped, and I slid my tongue over the stiff length of the sensitive side of his shaft, stealing a sharp hiss from him. Peering up to hold his stare, I worked my tongue in small, calculated circles, daring him to tell me to stop. Smiling at him in victory, I sucked the sensitive side of his cock between my teeth, holding his hungry glare. I leaned over, pushing the curtain of my hair away from my face to kiss the hard, etched lines of his abdomen with my tongue. He tasted like a sin that I wanted to know, like a tattoo on my soul, so fucking deep that he'd always be there.

His languid eyes emboldened me, making me want to learn every hard line of his stomach. I nipped his skin, biting just hard enough to leave a red mark, and his eyes narrowed, growing hooded with the show of teeth I'd given him. My tongue slid over the skin I'd pinched between my teeth as my hand tightened on his length, moaning hungrily when I released the skin.

"You're about to end up fucking wrecked," Torrin snapped.

I sat up slowly, sliding my hand down my belly to tease my core before pushing my fingers into it while he watched. My gaze flicked to his mouth, watching him sucking his lips clean while I shivered at the intensity of his fiery glare. I then lifted my hand to his heated mouth that scorched my fingers while he sucked them slowly, working his tongue around them without lowering his eyes.

I lifted his cock, and licked around the tip methodically. Torrin sat back on his elbows, studying me through heavily hooded eyes, capturing his bottom lip between his teeth.

Taking him into my heated mouth, I wondered at my brazenness with him. Normally, I didn't shed my inhibitions, but this male made me want to be bold with him. I wanted to make him powerless while I took his control away. I needed to see him brought down a peg and rendered to nothing but raw, broken need from my actions.

"Suck me, woman," Torrin growled, watching me gradually working him deeper between my lips.

His voice had bordered on rage and excitement, yet it was controlled. His body tensed beneath my touch, which wasn't what normally happened. Men normally softened against attention, growing weaker while I kissed them or pleasured their body with my tongue. Torrin grew harder, more demanding while he studied my lips and my movements. He didn't bend or become weak against my care, never shedding control.

I slowly withdrew him from my mouth, watching the fire igniting in his eyes with a silent threat of violence. He didn't want me to stop, and I didn't plan to either. However, he wasn't in control at this moment. I was.

My nails slipped over the rigid length, and he growled softly in warning, his eyes slitting to angry lines. I tilted my head, kissing the pulse at the base of his thick erection. His hand moved, gripping his cock before stroking it slowly.

Torrin ran his erection against my cheek, the large tip glistening with arousal. My head tilted further, dragging my lips over the stiff length while my tongue traced the veins, hyperaware of how hard his cock throbbed with his need for release. The heat of his stare burned all of my emotions, leaving them in a pile of dust on the sheets.

I closed myself off, pushing Alexandria away and

bringing out Lexia, the mindless warrior who waged battles strategically. I moved onto my knees, kissing the thick tip before I took him to his base without warning. His sharp intake of breath and the gasp of disbelief that escaped his throat intensified my need to bring this gloriously dominant male to his knees at my feet. Slowly, I pulled up while he watched me through eyes that burned brighter than the moon ever could dream of shining.

Sucking him deeper into the tight confines of my throat, I swallowed around him while holding his stare. He groaned while pumping his hips slowly upward, holding my head where he wanted it with my hair. My lips created suction, and my other hand released his cock to grab his balls, applying pressure to the tightening skin that sat below his throbbing length.

"Gods damn, woman," he said raspily, his voice filled with gravel.

Torrin shed whatever control he'd held, pumping against my mouth while he used the tight shaft of my throat that cradled him like a sheath.

I was fearless. I sucked harder, licking his soft underside while he fucked my mouth mercilessly. His hand wrenched my hair, forcing me back onto my knees to reposition us until I was on all fours before him. He was on his knees, pushing against my lips, demanding entrance. He thrust into my throat until he was cradled deep within it. He clenched my chin as harsh fingers angled my face, demanding my eyes hold his pale, wintery stare.

"You look so pretty sucking my cock. Now fucking swallow me, woman," Torrin growled, taking control from me while he leaned over, pushing his thickened length further into my throat. His hand slid down my spine, cupping my ass cheek before he squeezed it hard, slapping against the cheek once, causing my eyes to roll up and meet his heated depths.

I moaned around the thickness buried deep in my throat. Torrin's touch seared my flesh, causing it to tingle with heightened awareness. His palm slapped my ass again, and I gasped around his cock, groaning with pleasure while he studied my reaction.

The offending hand rubbed slowly, giving the reddening skin some care after he'd punished it roughly. Again his hand lifted, slapping against my heated, aching flesh. Instead of being offended or reacting as a normal, sane person would, I grew crazed with the need to savage his cock with my throat. His eyes glowed with banked heat as the muscles in his stomach tightened, and my legs spread, giving him unobstructed access to my most private parts.

He watched me while his fingers slid over the globe of my tender ass and pushed through the slickness that coated my sex. I wasn't just wet for him; I was drenched. Slickness coated my inner thighs, and his fingers slid into my body, moving deep without warning. I cried out around him, staring into eyes that danced with the knowledge of how fucked up I really was.

"I want to make you come," he admitted, searching my eyes, finding the denial burning in them. "You want to come, don't you?" he growled raspily, adding another finger.

My body clenched, sucking him deeper with the need for more while neglected muscles burned from being stretched. His voice was filled with need, and it unraveled the tightening in my belly.

I started to back up, but Torrin shook his head, abandoning my pleasure to take his. His hands gripped my hair until my scalp burned, screaming with pain as he used it to guide himself deeper into my throat faster.

"Fuck, you're so fucking hot," he grunted, thrusting his hips while I sucked harder.

My hand moved, sliding between my thighs to find my core while he noted what I did. His body was coated in a fine sheen of sweat, every sinewy muscle rippling with his growing release. He tensed, which was the only warning of his impending orgasm as he thrust deeper than any male had before him.

I swallowed as he filled my throat, then shifted away from him. Turning onto my back, I pushed my fingers through my arousal-covered apex. Slowly, I moved them until an orgasm danced on the edge while Torrin watched me. I removed my hands and balled them into fists while turning onto my stomach with my ass in the air. I screamed into the blankets from the pain that denying my need caused my aching cunt. My entire body tightened, throbbing with the need to finish. Pain gripped my sex, clamping and constricting with the orgasm's denial.

I was a fire burning out of control that charred my sensitive flesh and scorched everything in its wake. Hot tears stung my eyes. My body clenched and unclenched with pent up need. I threw my head back, inhaling and exhaling slowly before moving from the bed, heading for the cold bath.

Torrin had watched something personal unfolding,

and I hadn't meant to take it that far. I hadn't expected my body to be that turned on from giving him pleasure. Not so much that I'd need to force it to the edge and then let the pain sink in to prevent it from becoming that throbbing need that pulsed for hours.

I slipped from the bed and into the icy cold water of the tub, washing my body that was bathed in sweat from being turned on by the sick shit he did to me.

"Get dressed," he ordered, and I nodded without turning to see where he was.

Instead, I slid beneath the watery surface, washing away the pain that the refusal caused within my core. Embarrassment rushed through me, and regret that I'd let him see that happen ripped through me. Worse, frustration that I'd thought I could take control from him. He was a freaking legendary warlord, and I'd thought my stupid ass held enough power to take his control? Get a grip—but without it being around his cock in my throat.

Slipping out of the bath, I grabbed the drying cloth while he held his back to me. I didn't feel shame for what I'd done. I'd felt powerful, and I'd found a weakness within him. He needed to unleash his anger, and I wasn't afraid of what he wanted to do with me. In fact, his dominance was the only thing I liked about him.

Dropping the cloth, I grabbed my panties, slowly slipping them on while giving him my back. My pants went on next, and I gradually released the breath I'd held. Cocking my head to the right, I listened to the silence in the room. Turning, I found Torrin right behind me, so close to where I stood that he could have grabbed me if he'd wanted to do so.

"Finish dressing, now," he growled, moving past me to grab his clothes.

I pulled on the skintight top that compressed my breasts, making my form unpleasing. I reached for the scabbards that normally adorned my hips to house my blade and then lifted my attention to the male, silently watching me.

"I want my blades back," I demanded, daring him to argue.

"If you think sucking me off makes us friends or allies, you're wrong. You don't get them back until I decide you can have them back," he grunted, glaring at me. His stare dipped to my tongue, darting out from between my lips, licking over the swollenness he'd created.

"You're a bastard. You know I'm basically your bitch because you have my brother, yet you still won't trust me. Scared I might best you and leave you nothing more than a corpse for the monsters of your bastard king's kingdom to feast upon?"

Torrin snorted, trudging toward me. The look sparkling in his eyes caused my heart to kick up, speeding rapidly until the thudding of it echoed in my head. He stopped in front of me, and I stepped back, turning to move away from him. I couldn't think with him close to me, like the moment he was near, all coherent thought was sucked out of my head and replaced with dark pleasure that had no right to be there or surging through my veins.

I made it less than a step away from Torrin before he gripped a handful of my hair, jerking my body against his. He walked me backward, forcing me up against the wall, searching my face before locking his gaze to mine.

"Get the fuck off me," I hissed coldly. "You have no right to touch me unless I say otherwise. Don't think me sucking you off gives you any control over me. I know your kind, and I don't care for them or you, one little fucking bit."

Torrin froze in place, dragging his eyes to my lips before lifting them to hold my stare prisoner. His nostrils flared as we stood silently glaring at one another. His hand lifted without warning, pushing against my throat while his mouth crushed against mine. He consumed me, fucking my mouth with his tongue without warning. A husky moan slipped from my lungs, only to be captured by his starving lips.

His tongue plunged, caressed, and speared into my mouth like he was using his cock instead of his tongue. Taking my breath away, he fed it back to me while his hand tightened against my throat, forcing the air to dry up. His knee pushed against my apex, and I whimpered with what little breath he'd left me. My hands rose to his chest, and he pulled back, capturing them with one hand in a hard grip above my head.

Wintery eyes held mine, and he smiled cruelly. "You suck good dick, bitch. I didn't assume it changed anything between us, other than you allowing me to use your needy throat to plunge my cock into," he laughed icily, brushing his nose against the shell of my ear. "You don't know me or my kind. I'm the monster who enjoys making pretty girls scream and cry while they writhe in pain beneath me as I fucking devour their souls. You fight me, and it turns me on. Thank you for sucking cock like the good, dirty little bitch you are. Don't assume that it changes shit between us. You're my captive; I'm the one in charge. For the record, the only control you will ever have over me will be the control I allow you to *think* you have at that moment. Like when you sucked me off. You held no power, Lexia. You just thought you did because I allowed you to think it was possible. It isn't," he uttered, scorching my earlobe with his heated breath. His teeth nipped at it, tugging it before he moved his head to run his nose against my cheek.

My chest rose and fell with anger. I wanted two things to happen. I wanted this prick to suffer before he left this world, and I wanted him to fucking own me inside and out, leaving me dominated in a broken pile of need that would never be completely whole again.

"Now, do as you're told, so I don't have to punish you." Torrin brushed his lips against mine, sinking his teeth into my bottom lip, playing with it teasingly while running his tongue over the swollen tissue.

Releasing it, he stepped back all at once, which I hadn't expected. My knees gave out, and I slid to the floor at his feet, staring up at him through defiant eyes that imagined him pitted and roasting over an open flame.

"Finish getting ready. I'd get off your fucking knees. You look entirely too perfect on them. You're making my dick hard, bitch." He turned on his heel, moving toward the bed once more.

I stood without warning, moving toward him. He turned on me when I reached him. My foot rose rapidly, slamming into his groin before he could foresee the move. The moment he doubled over in pain, I lifted my knee, pegging him in the nose.

"You suck my dick, bitch," I hissed, seething with anger that fueled my rage.

I turned, rushing toward the door, but he grabbed me by my waist, tossing me across the room to bounce on the bed. Landing in a haphazard heap in the middle of it, I fought to regain air into my lungs. I gasped as he stalked toward me with anger, his muscles bunching with excitement at the idea of hurting me.

His hands clenched and released as he pounced, capturing me before I'd recovered from being onto the bed. I struggled against him, witnessing the intensity of his eyes as he hovered over me, shaking in anger. He pushed his hand on my throat and held me trapped against the bed with his viselike grip holding my wrists and the other holding my oxygen hostage.

"You are going to regret that, woman," he snapped coldly.

Torrin picked me up and placed me over his knees. One hand jerked my pants down seconds before the other landed on my ass violently. Shock echoed through my mind, and I screamed out while he spanked me painfully. I dug my nails into his leg, and he laughed darkly, still slamming his open palm against my ass. Moaning, I slowed my struggles as pleasure from his rough treatment registered. His hand paused while my ass lifted for the next strike, and my spine arched for him to land it against the red flesh of my ass. Fingers danced over the sore tissue, running slowly against the tingling skin that stung.

"Hurt me again in anger, and I'll do more than paint your pretty ass red, you naughty little bitch. I enjoy your fight, but I'm not into pain. I'm into giving it and listening to pretty birds sing for more," he growled, sliding his fingers through my clenching sex. I was more than turned on, which made me insane and unhinged, I was certain of it. "And you sing so pretty for me. Gods damn, you're drenched." He released me, pushing me off his lap onto the floor, smiling coldly as he peered down at me.

I turned toward him, fully intending to attack once more, but the sight of him cleaning my arousal from his fingers stopped me cold. It kindled a fire deep within me that rolled up to my nipples, pebbling them while it wrapped around them, sliding back down to flick across my clit until I shuddered. He smiled wickedly, watching my eyes growing hooded at the action. I could make out the hard muscle of his cock as he hissed, lowering his stare to where my thighs were slick with my heat.

He stood slowly, smiling as he made a sound like he'd tasted the rarest delicacy in the world. Hunching down, he pushed my wet hair behind my ear and sucked his lip between his teeth before releasing it.

"Fight it all you like, but you're just like me. You're a dark, twisted, sadistic bitch, and you enjoy me rough handling you. Lie to yourself if it helps you sleep at night, but your sex is soaked for me because it knows what I can give it. It wants what I can do, and so do you. You're not a good girl. You're a naughty one that craves someone who can bring you to your knees and break the thread of that fucking control you are forced to endure, day in and day out. It doesn't make you weak. It makes you strong. Which is exactly why you've never met anyone stronger than you who could take your control and force you to submit," he said huskily. Torrin grabbed my hair, but he didn't pull it. Instead, he pushed it away from my face, tucking it behind my ear before he placed a soft kiss on my forehead. "Come, they're waiting for us so we can head out before the storm reaches our location."

He'd spanked me, punishing me before his touch had gentled. It confused me, leaving me pissed off and turned on. I wasn't even sure what the hell had just happened other than he'd called me out, and he'd summed me up so hard that he'd reached in and withdrawn the truth from my soul.

No one had ever left me speechless or confused. No one had ever turned me on like Torrin had while pissing me off. I was either on the edge of moon sickness or losing my shit. One or the other had to be happening here.

"Come on, fix your pants, or I will," he demanded, lifting a brow while I just continued staring at him like he'd grown another head.

"I don't enjoy being hurt," I snapped because I wasn't certain what else to say. I felt like I had to argue that point. Right? I mean, shouldn't I be pissed that he'd spanked me and made me wet? It seemed oxymoronic, as though it shouldn't happen together.

"Fine," he chuckled while collecting his things without listening to my words.

"I don't," I argued obtusely, lifting onto my knees to fix my pants, finding my inner thighs drenched with arousal. Torrin's eyes latched onto the moisture, his gaze slowly rising to lock with mine. A sinful smile curved his delicious lips, and I rolled my eyes, standing to pull up my pants. "My vagina was trying to vomit at what you did to me."

What?

His lips twitched before he grabbed his pack, turning to look at me. "It must have been really sick to be *that* wet."

"Horridly so." I swallowed past the horrification over my word-vomit happening.

I followed him out of the inn, pulling the cloak I wore tightly around my body to hide the embarrassment that burned hotly, singeing my cheeks red. The others had saddled the horses and were waiting for us as we emerged from the doorway.

"I thought we'd need to send a search team in to retrieve you, two lovers," Zane stated, narrowing his eyes on me, hidden within the heavy cloak.

"I was getting my cock sucked by the lips of an angel with the enthusiasm of a demon."

I choked on air, turning to glare at him over my shoulder. Amo and Tabitha snorted, patting me on the back before Amo chuckled.

"That wasn't the kitty you were supposed to get the cream into, Lexia." She laughed, silencing it the moment I turned angry eyes on her. She lifted her hands into the air in mock surrender and shook her head. "I'm not judging. Not at all. You want to suck that dick, then you suck it really good!" she offered while the others laughed silently.

"Get mounted," I muttered.

"That's what you should do," Tabitha chortled.

"You're with me, Lexia," Torrin growled, causing the women to turn and look at him. Amo sighed dreamily as her owl, Scout, landed on her shoulder. Meanwhile, Tabitha reached out, patting Torrin's cock.

"Good boy, now aim lower so that her kitty gets some cream too," she stated, smiling up at Torrin, even though he'd leveled a chilling look at her that would have sent grown men running.

"Now, woman," he snapped, grabbing my arm to pull me with him while the others stared.

Chapter Eight

The Badlands were dried, dead vegetation and patches of swampland that spread between the mountain ranges. I'd gotten lost in my mind as worry for Landon and what Torrin had done to me, warred with my conscience and self-preservation. I didn't even know Torrin, yet I'd been brazenly wanton with him. It was so far out of my comfort zone that I might as well have been someone else.

Torrin growled, and neighing started beside me. It pulled me from my thoughts, and I turned to stare at where Chivalry had nipped the male sitting behind me on his leg. He tossed his white mane into the air, prancing beside us while snorting.

"What the fuck is his problem?" Torrin demanded crossly. Sliding his arm around me, he bared his teeth at my horse. His sneered growl and grip around my waist caused Chivalry to lower his head again, snapping his teeth toward Torrin.

"He doesn't like other men touching me. He also isn't impressed that I'm riding with you instead of him," I muttered, leaning over to nuzzle my irate, insanely-protective mount. "You're still the only boy I want to ride," I cooed, and he tossed his head, nodding as if he understood every word I spoke. "That's my guy, Chivalry."

"You named him Chivalry?" Torrin continued, and I rolled my eyes, even though he couldn't see the gesture. His arm pulled me back, and he chuckled against my ear. "Considering what you enjoy, I don't think he's the one you want to mount, little girl."

"Neither are you," I replied, resting back against him to search the area we traveled with curiosity.

I hated the Badlands. The dead vegetation reeked, and the swamp released poisonous gasses that smelled like rotting eggs mixing with death. We'd stopped long enough to cover our mouths to avoid vomiting. Even the warlord and his men had wrapped scented clothes around their nose and mouth to prevent inhaling the Badlands' toxic scent.

Massive cliffs marked each side of the flat land we traveled across. There were no trees to hide behind, nor bushes to relieve the need of my bladder. I could hear water rushing somewhere, which added to my urgency to ease my body's needs.

I squirmed on the horse, adjusting myself against the man behind me. Torrin loosened his hold, turning to look over his shoulder. I felt him tense, and the moment he faced forward, he issued orders in their language and kicked his horse into a dead run.

"Hold on, Little Bird," he warned, pushing his warhorse hard.

I didn't bother turning to see if Chivalry kept up, knowing he would sense the danger and follow me to my grave if the need arose. I'd raised him from a foal, training with him for years to make certain he was ready for the world we would enter together. I'd weaned him from his mother, raised him for battle, and he'd follow me to my death to protect me.

I stared out over the land for anywhere to take cover. Slitting my gaze, I took in the nothingness before turning, peeking back to watch as ghastly women flew toward us. Their mouths were hanging open, taking air into their lungs to screech and wailing their screams. I spun in the saddle, staring toward the haze that we rushed toward, and frowned. A thick mist was forming in front of us, which generally signaled other creatures created from the darkness were near.

"Where the hell are you running toward?" I demanded worriedly, furrowing my brow. No sooner had I asked him than we leaped and lunged blindly toward the sound of rushing water hidden within the mist.

I sucked in air moments before shockingly cold water bit my flesh. Horses and men followed us into the water blindly. The raging water rushed us downstream, fighting to take us beneath the rapids. I kicked against the current, barely treading water through the icy chunks that flowed around us, trying to remain above the surface. My body was spun, and something slammed into my head, sending violet lights blinking into my vision.

The water sucked me down even though I kicked, fighting the current to get my head above the icy grasp that tightened around me. Something moved toward me beneath the surface, and I screamed, wincing in pain as a horse's hoof met my head, causing a heaviness to take hold.

I sank weightlessly, unable to stay afloat or swim anymore. I watched a dark blur coming toward me, and wintery eyes held mine. Torrin's arm wrapped around my waist securely as he pulled me toward the surface of the water, powerful thrusts of his legs against the water shot us upward.

We breached the surface, and I coughed violently, throwing up water. Torrin turned me in his arms, forcing my back against his chest while he took us toward the shore on the opposite side. He made the swim look easy, pulling me out of the water like a drowned fish to drop me on the river's bank. I turned over, throwing up as my stomach rebelled.

My attention moved around the crowd, counting feminine forms that also were tossing their guts up. My eyes swung back to the river we'd escaped, and I frowned at the black, oily water filled with darkness.

"You fucking dunked us into poison?" I hissed accusingly.

"It was better than being sucked to death by evil bitches who feed on your fucking soul, wasn't it?"

"I could have died!"

"But did you?" he shouted, and I blinked slowly, glaring at him.

My head whipped around at the sound of horses in distress. Chivalry was barely above the water, fighting to stay afloat. I jumped to my feet, rushing toward where he went under the surface. I didn't hesitate at the shoreline, leaping into the icy, poisonous water to get him out. I kicked my legs, grabbing his mane as someone else broke through the water, wrapping arms around Chivalry to pull him up.

We broke the surface together, Torrin holding Chivalry, whose eyes were rolling wildly as he made panicked sounds of distress. Once we were on the shore again, I patted him down, gasping for air as the water's oily substance clung to me. Men surrounded us, speaking to Torrin in their foreign language while I rubbed feeling back into Chivalry.

"They'll take him to rest with the other horses," Torrin announced, yanking me with him to where his men were building a fire and setting up tents.

I sat on a log beside Amo, who turned wide, terror-filled eyes toward me. Her long, caramel-colored hair was stuck to her body in clumps, and her vivid green eyes had grown pale with the chill. We all shook violently, which I wasn't convinced was only from the icy plunge we'd taken. It was more likely the poison was sinking in through our flesh, inducing sickness.

We sat beside the small fire, unable to stop the trembling that was becoming more like convulsions as they finished the tents' preparations and rolled out bedrolls. Everyone was soaked, and the longer we sat around, the worse the chill grew.

My attention moved to the opposite side of the bank, focusing on the wavering figures that paced the ground, unwilling to enter the water. It wasn't because they couldn't swim, because those evil whores could fly.

So what prevented them from coming across?

"That's interesting," I said through chattering teeth.

"Yes, it's almost as if they fear whatever is within the water," Amo pointed out. "I for once agree with them; this sucks."

We watched in silence as one banshee got close to the water's edge, and something reached up and sucked her below the surface. I blinked slowly, sliding my eyes to Torrin, who glared at me with a cocky smile playing on his lips. I shivered violently, slowly meeting Amo's and Tabitha's horrified, wide eyes.

Creepers had been within the water, which meant Torrin and his men were somehow immune to their notice, or we'd all be dead right now. Either that or the creepers were afraid of the men and had scattered the moment we'd entered the murky depths.

Worse than that, it meant we couldn't escape through the water alone. My lips pursed together tightly as I took in the scene. Slowly, I turned back to where the banshees had all slunk away from the edge, hissing and spitting as the slimy creatures that lived in the swamps of the Badlands crawled over the bank, sputtering and gasping while hunting their next meal.

The creepers reached the ghastly figures that let out ear-piercing screams, doing little to dispel their attackers. Creepers were immune to banshee screams, having no ears to hear their shrieks of terror that froze their victims in place while fear rushed through them. Banshees could also foretell death, but these were no longer among the living that had the ability.

A hand touched my shoulder, and I jumped, staring

up at Torrin while my chest rose and fell from being startled. He smiled softly, his eyes heating while they slid to the outfit that hugged me like a second layer of skin from being soaked. My cloak had been swept downstream, which meant it was going to be a very chilly ride for the duration of the trip.

Turning toward Amo, my second-in-command, I clucked my tongue twice, and she nodded while I got to my feet. My focus returned to Torrin, who narrowed his eyes on me before looking down at where Amo studied him.

"The fire is to ward off the creepers, but it won't do much to dispel the chill. I suggest you all find someone to bed down with tonight," Torrin announced in a clipped tone, nodding toward the furthest tent. "You're with me, Moonflower."

My eyes darted back to Amo and the others, nodding with the orders I'd just given. Once we were inside the tent, I studied the fur bedroll. One bed, again. Frowning, I crumpled my brow while Torrin moved to his pack, pulling out a jug of whiskey. He placed two pewter cups onto the ground before he filled them full of the amber liquid.

"Drink and then get out of your wet clothes before the poison sinks further into your flesh. You're going to need to drink this too." He grunted, holding out a vial that had shimmering liquid in it. "You drank half the fucking river before I pulled you out."

"What is it?" I questioned, and he canted his head to the side, glowering at me.

"It's a tonic that expels the toxins through your skin.

You'll more than likely sweat it out, but this will ensure that nothing remains in your system to cause you issues. I don't have time to deal with a sickly woman while we move deeper into the Darklands."

Torrin stood, handing me the vial before he started removing his clothing. My eyes slid over the bronzed flesh as I pulled the stopper from the vial. Sniffing it, I recoiled from the pungent scent while turning up my lip. I groaned, scrunching up my nose before I placed it against my lips, taking a drink. I gagged and was grateful when Torrin handed me the whiskey. I gulped it down, frowning when I noticed he had stripped down to nothing.

"I have to pee," I exclaimed.

He grunted softly, shaking his dark head before his eyes lifted to lock with mine. He grabbed a pair of lounge pants that hugged his powerful thighs tightly and nodded at the flap. I followed him to the far side of camp, where dead logs covered the ground.

I waited for him to turn around and away from me, and he smirked. "I've seen you naked, woman." His arms crossed over his chest like he intended to continue watching me.

"So you have, but it's the gentlemanly thing to do, turning around for a woman to relieve her needs in private." I watched the challenge burning in his eyes before he allowed my request, giving me his back.

I squatted, quickly relieving my bladder that had been complaining for hours. Rising, I pulled my pants up and started toward Torrin, only to stop dead in my tracks. Chills raced up my spine, and my body stilled completely.

Torrin still faced away from me, not feeling the danger near to us. Tears gathered in my eyes, and everything within me screamed. My blood chilled to ice, and my heartbeat pounded in my ears as mist covered my skin, immediately freezing where it gathered. My eyes no longer blinked, and my hair hardened with the icy grasp of death.

"Bloody hell, woman," Torrin snapped, turning to look at me where I was slowly freezing to death. "Wraiths," he whispered, clucking his tongue loudly while his eyes slid over my shoulders, and he launched himself at me.

He took me to the ground, hard. My body rebelled from the pain his heat created against my frozen flesh. His mouth brushed against mine while he peered into my eyes, which continued to freeze. I was going to freeze to death! I couldn't even scream or speak with the ice that filled my throat while my lips turned blue.

I could hear the feet and blades that drug across the ground as the dead moved toward us. Wraiths were one of the few creatures we couldn't stand against to protect ourselves. They were newly dead beings, killed by nightwalkers, and raised from their graves by dark magic to hunt the living. They spread ice through the air in the form of a fine mist that clings to the skin of their victims. The wraiths freeze their prey in place, easily reaching them during their painfully slow death march, unhindered by their sightless eyes.

Their inhuman moans and howls filled the air while hundreds of feet barely lifted while they made their way toward our camp, driven by their sense of smell and our living scent.

Torrin covered every inch of me with his body. His hand lifted, enveloping my mouth, and I realized I was moaning softly. My consciousness was slipping, fading to nothing as my blood thickened to frozen sludge in my veins. Torrin's eyes filled with worry, and his dark head lifted before he pulled me up with him, rushing toward the tent.

The moment we entered, he stripped me down to my skin, shucking his lounge pants to fold us into the blankets. His enormous hands rubbed my body down as he studied my face with worry burning in his eyes. I whispered no words as the hissing of the monsters outside the tent grew closer to us. His hands warmed me, rubbing life back into my body.

It wasn't enough. My eyes wouldn't close, which meant I was going to die, staring at the hottest man I'd ever encountered. I wanted to laugh hysterically at the irony of it, knowing that upon death, I'd embarrass myself as all bodily fluids released. Thank the gods I'd just peed.

Torrin's mouth lowered to mine, claiming it even though I wasn't kissing him back. His fingers slid through my sex, and I almost groaned, but the air wasn't filling my lungs. He pushed into my sex, and I blinked, frowning as my body started pumping blood while pleasure rushed through me. His eyes smiled, and I blinked past the icy layer that had grown over my mine.

"Breathe for me," he whispered so softly that I wasn't sure I hadn't imagined the words. He stretched my body, and I arched, while his other hand lifted my head for him to claim my mouth in a hungry kiss.

Screaming sounded from outside, and he paused, lifting his head toward the tent flap. A single tear escaped me as a bright light burst through camp. Torrin's eyes met mine, and I closed them against the grief as one of the moon-touched succumbed to death.

The sound of slurping and snarling exploded, and Torrin pulled me against his chest, drawing the blankets over our heads to hide our body heat from the predators. His fingers withdrew, and his lips brushed against my cheek. I took solace in his embrace, allowing his warmth to lull me to sleep.

I knew that when I woke in the morning, I'd collect a pile of moonstones. A single pile of rocks is all that's left when we die. They are useful in dispelling the darkness from reaching toward the moon-touched tower and village.

Torrin continued touching me, running his hand over my arm to dispel the chill of the dead. His body against mine was like a fire, burning my skin until it itched from thawing.

"Sleep. You're safe now," he whispered into my ear.

Chapter Nine

By morning, the storm trailing us had finally caught up. Stepping from the tent with a heavy heart, I watched the others as they did the same, escaping the hold of the men to see who we'd lost during the night. We all flicked our gazes over each other with uneasiness and worry. My throat constricted, and my chest tightened while I counted heads, searching faces, and then paused.

"What the hell?" Amo asked, her green eyes searching the faces once more while her finger counted those present.

"Everyone is here and alive," I muttered, sliding my attention around the camp until a small pile of moonstones caught my eye. I moved toward it, crouching to run my fingers over the smooth surface of a stone. "They are small, so this is from someone younger than us."

"That makes little sense," Tabitha grunted, scratching the back of her head while smothering a yawn.

From the look of her hair and disheveled clothing, it was apparent she'd spent most of the night in the throes of passion. Sometimes I seriously hated myself for the vow I'd taken, but I owed the girls I lost at least that much. I'd messed up. I'd lowered my guard and had focused on my needs instead of those who depended on me to keep my head straight and on the mission.

I picked up the stones, holding them to my nose before the frown deepened as pale eyes locked with mine. Sliding my attention to something safer, I shook my head.

"No idea who it was or why they would be this close to us. They were within the Darklands, which means someone sent them," I stated, and Amo pursed her swollen lips.

I scanned my team of women and rolled my eyes as a groan expelled from my lips. I was the only one who hadn't succumbed to the debauchery of my baser needs. Holding out my hand, I offered the moonstones to the obscenely virile male who had saved my biscuit last night. He accepted the stones, holding them in his hand.

"You're right. They were young, and probably unclaimed by the Order of the Moon," he rumbled huskily. "Most likely on the brink of puberty, judging by the lack of stones left in death."

Stones.

Left.

It pissed me off that even in death, we would still be left to work for the Order, not that I'd ever audibly complained about it. No, because that would be considered treason, and they would execute my entire team.

"So, last night," Amo started, and I blinked at her, shaking my head.

"I don't want to know that you all got laid and that my kitty didn't get creamed."

"Well, I mean, that wasn't where I was going with it, but you're close enough to the time where you could forgive yourself, asshole."

I peered up into pale green eyes and nodded. "I could, but I owe them the entire four years," I argued.

"You didn't even like Sarah. She was a total weak link and a bitch to boot," Tabitha returned, and I moved my attention to Torrin, who noted every word.

"I took a vow of punishment. I intend to honor it no matter how much my kitty wants his cream," I stated, realizing my error the moment it had slipped from my tongue. "Whoever *he* may be when I finally release myself from the oath."

"There are more stones further from camp," a warrior stated, striding toward us, his midnight-blue eyes lifting to mine, then sliding to Torrin's with unease. "There are several piles of them, unfortunately. I'm guessing the wraiths fed gluttonously last night, which means they should be sated for now."

"How is that possible?" I countered, watching the men's faces shut down all emotion. "Nothing? Just going to let us assume the worst?" I asked, watching the anger sizzling in Torrin's stare.

I shouldered past him, moving toward the horses while my team stood around watching me. Once I reached Chivalry, I nuzzled his neck, brushing my hands against his flank while he neighed loudly, tossing his mane around. He offered comfort from the turmoil in my mind.

Why would there be moon-touched people here? And why would they be stupid enough to be out in the darkness as the moon rose? The day was iffy enough for the moon-touched people, but add in the darkness of night, and you could count on the monsters unleashing to feed.

That's what happened in the Badlands. It was why the moon-touched stayed far away from this place. Not to mention, we'd been banned from entering it. Sure, we were still close enough to the border that the moon-touched could have slipped in and lived among the cliffs, but they would have had no chance of remaining alive if they'd lingered here that long.

I felt Torrin behind me but ignored him as he saddled his horse. I bristled, not being able to understand what had befallen the others. I knew wraiths had consumed them, but why were they here, and had they followed us? Had the Order of the Moon sent someone to spy on us to ensure we finished our mission? It was possible. It would be stupid on their part, especially without warning us first.

"I need to go figure out why other moon-touched were here last night." I turned to find Torrin inches away from me.

"No, you don't," he argued, handing me his cloak. "Put this on and cover up your fucking hair."

"Why?"

"Because I fucking said to put it on, woman," he demanded, daring me to challenge him.

"Put it on your fucking self, asshole," I muttered, turning back to Chivalry.

Torrin grabbed me from behind, yanked my arms behind my back, and shoved me against his horse's flank. I yelped as he held me there, sliding his mouth across the back of my neck as he whispered.

"If you want to be rough-handled by pissing me off, it's one thing…" Torrin growled, and neighing sounded behind us. I turned, watching him shake his arm violently to remove Chivalry's teeth from his forearm. Smiling at his anger, I winked at my horse before concealing it as Torrin turned back toward me.

I clucked my tongue, and Chivalry released Torrin, his anger palpable in the air. He crackled with it, and yet he didn't strike my horse. Instead, his hand lowered, pinching my ass, and I gasped and ground my teeth together.

"You need to get your fucking horse under control," Torrin seethed, his teeth skimming against my throat. "He's as wild and unpredictable as his rider."

"He better be; I trained him myself," I muttered. "You done yet? I'm getting a little more horse than I want, and mine is probably about to attack yours for having his scent on me."

"Put this cloak on, now. You don't want to be visible when we pass the nightwalkers or the others that will fight to suck that light from the marrow of your worthless bones. I never agreed to protect you. The choice is yours," Torrin snapped, tossing his heavy cloak toward me.

I turned, staring at the others who waited to see what I did. They wore their cloaks. Mine was the only one lost to the river's rushing current. I pushed my arms through the sleeves to pull it up over my hair.

Torrin watched me in silence, but there was something ravenous in his stare. He pulled me closer by his cloak, pushing my hair into the hood before he leaned over, dragging his lips over mine while everyone watched. I moaned, then slapped his cheek in embarrassment as the girls groaned.

"This is why her kitty never gets fed. She's never getting laid like this," Amo grunted, and the others agreed, much to my chagrin.

"One day, someone is going to make it scream, and she's going to end up tying him to a bed and never letting him up from it," Tabitha snorted, scowling.

I blushed, hating the heat that burned my face while they talked about my pathetic, obsolete love life. Even before I'd taken the vow, it'd lacked fire and everything else. I'd always been the last one to end up with whatever male they'd left free for the night. Amo said it was my resting bitch face, that it made me unapproachable. Tabitha said it was the angry vibes I gave out, and that I was defensive about who I let get close to me.

I was thin and lacked the luscious curves that men craved. I wasn't outgoing and didn't enjoy being boisterous like the others. I was always on guard because if I wasn't, people died. My demeanor was shielded, having never met someone who hadn't wanted something from me. My eyes were almost always narrowing on people while I determined if they were friend or foe. I simply didn't have the inner beauty others held. They were light, and I bordered on the shadows.

I waited for Torrin to give the order to mount, but he didn't. Instead, he lifted me without warning onto his horse. I grasped for the mane, frowning when he mounted behind me. The sky rumbled, and we both looked up as rain began falling.

Torrin's deep exhale told me he wasn't looking forward to riding without the heavy cloak to guard against the elements. I turned, unclasping and removing the cloak, then handing it to him. Grunting, he accepted it, wrapping it around him and me while he pulled me back against his body, which dwarfed mine, enveloping me in his warmth.

"We will ride until we reach the Darklands," he said against my ear, causing me to shiver from the heated breath that fanned the shell of my ear. "If you grow chilled, let me know."

"You're very hot," I stated and felt his lips curling into a smile against my ear. "You know what I meant," I amended as the horse started forward, and his arm tightened to hold me.

"You burn hot too, Moonflower," he whispered thickly, and I swallowed.

I let my body relax against him, listening to the world around us while we traveled. I was further south than I'd ever been. The passing countryside, while barren, was eerily beautiful.

The rain pelted down on us, drenching us through the cloak until we were both miserable from the chilled air. Hours moved by, and the countryside turned from barren land to rolling hillsides. Large waterfalls crashed over the cliffs, filling huge glowing pools of water that exposed light from the earth below it.

The deeper we went into the Darklands, the lighter it became. The landscape was strangely changing, and I hadn't expected it to be pretty. I turned as something flew above us, and my eyes widened as a large, colorful bird squealed loudly, dropping from the sky to fly beside us. Chivalry reared back, bucking in warning, but the bird ignored him, landing on his back.

Torrin clicked his tongue and held out his hand as the large bird leaped from Chivalry's back to Torrin's arm, where I noticed the vanguard where the bird could perch. Torrin's arm released me to unroll a length of leather parchment from the bird's leg. My eyes scanned the message.

Stop playing with your cock and get back here. Your newest conquest is driving me crazy with her need to be ravished all night long. I think she prefers the pain to the pleasure, asshole. You wanted this courtesan; get your dick back here to satisfy the needy bitch. ~Signed, Your not so happy, King. P.S. Don't hit that moon-pie pussy without me, asshole.

Torrin snorted, crumpling the message up before he reached into the saddlebag and then leaned forward. My eyes studied the bird before dropping to his reply.

Keep her there and try spanking her. She purrs when you make her ass red. Karina also adores being taken from behind, hard and fast. Pull her hair, asshole. She's there for a reason. You're going to like Alexandria. She's wild and sucks a mean cock. ~Signed, Went to get the bitches you sent me to get, asshole.

I swallowed past the anger burning in my throat. Torrin was rumored to be over five hundred years old, yet he replied to the king like a tavern boy trying to land free pussy for the night. He rolled the scrap of leather up and secured it to the bird's leg, lifting his arm as it took flight. It flapped large, colorful wings to gain altitude before it shot through the sky above us. He pulled me back, and I allowed it, pretending not to know what he'd just written. Most people didn't know the Night King's ancient language, but I'd been taught several languages for my position.

Torrin had purposely been using it to exclude us from their plans, but I'd understood every word he'd said, every order he'd given his men. I'd been privy to everything they'd discussed without him ever knowing. I could play dumb for as long as I needed since it helped me learn their plan without playing my hand.

The lights of a town came into view, and I exhaled. I was more than ready to unfold from the horse and stretch out my aching limbs. Plus, we were all drenched from the constant rainfall that didn't seem to let up anytime soon.

"We'll stop for the night here," Torrin announced in a language I could understand, turning to one man, who moved in beside him. "Go check out the inn. Make sure none of the nightwalkers are visible. If they are, send them away under the king's orders. Anyone else within the tavern needs to be aware to hold their tongues in the presence of our current company."

I did a double blink, turning toward one of the men, who observed me. His lips pulled back from his gums, and serrated teeth became visible before he nodded to

Torrin, heading off to do as he'd been ordered. My heart slowed, and I used my senses to scour the town as far as my sight would reach.

Within the shadows were several nightwalkers, who were moon-touched creatures that had turned to the darkness, allowing it to slither into their souls, expelling the light. Bloody hell. They were ravenous beings, starving for the light they'd once held and given up. Torrin was walking us in like dinner to a starving village of turned beings.

Chapter Ten

The inn was clean, with creatures that seemed normal, or as close to it as you could expect this deep into their territory. This one didn't have people itching to touch us, but then Torrin and his men weren't allowing them anywhere near us, either. Ale was brought to the table by his men the moment we'd taken our seats. A boisterous singer with a stringed instrument was singing a lusty tune as she flirted shamelessly with the men. Peering into the shadows, I studied a few of the patrons watching us with hunger burning within their gazes.

Nightwalkers.

I shivered, dispelling the chill that clung to my skin while I sipped the ale. A barmaid had shown me to a room with Torrin, where he'd allowed me to change. He thought, by standing watch over me, it would prevent me from escaping him. My dress was short, but then I hadn't had time to wash the lightweight leggings I usually wore. I'd asked Torrin for soap and water, only to be told that

I could do my laundry once we reached the palace in the next few days.

My bare legs seemed to have gone unnoticed as the rest of my team appeared in matching outfits. Torrin pushed me into the corner of the table against the wall, and my girls piled in around me. He tapped his fingers on the table as some men bowed at the waist, holding a hand out for the girls to join them in a dance.

I smiled, watching Amo bypass one warrior for another who had a darker complexion and was covered in tattoos and markings. His emerald eyes slid over her with a hunger he didn't bother to hide. Silently, I watched as they began dancing to the song. Others joined them until only Torrin, and I remained at the table. I'd had four cups of ale before Amo returned to the table, holding out her hand for me.

I looked at Torrin, and before he could protest, Amo yanked me from the table and pulled me onto the dance floor with her. Her arms wrapped around me, and I stiffened, laughing as she slowly kissed my ear.

"I'm not hitting on you, promise. However, I'll get your kitty going if it means finally being able to talk without ears hearing us," she chuckled, causing my eyes to sparkle with mirth. "There are nightwalkers everywhere, and I am pretty sure that the warrior who spent three hours eating my pussy last night was one of them."

"The entire town is filled with them, too," I muttered, resting my chin on her shoulder, and my eyes locked with Torrin's as he watched us through a narrowing glare. "They have Landon, which means we have to continue to play along until we can either determine his location or get eyes on him. I also saw the Book of the Dead in Torrin's memory, which means they may know where the Sacred Library is hidden."

A warrior pressed against my back while another slid his arms around Amo. I turned, and the violet gaze that held mine took my breath away. He spun me around without warning as the music changed, becoming a fast, frenzied song that had him moving us around to the sexy beat. His body was hard lines of sinewy muscle, and his scent was exotic.

"I'm Roland, woman," he said huskily.

"I'm Lexia, not *woman*," I returned, allowing him to spin us around the dance floor before his hand left mine, forcing my knee to bend as he brought it up against his hip. He dipped me back slowly while his hand slid over my exposed thigh.

"It's nice to get you away from my captain, finally. You seem unfazed by his attempts to seduce you," Roland continued, righting me as he watched my face for any signs that he might have entranced me.

"I don't think anyone could be unfazed by Torrin, ever," I grunted, pushing Roland away from me as the song ended. "If you'll excuse me, my girls are about to let loose, and I intend to do the same."

I joined the girls, danced to the song's beat as it ramped up in tempo to a jig, one we had danced to a million times before. I settled between them, moving my feet while they followed my lead. We danced until the song ended, and then a new one began, a slower, sultrier song that had us swaying our bodies seductively, making our blood heat with need.

I searched for Torrin, finding him studying how my body moved to the stringed instruments that lured us in, holding us prisoner. The song flowed through us like lava pouring from a mountain peak. I slid my hands down my body, watching as heat pooled in his icy stare, sending more warmth to my core with the look of hunger burning in his.

I smiled impishly, knowing that my moves were igniting a fervor within him that burned violently. Lifting my hands back up my body, I closed my eyes, spinning to the beat while I pushed my fingers through my hair, remembering how Torrin's hand felt in it. A throbbing pain started in my belly, pulsing with the need that had remained dormant until he'd made my body come to life with his touch.

Celibacy hadn't been harsh or as bad as I'd thought it would be at first. Also, there was a sense of freedom that came without needing to drink the moon berries that prevented life from taking root in my womb.

It also kept me from enduring the pain they created, once swallowed. It had actually been easy since I hadn't had an issue ignoring men, not until I'd met the warlord who consumed my mind and awoke the darkening need of desire within me.

I was lost to the beat, swaying and moving until arms wrapped around me and yanked my body against a hard, muscular frame that caused my pulse to jackhammer. Torrin lifted my chin with a single finger, bringing his mouth against my ear before a whispered breath fanned against the sensitive flesh.

"You're teasing me past my limits, woman," he growled huskily. "I don't enjoy sharing my toys with other men, either."

"That's not the rumors I've heard. In fact, most state you often share your pussy with your king. I, on the other hand, don't plan to be shared with anyone." I laughed huskily, enjoying the slight buzz I'd caught. "And you don't get to tell me who I can and can't dance with. I couldn't give two rats' asses about your limits, Torrin."

His hand glided up my spine, sliding through my hair, twisting it back without hurting me. His mouth moved over my throat, sending heat rushing through my body while he teased me with his scorching lips. Teeth scraped over my pulse, and he chuckled darkly with my reaction to him.

"You'd be in heaven with two mouths ravishing your body. Two cocks pushing into your tight holes that have been neglected for far too long. I bet you'd make the most delicious sounds as we pounded into your body until you were nothing more than a sobbing, quivering mess that couldn't move once we'd finished using you."

He held me against his thick erection, pulling back to show me the heat burning in his wintery stare. He smirked, turning to the men who had drifted around the girls, slowly dancing with them while Torrin and I stood still on the dance floor.

"Come, we're going to retire for the night," he growled, pulling me toward the long, steep staircase that led up into the sleeping quarters.

"I was having fun," I protested, shuddering against the idea of being at his mercy in a room alone once more.

"You were teasing me with your slow moves while you touched all the places I want to drag my lips across.

If you like, you can dance for me in our room, naked. I prefer you naked, after all. I enjoy knowing how wet I make you."

I snorted, stopping on the landing to peer out over the dance floor where the girls were grinding and moving against the men. They looked erotic, gyrating, and pulsing against the warriors who were, in fact, our enemies. I scanned the room, noting that men stood within the shadows, guarding the place against the nightwalkers.

Hands landed on either side of me, caging me in against the railing as Torrin's mouth skimmed over the back of my neck, dragging from my shoulder to my ear. "Does it piss you off that they willingly fuck my men? I've been told your girls are rather—wild with them. Amo especially sheds all her inhibitions and enjoys taking more than one man into her body."

I bristled at the fact that he thought we were loose in morals, or worse, whores. I turned in his arms, brushing my mouth against his lips. Teasingly, I nipped his plump bottom lip between my teeth, moaning as I cupped his hard erection. I tightened my hand, and my teeth pulled his lip before releasing it.

"Don't confuse the fact that we're fucking your men with weakness. Pussy has power, and right now, they're using it to lure your men into a false sense of power over their delicate sensibilities. We're trained to use all of our body, and that includes our nether regions. Amo has your men eating out of her flower petals, literally. They're assuming she's some fucking damsel that needs protection, when in fact, she's a cold-blooded killer. She could ride a cock while slitting a throat, and she would even finish after her victim has bled out beneath her. Tabitha has sucked a cock while shredding the vein in it with her teeth. She loves the taste of blood and rubbing it against her swollen clit after she's finished her job. We're not whores, Torrin. We're assassins, willing to play dirty to lure our prey into a false sense of strength and masculinity before we end their pathetic fucking existence."

I ducked beneath his arm and started toward the bedroom we'd be sharing. The moment I opened the door and passed through it, Torrin yanked me from behind and slammed me against the wall, caging me in with his massive body pressing against mine. His hands lifted as I tried to push him away from me. Forcing them above my head, he pinned them to the wall with one hand. The other wrapped around my throat just hard enough to show me who had control.

"If your girls harm my men, I'll slaughter them while you watch me ending their lives. You, on the other hand, would end up caged in a dungeon for my enjoyment. Do you think we're not aware that you're all murderous whores who use your cunts to end lives? I know everything about you and your little band of bitches that traipse across your lands, killing those you feel have endangered others."

"You don't know anything about me!" I hissed, watching his lips curve into a lethal smile that promised pain.

"Alexandria Helios, chosen to lead her Moon Clan unit. The last remaining Helios female of her entire clan," he stated, holding my angry glare. "You're skilled in archery, unequaled in marksmanship, and unmatched in swordsmanship by any assassin before you or after you. You're skilled in tonics, healing, magic, and your skin is lighter than any they've seen before you, meaning your blood is purer than those within the Order of the Moon. You lost your virginity at nineteen and weren't called by the moon to breed until you turned twenty-three. The male who chose you as his mate fell in love with you, yet you declined him, and they sent him away. You earned three immortal marks of strength, power, and one thousand kills before you turned twenty-five. That alone is an accomplishment unheard of for someone with a pussy." Torrin watched me through chilling eyes, his lips moving as my heart thundered, knowing that the things he'd spoken of were only known by those within the Order or by Landon.

"You were chosen to lead your group before you could even speak full sentences. They trained you for war by the most skilled warriors within the Order of the Moon. You think you aren't as beautiful as the others you ride with, choosing to allow them to pick their lovers first. Then you take whatever they leave at the end of the night, and you fuck hard. You fight on and off the battlefield, but you find men lacking. It isn't because they're unskilled lovers. It's because you're dominant and demanding, and they don't know how to handle you. I do," he growled, releasing my throat to push against my aching pussy. "You're always in control because those beneath you depend on you, to never relinquish it, ever. You have not met a man who can give you what you crave, which is to quiet your fucking mind so that your body can find release. You have no control right now, which is why you're so fucking wet for me, here," he stated, pushing my panties aside to slide his fingers through the wetness of my arousal.

I swallowed hard, staring into his frosty, pale blue eyes that burned bright while he watched me coming to the reality that he was right. He *knew* me. He hadn't sought out just any moon-touched riders; he'd hunted me down on purpose.

That told me more about the situation than listening to Torrin speak to his people in a language they assumed I didn't understand or comprehend. He also had no clue what languages I was fluent in since that wasn't in my files.

"Let me go, now," I seethed, watching as he shook his head.

Torrin's fingers pushed into my body, and my muscles clamped down hungrily against him. My entire body burned with the singular focus to come undone around him. My spine arched into his touch, and I closed my eyes against the multitude of sensations that ripped through me. I rocked against the fingers, sliding in and out of my body until his mouth crushed against mine. Torrin released my hands, and I moved them to his hair, holding him against me while his scorching kiss left me gasping for air with oxygen-starved lungs. I moaned hungrily against his mouth as he lifted my rear with one hand, never withdrawing his fingers from my body while he walked us to the bed.

Laying me down, he stared at me while lifting his shirt up and over his head. His eyes held me prisoner while my mind slowly came back. I shook my head, and he turned, moving away from me to an enormous desk that had a thick, leather-bound book. His hands rested on it while he faced away from me, fighting to calm the urgency rushing through him.

"Bathe and go to bed before I forget you took a vow of celibacy, and I bury my throbbing cock in your tight body. You make it difficult to ignore your needs when it's running down your thighs, woman. I have some work to do. I suggest you bathe quickly before I finish."

He continued to face away from me, gripping the desk firmly. The muscles in his shoulders bunched with tension, straining against the need to give in to the chemistry happening between us. My attention shifted to the window where the moon was shining. I knew I'd be called to the moon this time. That meant I would be with Torrin during the mindless mating need that took control.

Slipping from the bed, I silently shed my dress and moved to the large, opulent tub that had been filled to the rim with steam wafting from it. Beside it on the table were small glass vials of soap and candles that burned with a soft glow, filling the room. In front of the tub was a crackling fire that soothed and removed the chill that remained within my bones. Citrus lingered in the room, and it calmed my senses against the sexual assault that was rocking through me.

Shimmying out of my panties, I slowly stepped into the tub as a moan escaped my lips. Settling in, I leaned back, watching the dancing flames in front of me as the sound of pages turning fought with the crackling and snapping of the fire that licked the wood. Sitting up, something in the fire caught my eye. I leaned forward, which brought my ass out of the water.

"There's something in there." I swallowed, watching the tiny creatures that crawled on the logs, dancing within the flames. Fire fairies? I smiled, turning wide eyes toward Torrin, who watched me with lust in his gaze, burning hotter than the fire.

"Fucking bathe, woman," he growled, sitting back in the chair as his nostrils flared.

Sulking, I sat back in the tub and washed my body quickly. I worked the shampoo through my hair, grimacing when I discovered there was no conditioner to make brushing my hair more manageable.

Stepping from the water, I wrapped the drying cloth around me and went to the amber decanter of whiskey. After pouring two glasses full, I padded to Torrin, offering him the second glass. I waited for him to drink it before indulging, uncaring that if someone had poisoned it, he'd have died from it first. Someone had to be the sampler, right?

"Are you planning to bathe too?" I asked, noting his brows pushed together as he watched me drink the alcohol.

"Not tonight, no. I've given your laundry to the hostess to wash. I figured it was safer than you riding with me without panties."

"Indeed," I chuckled, sitting in the other chair while sipping the drink.

The liquor tasted different from what the last inn had served, but it was wet, and I was thirsty. My eyes slowly feasted on Torrin's powerful body while he studied me. This legendary warlord boasted of strength in everything he did, and there was a cunningness in his gaze that bothered me.

I knew he was playing me. That much was evident from the words he'd spoken to the others and his king. Torrin was used to getting what he wanted, and that was currently me. He had women falling at his feet, which wasn't my issue. I didn't care how many women he had because I didn't intend to get attached to him.

My mission was simple: find the library and my brother. And then get as far away as possible from this man and his king. Torrin assumed he'd caught us, and while I hadn't expected to end up at his feet, it worked out in my best interest. If it hadn't, I'd already be gone. Hell, I'd have been gone the moment he got too close to me.

I'd already worked out an exit plan from this inn, but that wouldn't get me any closer to finding Landon or the library. I'd seen Torrin's memories, and I'd seen within his mind the book that could have only come from the library. That meant either he'd been within it, or he had someone who knew the location.

"You're plotting," he stated, narrowing his eyes on me as I lifted the cup to my lips.

"I'm deciding if you'd be worth bedding when the moon calls me in a couple of days. If I decide otherwise, I must find another male in which to unleash my sorely neglected pussy."

His lips twitched as his eyes pooled with heat. "You assume I'd allow another to fuck you after tasting you?"

"I assume the male who ends up in bed with me is my choice, and only mine, to make. Unless, of course, you believe you can force me to accept you as my lover." I stated, lifting the glass to my lips as my eyes grew heavy.

I looked into the glass, frowning before setting it down on the desk. My body grew heated while he watched me. Smiling roguishly, Torrin steepled his fingers in front of his mouth. I stood and moaned as the chair brushed against my thigh. Turning, I looked at him before shuddering violently.

"Moonflower-spiked whiskey," he explained, watching my hand slide to my tingling nipple. "Aphrodisiac to your kind; normal whiskey to mine," he muttered, his eyes heating while they dropped to where my hand was smoothing over my flesh.

Moaning exploded from the surrounding rooms, and I groaned. "You didn't think you should tell me?" I questioned, stifling the urge to rub my fingers against my core that pulsed with a sharp, painful throb. My skin grew hypersensitive, and the drying cloth was too tight and offended everything within me.

"You're a big girl, Alexandria. I assumed you wouldn't drink whiskey from strange places without asking what was in it first. I was wrong."

"I *assumed* it was just whiskey," I whimpered, grabbing the chair to keep my hands from moving to the wetness pooling between my thighs.

"You *assumed* wrong." He shrugged, grabbing the leather-bound book to continue reading. "You're about to be in immense pain since the whiskey imitates your moon's call, which is why it's in every room of the *brothel*."

"I thought it was an inn!" I shrieked, bending over to place my hands on my knees as a wave of scorching heat rolled through me. *Shit!*

"You should stop assuming things. You're not in your world anymore, Little One. You're in mine. Here, we enjoy sex and crave the intensity that comes to your kind naturally when you're moon-touched and called to answer it."

"It's a *breeding* thing, not a sexual encounter for fun," I ground out, dropping to my knees while he smiled. "It's also very painful when it's denied, asshole."

"So we've been told. However, most of the women who indulge aren't celibate, Alexandria. They're also not inflicted with the power of the moon, as you and your girls are. More often than not, they're from a watered-down line that has gone unnoticed by your order. Or they're deserters who have refused the moon and sought out the darkness. Most who visit this establishment are women, and the ones drinking the whiskey are men who have ignored the call to join the Order of the Moon."

My body was covered in a fine sheen of sweat. My eyes rolled back in my head as my nipples hardened, and everything within me grew taut with need. My head dropped forward, bowing before him as my hands went flat against the floor. The pulse in my core throbbed violently, and soon it would become a pain that cramped in my belly.

Standing took effort. Moving to the bed to curl into a ball was torture. I lay on the mattress, spreading my legs apart to keep my thighs from brushing against the needy, burning flesh of my apex. I fisted my hands in the blankets and parted my lips for the moan of raw, sexual need to escape the confines of my throat in a sorrowful sound. I could do this; I knew I could. I'd done it before, many times.

I'd ignored the need to fuck everyone close to me with a red-hot urgency that ended in debilitating pain if dismissed. I'd disregarded it for four years, and the fact that I was mere days away from ever having to deny the call again, only to end up in some induced reproduced version of it, pissed me off.

I felt Torrin's heated eyes on me, noting the way my hips moved while my sex lay exposed, drenched in arousal, dripping from the drugged whiskey I'd drunk. Moans were coming from all around our bedroom. Each of the girls had probably partaken in the whiskey, too.

I wasn't stupid enough to believe they'd simply ignored it happening. No, Torrin's men observed us drinking their watered-down version of the known aphrodisiac. They'd allowed us to drink it, showing us that even though we'd been sneaky about the seduction, they were in full control. Now they would show us viscerally who was in charge, and they'd do it through orgasms. Fucking great!

Torrin's hand touched my body, and I curled into the heat it offered, peering up at his wintery eyes that promised relief. A single finger trailed between the valley of my breasts, stealing a moan from my lips. His dark head leaned over as his teeth clamped onto one nipple. Groaning loudly, I moved my hips with an invitation. The thrust of them was unhurried, while his tongue flicked my nipple leisurely.

His other hand gradually slid between my thighs, cupping my sex before leaving my neglected clit untouched. Three fingers danced against my opening, and I held his stare before they moved, sliding down to where I was writhing against them with need.

"It's also more potent than your moon's call to breed. The men use it to keep aroused, to sate the women's hunger who come here to experience endless, unbridled passion. You will not win this fight, I'm afraid. You will not endure pain, just a raw need to find release any way possible."

"I've endured worse," I whispered through dry lips.

"I know you have," he agreed. "I could give you relief, or you could try to ignore it. You could also come with me into my dreamscape, and I could give you relief there, which won't be real, but it would be enough to fool your mind into thinking you're finding release."

"I am not going into your dreamscape," I groaned, feeling him pushing into my body while I shuddered so violently that I almost came.

Torrin sensed how close I was, withdrawing from my body instantaneously. "I'm trying to help you keep your oath, woman. You're about to lose control; I promise you that. I'm giving you the option not to lose it here and come with me into my mind."

"You planned this, didn't you?" I accused, rubbing myself against his leg like a dog who was trying to establish dominance. I was so going to kick his ass when I stopped *writhing*!

"No, but I didn't stop you either. From the sound of things outside this room, neither did the other women. Unlike you, they seem to be enjoying themselves *immensely*. I could always go find one who is interested in being shared and given unimaginable pleasure."

"I hate you," I groaned, turning onto my stomach to dismiss him. My hips spread apart, and my hands twisted in the blankets. Burying my face into the pillow, I whimpered. My ass lifted with need, and Torrin growled, slowly sitting back to watch me gyrate my ass.

I squeezed my eyes closed while violent waves of lust rolled through me. I was soaked in need, arousal painting my thighs while Torrin stood at the edge of the bed, watching. I felt him moving away to return to the desk.

I focused my mind on one thing, and that was where Torrin was and why he wasn't within me, driving me to the abyss of pleasure that his body could give me.

Hours passed, and wave after wave of need sent me wafting on the swells of the ocean. One minute I was inside the room at the inn with him, and the next, I stood in a large, opulent bedroom that had been in Torrin's memories. Slowly, he turned, facing me with a dark smile lifting the corners of his mouth.

"About fucking time, woman," he growled.

Chapter Eleven

I swallowed hard past the dryness of my mouth as Torrin stepped out of the shadows. His body was covered in sweat, which forced my attention to latch onto one droplet, following it down the V-line of his body before slowly rising to hold his wintery gaze. Dark, seductive tattoos pulsed on his bronzed flesh, capturing my attention as a loud whispered groan of sexual need escaped my throat.

"If I find release within your dreamscape, does my body also live it outside of here?" I asked, needing clarification.

"You won't experience a full climax if that is what you're asking," he stated, his eyes sliding down my body. "You will still feel the need for release, but it will stop that throbbing ache in your soaked, *very* delicious tasting cunt that you've left needlessly neglected."

I groaned, clenching my fists tightly at my sides.

Tearing my stare from his, I looked around the empty room. In his mind, I was in a dreamscape that allowed him to do whatever he wanted with me. I wasn't sure who had brought me here, him or me? Did I necessarily care? *No.*

Slowly, I moved to the table that the book had been on, leaning against it, rolling my head on my shoulders. He'd brought me to a room that whispered of sin and lust. I was beyond caring about how we had ended up here, as long as it happened.

Heat enveloped my back, and before I could turn to face him, he slammed me down on the table. My hips bit into the wood, and I whimpered at the full control he held. His foot parted my ankles, and I gasped the moment his hand landed against my backside.

"That's for making me wait to taste you," Torrin growled raspingly, leaning over my body to trace kisses down my spine. His hand landed again, and I cried out loudly, rocking my hips for his touch. "That's for driving me insane with the need to be in this tight body." Again, it slapped against the round globe of my ass as his nose brushed against my ass cheek. "That's for dancing with another male when I wanted it to be me against your pretty curves."

His tongue slid through the sleek arousal, sliding from one end to the other. Torrin flicked my clit hard with his tongue before sucking it into his mouth and pushing his tongue against my opening. His hand still held me down against the oak table. I could barely breathe past the pleasure his mouth forced upon me.

His fingers entered my core, and I clenched down tightly around them, needing more than Torrin was giving me. I bucked against them, fighting the hand that held me down on the table. A deep rumbling sound from his chest sent vibrations pulsing against my sex. I cried out with need, feeling arousal drenching my sex with readiness. Torrin stood swiftly without warning, turning me toward him with only his controlling hand at the back of my neck.

My mouth crashed against his in an earth-shattering kiss. His hand held me at the base of my skull, forcing my mouth against his while he walked us toward the large, dark bed covered in midnight-colored silk. I pushed my hands through his hair, holding him tighter against me while my tongue speared into his mouth, thrusting in to capture his tongue while I showed him what I needed from him. His other hand lowered to my ass, lifting me easily to grind my body against his.

Slowly, he settled me back onto the silken sheets, staring down at me with ribbons of lust and need glittering in his stare. His hands captured my legs behind the knees, and he pushed them up against my shoulders, allowing his greedy mouth full access to my pussy. He didn't devour it like I craved for him to do.

Instead, his heated gaze took in the arousal coating it, beckoning him to indulge in sin with me. The look in his eyes was pure hunger, splattered with stars of intoxication that begged him to get drunk on me. His face darkened with savage lust, and then he was there, devouring me with urgency.

Tongue deep into my core, Torrin growled wickedly while holding my hooded gaze. My moans were loud, unleashed from the ability to cry out for him without being heard. I released the cries that exploded with his name on the edge of my tongue, pleading for more. My body started to unravel, but he paused, stepping back to watch me as he sat up.

"You don't come unless I say you can. You don't have any control here, woman. You're at my mercy, right where you belong. Now, get up and get on your knees. I intend to fuck your throat, and then if you've been a good girl, I'll let you come before I wreck your pussy."

I stood, glaring at him with defiance, and he smiled, daring me to argue as anticipation mixed with excitement filled the room, crackling with the intensity of it. Torrin stepped back as I climbed from the bed, dropping to the floor to stare hungrily up at him.

Silently, he pushed his pants down his narrowly tapered hips, freeing his thick length to my starving gaze. My tongue snaked out, licking my lips while he groaned. The moment he stepped forward, I reached for him, but he shook his head.

"Hands behind your back, and don't touch me unless I say otherwise, Lexia. In this room, if you do as you're told, you'll get rewarded for being good. Do you understand me?" Torrin asked, and when I nodded, he bent, gripping my jaw painfully. "Use your words, little birdy, so I can make you scream for me."

"Yes," I whispered huskily, shocked by the sultry tone that escaped from my lips.

Torrin positioned himself in front of me. His breathing grew harsh and labored as he pushed his cock against my lips, holding my gaze.

"Open your mouth and suck me off, woman," he purred, watching my mouth do as he'd demanded. He stroked my hair before sliding his fingers through it, fisting it while he watched me. "Breathe," he demanded, and I did.

The moment I exhaled and took in the air around his thickness, Torrin thrust forward. I moaned around him, fighting the fullness he created in my throat. His girth blocked my airway while he used my throat to sheathe his impressive cock. His breath hitched as he used my hair to guide himself deeper. He thrust deeper, then growled as he held my head still, and I felt hot spurts hitting the back of my throat. All at once, he withdrew, and I chased him, needing him to fill me any way I could get him.

Torrin didn't allow it. Instead, he picked me up from the floor and kissed my shoulder, biting it softly while I groaned. His fingers slipped between my thighs, tracing the soft folds with the tips.

"I love how wet you get for me," he growled, turning me around before he pushed me backward onto the bed. I gradually backed up while he watched me, and I wondered what he'd do if I made him fight to take what we both needed, wanted. "Spread your legs and show me what belongs to me."

I groaned past the swelling in my throat. Slowly lifting my knees, I let them drop open, watching Torrin's eyes glow with wickedly dark desire. He moved onto the bed, prowling toward me. His dark head lowered, nipping one nipple before the other, chuckling at my response to his heated bites.

His heavy erection pulsed at my opening as he continued towering over me. He fisted his hands on either side of my head, caging mine in, while his ice-blue eyes sparkled with excitement as he tensed.

My breathing grew shallow, need driving my hips to rock against the tip of his cock while he studied me. I needed him. It ached within me with ardor, sparking until it was an inferno of lust that had me moaning loudly. I whispered his name on my lips as he remained still, watching me until I shuddered against him, pleading for him to enter my core.

"Do you want that?" he asked gutturally, his voice running over me like gravel.

"Yes," I breathed, unable to deny what I craved from this warrior who watched me with the eyes of a predator. Fire blazed in my belly, and my entrance soaked with need. The blush of awareness started to spread, and his mouth lowered, sucking my bottom lip between his until he bit into the plump flesh, and growled. "I need you, Torrin."

Torrin shivered at my declaration, pulling back. He peered down, staring at where he rocked against my entrance. His gaze watched me while he pushed a single inch into my body. I gasped, lifting my legs while my ass arched, knowing I wouldn't fit him into my body without being positioned to take his length.

He entered me painfully, even though he wasn't even in my body yet. He grinned, staring down at where my body clenched and tightened while muscles ached, screaming from neglect. He'd only added the tip of his cock, and my body was a mass of burning tension, aching from being stretched.

Torrin withdrew, sitting back on his knees before his mouth lowered, lapping against my core while I sat shocked that he'd withdrawn. I tried to sit up but could not. He curled his arms around my thighs, jerking me closer as he used his tongue to fuck me. My body tensed, and the moment his nose brushed against my clit, everything fired up all at once.

I screamed as the orgasm rippled through me, starting in my toes, moving into my thighs, and spreading through my belly to end in my fingertips that dug into the blanket. I twisted the sheets with my hands, fisting them as my entire body trembled without warning. It was like everything within me had felt Torrin, felt the violence of the earth-shattering climax that rolled through me in wave after wave of passionate pleasure.

My core tightened as Torrin pushed his fingers into me. He watched as he held me in the throes of the release shooting through me. Every thrust forced me to climb higher, cresting the peak as light burst into my vision. I screamed his name on repeat as if it were stuck on my tongue and would never leave it. Galaxies erupted as blinking lights, and my hips bucked harder, begging him for more while he sucked my clit. Torrin fucked me with his fingers in a steady beat that mirrored the ragged breathing that expelled from my lips. Every thrust forced the orgasm to burn brighter, boiling through me until his scent filled me, and I fought to get away from the pleasure he created.

Pain entered my mind, and he lifted, mouth glistening with my arousal coating it. Torrin tilted his head, showing me darkening eyes while the smile turned cold and unfeeling. Obsidian darkness flooded his irises, and he climbed up my body, claiming my lips hungrily while I lay spent and unmoving. He growled, leaning his head against my shoulder to nip at my collarbone before he lifted his stare, exposing wintery-blue eyes that cooled the fire he'd created within me.

"When I take this pussy, it won't be muted or within a dreamscape. I want you to feel every inch of me stretching your tight body as I fuck you. I want to hear you scream and watch your pretty eyes filling with wonder and pain as I destroy every part of you, Lexia. Now, wake up because it's time to go, and I'm fucking exhausted from you ignoring the need to come all night. I have to applaud your strength and merit; you're committed to the oath you took. In two weeks, you will be mine."

I sat up in bed, searching the room for Torrin as I took in the familiar brothel. He sat across the room in a chair, staring at me through the shadows, with a smile playing on his sexy mouth. I gasped as a tremor of lust shot through me, my hand sliding down to where my sex was still soaked with need, but it wasn't swollen from his mouth or red from being pleasured by his rough, unshaven face. I sucked my lip between my teeth, watching him licking his lips while his eyes sparkled with naked hunger.

"You didn't fuck me. Why?" I demanded.

"I told you why, woman."

"You remember everything that happened in there the same way I do?" I asked, blushing to my roots with how insane I'd been with need.

"Everything, including how you were begging me to fuck you," he rasped, his voice moving over me like honey warmed over a fire. "I even remember how wet you got when you came against my lips. You were crazed, screaming my name like I was your savior, and you were a follower who worshipped me. Now, I suggest you wash off that pretty pussy, because you're soaking wet, and I doubt there's anyone here who didn't hear you screaming for me inside this brothel. I'm pretty sure that everyone assumes you broke your oath since you screamed my name to the rafters. If I'd been a better man or cared to, I'd have covered your pretty lips. But I'm not, and I didn't. I enjoyed my name coming off your tongue as I ate your greedy pussy as it came so hard I actually fucking felt your arousal dripping down my chin."

I swallowed past the tremor of need his words created, hating that my body ached, and my nipples hardened from the silkiness of his tone. I couldn't even argue that I hadn't wanted it because I had. I'd never come so hard in my life, and if that was muted, then I needed him more than I needed the air feeding my lungs.

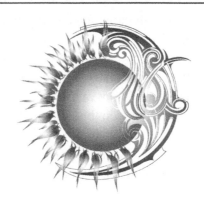

Chapter Twelve

The ride was filled with an uncomfortable silence, yet it was almost deafening as we moved deeper into the Darklands. I surveyed the rough terrain, memorizing how we traveled through it, free of attacks on our lives by creatures. We'd been riding for hours before we encountered anyone.

We dismounted, and I was told to stand with the women while Torrin moved to a group of men approaching us. Behind them was the wall that divided us from them, dark from light. Sliding my gaze around the high guarded wall, I frowned.

"That's a problem," Amo chuckled. "You got fucked last night?" My head spun at her change of topic, which I was certain she'd done on purpose.

"No, I didn't. I know that is a problem. Find a weakness because it has to have one. We need to know what it is, so we don't end up stuck behind it for longer than needed," I returned.

"I heard you screaming Torrin's name at the top of your lungs," Tabitha ground out, her eyes slowly searching the wall. "There, far right. That's a crack, and with a little help, the wall should come down easily."

"I was in his dreamscape, and he gave me release after I partook of the moonflower-spiked whiskey. I am pretty sure they were showing us our weaknesses. I think we should be more careful about the food and drink we consume."

"Back up, dreamscape? How is that any different from just fucking him?" Amo asked curiously, with no judgment in her tone.

"Because my body didn't find release," I supplied while blushing. "My mind, however, had the longest, most intense orgasm of my life in that place."

"Did he fuck you?" Tabitha asked and turned as the other girls listened. "Lexia, come on! You're the only one clinging to that oath, and we're all left to deal with your painful screams when the moon calls you. Give us the goods!"

"No, because he wants me to be fully aware when he takes me," I admitted, watching their eyes get large and wide as they nodded. "I think he may be man enough to sate whatever is wrong with me that keeps me unsatisfied."

"You are missing your mate," Amo announced. "That's why you can't come with some boring ass dick. You're a forever kind of woman. You cling to the idea that sex should mean something more than just basic needs," she scoffed, buffing her nails on her chest while looking at me pointedly.

"Like I'd get a mate, asshole? No, I'm not anyone's mate. Could you imagine being saddled with me? The poor prick would probably off himself before allowing me to claim him, anyway." I breathed and then noted Amo's eyes had moved over my shoulder.

I turned, staring into the frosted glare of the male who had been silent behind me for most of the ride. Hell, Chivalry had even kept his distance from Torrin, choosing to nudge my leg instead of his. I wasn't sure what had changed, but something had. He'd been cold and distant the closer we got to the gate guarding the way into the Kingdom of Night.

Maybe it was because Torrin thought he'd subdued me with his mouth and was no longer interested in me. Or maybe it was because he'd never been interested in the first place? I shook it off, waiting for him to speak, but something chilling passed in his stare, causing me to swallow down the urge to step back and run.

"We will bring your horses into the kingdom through a secondary route. Their coloring will cause issues, and I'd rather not waste any more time in reaching the palace than necessary," Torrin stated, nodding to the men who moved in to retrieve the white stallions.

My eyes slid to Chivalry, who reared back as the guard approached him. My heart thundered in my chest, realizing he was cutting off our escape while disguising it as a need to reach the palace sooner. I wasn't stupid enough to fall for it, but arguing wouldn't stop it from happening.

I walked toward Chivalry, ignoring the guards who

tried to push me away. Holding out my hand for my horse, I exhaled as he calmed and sidestepped toward me. As I clucked my tongue, he soothingly placed his muzzle into my palm. He rubbed it against me, neighing his displeasure while I exhaled again slowly.

"You'll be okay, sweet boy. I will meet you there and feed you the best oats in the world. Be my good boy, and I'll come to see you as soon as we arrive," I cooed, leaning my head against his neck. "Keep the others calm and tell them we are safe and on our path."

"You speak to the animal as if he understands, crazy woman," the guard snorted, and I smirked, watching Chivalry shake his mane and prance around.

"They're much smarter creatures than you think they are," I returned icily, leveling the guard with a chilling look. "Should anything happen to my boy, I will return to take yours," I warned, lowering my icy stare to his dick. "And I'll do it while you're still alive. See that Chivalry is treated well, as he is very important to me." The guard laughed coldly, glaring at me as I turned, walking past Torrin, who narrowed his eyes.

I stood with my group, waiting for the men to take us into their territory. Amo's owl, Scout, left her shoulder and flew around us, squawking his displeasure as Amo waved him off. My heart hammered in my chest as I felt Torrin standing behind me, and my eyes slid to Amo as the men moved in around us. Inhaling, I sucked my lip between my teeth, closing my eyes as my heart echoed in my ears, pounding like thunder.

"They need to be wearing cloaks," Torrin announced, and I watched as the girls were covered in them by the men behind them. "Here, woman," he growled when I failed to turn away from the look in the men's eyes.

I felt the cloak on my shoulders, and with it, magic wafted through me. My body grew pliant, and my mind turned numb. Torrin picked me up and moved toward a waiting wagon. They brought the others and deposited beside me in the same ale-scented wagon. I growled, staring up into Torrin's eyes while he glared down at me.

"Can't have you remembering the way back, now can we?" he asked, smirking as I moaned. "Sleep. You're going to need your rest."

My eyes grew heavy as Torrin touched my cheek with his fingertips. He smiled coldly, his eyes appearing black as I blinked, fighting sleep. He lowered his mouth, whispering against my lips.

"Stop fighting it, little warrior. It's spelled with your potions. After all, your people use it on each other more than they do us." *Us?*

I rocked in the wagon, hearing my team moan around me as they, too, fought the pull of sleep. *Mugwort and lavender.* He'd used our tonics to render us paralyzed and unable to stay awake. Lips touched mine, and teeth nipped playfully as he growled huskily against them.

"You'll wake up where you're supposed to be," he stated, standing back before nodding to someone.

The wagon started forward with a jerk, and I stared up at the sky, watching the wall as we passed beyond it into the lands of the Kingdom of Night. Only they weren't dark. Light illuminated the skies, but the glow came from the ground. My heart stopped as I realized why he'd put us to sleep before going past the wall.

They lined the entire inside of the wall with moonstones. It was built with the remains of the moon-touched people, and they had attached thousands of stones to the wall. Tears burned my eyes, pricking them angrily. I closed them, succumbing to the potion, I'd brewed myself.

Someone jolted me awake and then yanked me from the wagon. My heart flipped in my stomach as I fought off the hands that held me. I couldn't hear, couldn't feel anything other than weightlessness that told me I was being carried and rushed into some type of dwelling.

"Stop fighting me, woman," Torrin snapped, and then it hit me.

An icy chill rent the air as moaning exploded in the distance. *Wraiths.* I pushed down the fear, still paralyzed by the potion and unable to move. My eyes took in the shadowy walls of the structure, noting they were made of stone. On them were pictures that looked as if a small child had drawn them. My team was brought in behind us, and then Torrin began issuing orders while he lifted me, carrying me over his shoulder like a bag of flour.

His hand landed on my ass, or I assumed that was what patted my backside as the prickling sensation of my spine awakening, irritated. My legs burned and itched with the life flowing back into them as they woke with the sensation of fire ants biting them. I wiggled my rear, and Torrin's hand landed on it harder.

"We're surrounded by wraiths, Lexia. Stop moving and stop fighting me. We're in an abandoned home, which means there are no wards or moonstones to prevent them from entering."

Well, that was stupid of him.

"I'd have taken you into the village, but they're rather—unwelcoming to your kind. Now, be a good girl and hold still. No noise, or we'll be tossing some of you to them so that the rest of us can escape unscathed."

I bristled, wanting to slit his throat and ride his mouth at the same time. I was seriously kicking his ass the moment I could move, and no longer surrounded by the one creature that could actually kill us. Torrin placed me on a bed in the attic, and I watched him from the moldy thing while the women were brought up behind me. The men placed moonstones at the attic entrance and then crawled back to sit beside us.

Torrin's hand slid into the cloak I still wore, tracing circles on my skin, peering down to smirk at me. I studied his thick lashes and the way his icy gaze was swirling with something sinister. I'd miscalculated his strength and intelligence. That was a huge problem. Torrin's hand slid into my shirt, rolling my nipple between his fingers before something crashed downstairs. No one moved or made a sound as the dragging of blades echoed through the lower floor of the house where we'd hidden.

Neighing started below, and the horrifying sound of horses being consumed filled the air. Normally, wraiths didn't feast on animals, preferring two-legged creatures to four. Torrin's cheek pulsed as anger and regret burned in his stare. My heart released a soft thump, grateful that Chivalry hadn't been down with the horses. My eyes closed, shutting out the sound of slurping as the wraiths sucked the marrow from the horses' bones.

We were fucked, and not in the fun, delicious way I'd hoped to be. I had a feeling we were walking into a hornet's nest and about to be thrown into something dark and twisted, which meant I wasn't any closer to finding my brother or the library.

Torrin leaned over my body, staring at the door as his men built a wall in front of us. The temperature began dropping, and scraping sounded before something exploded, and the entire house shook violently. I stared up at Torrin in abject horror as the floor beneath me crumbled.

"Fuck," he snapped, grabbing me to envelop me with his heavy frame. No sooner had he rolled me, trading positions, the floor caved in, and everyone went sailing toward the ground, which was covered with wraiths.

Chapter Thirteen

There were times when you knew how bad things are about to get. And then there were those rare times when you realized exactly how *fucked* you were about to be. I knew it would be terrible as we dropped toward the ground with the house crashing down with us.

When we'd landed, Torrin took the hit against the ground and then rolled me beneath him to protect me from falling debris. Once the house had finished crumbling around us, Torrin left me on my back before he withdrew his blade, igniting the weapon with his magic. His men moved into action, fighting the wraiths that swarmed us immediately, drawn by the scent of our blood.

I stared up into the darkness, my body filling with terror from the nearness of the monsters surrounding us. My eyes were frozen open as frost covered my thick lashes, and air refused to fill my lungs, creating a ragged breath that stuck in my throat. Something slammed against my side, and I jolted. The soulless, silver eyes of a wraith met mine before he lowered, sinking his teeth into my arm. Pain sliced through me, but I couldn't cry out to alert Torrin.

I was going to die, and that realization sucked.

Something slammed into the wraith, making the pain lessen a fraction. Torrin peered down at me, sending his blade back between the creature's torso and body. Then something shattered close to us, sending shards of glass raining down on me, or worse, shards of the wraith. I watched it move to the side where my eyes couldn't follow. Pain shot through my thigh before a loud slurping noise filled the air. More pain sliced into my side but stopped as the blood turned to sludge within my veins.

The iciness in the air promised rest as the wraiths fed upon my body painlessly. Strangely enough, I felt at peace, knowing the end was near. Blinding light shot through the rubble of the house, and I sensed my sluggishly beating heart tighten with the pain of the loss. The wraiths howled, screeching against the light that momentarily blinded them.

Consciousness began to slip away, and I smiled inside as nothingness entered my vision. Something liquid gushed from my side, and a sliver of pain pierced my breast before swords were slamming into the wraiths feasting on me.

"Bloody hell, get them up!" Torrin shouted, but the sound was muted.

Everything was muted.

The pain I'd had.

The fear I'd felt.

The fact that we were *dying*.

The peace was—nice.

I'd expected to feel it all, but nothing came. There was just calmness in accepting what was happening and that I held no control over it anymore.

Hands grabbed my arms, and I was dragged away with wraiths still feasting on my body. Torrin dropped me, sending his blade through them as more light exploded around us. I was picked up, and then Torrin rushed me away from the howling wraiths as more light ignited, a telltale sign that another one of my sisters had died. He cradled me carefully, staring into my frozen eyes while he issued sharp commands, and then he rushed toward a house that had a light glowing from within the dwelling.

Inside, he shouted for a healer, but no one answered. His eyes looked around in a panic, cussing violently while he moved me to the fireplace, abandoning me next to it. Igniting the flames, Torrin withdrew his blade, turning to rush back into the fighting.

My eyes thawed first, and I turned my head to stare into Amo's sightless, cloudy green eyes. I crawled and fought to make my body work. I struggled to get to my best friend, who had white lines running down her face. Screaming in frustration, I forced my body to move, shielding hers with mine while tears slipped from my eyes.

Like me, Amo was covered in bites from the wraiths, which meant poison was slowly killing us even though we'd escaped. My tears slid over her frozen face, and then something pinched me. I lifted to frown at her pink fingers.

"Don't die, please," I whispered through my cracked lips that oozed blood from being frozen shut and then jarred open with my words.

Lifting my gaze, I took in Tabitha and a few others, who were all slowly thawing out deeper within the house. A hissing noise sounded behind me. Turning, I discovered a wraith slowly inching toward us. The others were still too frozen to respond, and the worst part was, so was I. I watched it slowly dragging its feet across the floor toward us.

It dropped to the floor when it reached me, sinking its teeth into my thigh. Something silver flashed before my eyes, and I lifted them to find Torrin dropping to his knees to place his hand over the bite mark on my side. My head turned, staring at the wraith that lay lifeless on the floor beside me, in two pieces.

"Go find a healer, now!" Torrin demanded, and the sound of feet padding across the floor filled the home. "Get the moonstones and place them around the house," he growled, and his eyes locked with mine. "Although they're dead, they can still serve to keep you alive. You're a fucking leader; act like it."

I hated he was right, but knowing I'd lost more of my team stung my eyes with unshed tears. My heart tightened as my throat clenched, threatening to seal. Torrin witnessed me fight the need to get up and go to them, even knowing I was badly wounded.

"Stop fucking moving," he warned vehemently. "You're bleeding out. The wound in your stomach is deep and gushing your life essence onto the floor of a brothel. This isn't how you die, Alexandria. You lost five women, which means the others need you to survive.

Without you, they're dead at the end of my blade. Do you understand me? I will fucking kill them if you die."

"Fuck you," I shivered, and he smiled.

"That's my girl. You get pissed. Do whatever it takes to fight. You hear me?" He pushed down on my side, and I gasped, turning over to spew what little food I'd eaten as the pain became too much to bear. "I need the antidote now!"

A commotion started at the door, and then the room flooded with people. Torrin stepped back as a woman moved forward, grabbing my chin before something horrid tasting was forced down my throat. I gagged and then groaned as she held her hand over my mouth.

"You drink it, child. You hold it down, or you are dead, do you hear me?" she demanded, her sharp chocolate-colored eyes holding mine. "She's going to bleed out."

"That can't happen," Torrin argued. "The king needs her alive. Do *whatever* the hell you have to do to make sure that doesn't happen."

"Look at her body. It's ravaged in poisonous bites. She is gushing blood all over the floor, and it isn't something even I can prevent if her Moon Goddess seeks to take her from this world, Torrin."

"Don't let her die," he commanded like she was a warrior on a battlefield instead of a healer he could order around. Torrin's knuckles brushed over my cheek. "Stay with me, Lexia. The fierce assassin doesn't die from a wraith bite. You're stronger than that, understood?"

"You're not a god, Torrin," I whispered through

chattering teeth.

"Not yet, no," he replied, his lips tipping up into a roguish smile.

"That's rather cocky," I muttered, watching his eyes sparkling with mirth.

The healer snorted, pushing against my side, which caused nausea to roll through my stomach, churning it until it burned the back of my throat. I gagged at the taste while Torrin pulled me into his lap as the woman continued to examine us, shaking her head before she started tending the wounds.

"If she's arguing with the likes of you, she may yet survive."

Torrin smirked, pushing hair away from my face while she applied a moss-like covering over the bite marks. I didn't have the heart to tell him that no moon-touched person had ever lived through the bite of a wraith, but I also didn't want to die alone.

Another vial was pushed against my lips and tipped up. I drank it, staring up into Torrin's icy gaze as the tonic sent heat rushing through me, colliding with the iciness that filled my limbs. I really didn't want to die here, but it wasn't looking as if we'd get a choice in the matter. Torrin would probably collect my stones and rub his stupid balls with them if I died.

That meant I had to fight. I had a mission to finish, an entire race depending on the cure for moon sickness. I was a warrior, one of only a handful of assassins with the skillset to accomplish this goal. No, Torrin was right, which pissed me off. This wasn't how I died. I'd fight, and I'd see this through. I had to survive because Landon was somewhere in this kingdom, and I intended to find him and save him from the sickness, no matter the cost.

Chapter Fourteen

My eyes were heavy, and my body felt fragile and weak as I came to from the nightmares plaguing my dreams. I pushed up from the bed, searching through the shadows of the room. Struggling to get upright, or at least into a sitting position, took effort. The door opened, and Torrin entered, moving toward me as I tried to stand but fell into his arms.

"You're not healed enough to be up and moving yet, woman," he growled, settling me back into bed.

"I need to see who lived," I demanded, and he winced. "They're my family!"

"You lost seven, Alexandria. I'm sorry, but they couldn't be saved. Most died before we could get them away from the wraiths. Amo survived, though," he offered, and I turned away from him as pain sliced through me violently with the losses.

"We shouldn't even be here," I whispered, sucking

my lip between my teeth and biting it to null the pain inside of me until I tasted blood.

"But you are. You intended to come into our kingdom one way or another. You knew there would be losses," he stated, pushing the hair away from my face. "You didn't scar, not badly anyway."

"Do you think I care if I scarred?" I snorted, turning angry eyes on him. "Seven people lost their lives because you drugged us, Torrin."

"So it's my fault?" he scoffed.

He stood, pacing beside the bed before he stopped and stared down at me, with anger humming palpably through the room. I turned onto my side, forcing my body to the edge of the bed to sit up. Dropping my head into my hands, I shuddered. My stomach churned, and my heart thumped against my ribcage. My head spun with guilt, and my eyes lifted to hold his.

"It's your fault we're here. It's also my fault because, as their leader, I failed to assess and see the possibility of this outcome. I miscalculated and didn't count on treachery before reaching the kingdom."

"So what now, Lexia? You go into seven years of self-suffering because you couldn't control the situation? That's not how this works. You were captured, held prisoner, and drugged. You want to blame someone, blame me."

"Just shut up," I groaned, hating the pang of self-loathing and grief that rocked through me.

"You need to crawl your tiny ass back into that bed. You're not healed enough to be out of it yet. It's only been three days since the attack. The poison from the wraiths held you in a high fever that only broke this morning. You need to allow your body to heal and rest."

"I need to see them, Torrin," I argued, but he ignored me.

He forced me into bed, lying on his side next to me. He gazed into my grief-stricken eyes with understanding, sending more pain rocking through my body to wrench my heart tightly.

This man led legions into battle, and while he'd probably lost thousands of men and women, my team was brought up together since the moment the Order took us away from our families. We were sisters, raised to fight together, to do everything together, so we were better *together*.

Torrin's hand lifted, pushing the hair away from my face while slowly exhaling. One minute I was in bed with him, and the next, we were standing in the ruins of the house that had exploded. I shivered against the heat, touching my back, and turned, peering over my shoulder into a dark, angry stare, no longer the color of freshly frozen water.

"Tell me what you could have done to prevent this," he stated, nodding toward the slow-moving wraiths converging on us from his memory.

My body was on the ground beneath his, and I winced at the sight. Torrin's arm was twisted and mangled as the house peppered his back with fragmented pieces. He'd been wounded, yet he'd still fought to save us and protect me.

Torrin shoved aside my body as he rose to his feet,

defending me while I lay unmoving, frozen in the terror created by the wraiths. The first one fell on me, gnawing on my arm, which made bile fill my throat, threatening to spew past my lips.

I stepped back, only to have Torrin wrap his arms around me, holding me tightly and securely. There was an entire army of wraiths, larger than any horde I'd ever witnessed before, moving around us. The sound of their feet sliding across the frozen tundra sent my blood pounding in my ears, thundering deafeningly.

Fear spiked in my mind, and the need to run from what was happening echoed through me. My mind gripped hold of the panic I'd felt lying unguarded on the ground, exposed during the attack.

"They can't hurt you, Alexandria," Torrin murmured against my ear. "I have you, and you're safe with me. It's just memories."

His arms tightened more as I saw Torrin move to take the head from the wraith, sucking the light from my arm, mangling the flesh to get deeper. Torrin's dark head lifted as one of his men howled, going down beneath several wraiths attacking him all at once. He didn't move to save the warrior, choosing to take his head instead.

I'd faced that choice once before. It wasn't an easy one to make, but Torrin hadn't hesitated. He swung his blade while his men formed a circle around us, doing everything within their power to protect our prone bodies from being eaten. Wave after wave of wraiths rushed forward, and Torrin's men continued fighting for us, and even though a few got through the circle, they held. We'd survived against insurmountable odds.

Torrin turned, his body twisting as he sliced through the wraith gnawing greedily on my torso. The swing of his sword was sure and swift, rushing down against the wraith's middle. Light exploded, and my eyes swung to the body in the middle of the circle. Carla was conscious, a dagger protruding through her chest as she sacrificed her life for us. Light burst, forcing the monsters back as she shattered.

One of Torrin's men dropped to his knees, dead on top of Erin. She took his blade into her blue, frozen hand and slid it into her chest as her eyes slid to the woman on the ground beside her. Kate grabbed the warrior's other blade, exhaling as she forced her hand to close around the hilt before she thrust the dagger into her heart, pushing the wraiths further back yet.

All seven of my warriors had committed suicide to drive the monsters back, giving the warriors a chance to escape with our unmoving forms. Tears swam in my eyes as I watched them, making the ultimate sacrifice to provide us with time to flee and sustain life. A sob left my chest, seeping through my lips.

My chest tightened, compelling my throat to choke down the tears that tried to slip free. Torrin and his men lifted us, moving through the debris of the house that had crumbled beneath the starving wraiths. I'd seen enough and knew that there had been nothing I could have done.

Turning in his arms, I groaned at the sight of Torrin's dark eyes, noting that he watched me taking in what he was. Torrin was of the darkness. He was a creature that had succumbed to the promise to live within the darkness by accepting its seductive lure. Thin, black veins covered Torrin's fingertips that lifted, cupping my face with worry. His black eyes were surrounded by tiny veins that pulsed through his face, but where others looked evil, he looked—*sexy*.

He might be a monster, or a creature I'd be forced to kill, eventually. Several rumors surrounded the Kingdom of Night's people, whispers that they were derived from the darkness that allowed them to live while swallowing up those of the light. I'm guessing that Torrin was among those who had welcomed darkness in but didn't feed on the light within others. Nightwalkers and similar creatures fed gluttonously from moon-touched people. The thing was, Torrin didn't scare me. He excited me.

I cupped his cheeks, and his nostrils flared. His dark eyes watched me as if he expected me to scream or fight his touch. He'd saved us, and regardless of what he was, he was the reason we had survived. He'd chosen us over the lives of his men. He could have easily fled. Torrin had decided to stay and protect us and to save us.

I lifted on my toes, brushing my lips against his. He growled hungrily, watching me claim his mouth in a soft kiss. He didn't move, didn't react as I slowly kissed him with trembling, heated lips.

"You saved us, and for that, I am eternally grateful, Torrin," I admitted, breaking him loose of whatever hold had restrained him, and he kissed me hard and fast.

Torrin bent, sliding his hands behind my thighs to hoist me up against his solid frame. I wrapped my legs wrapped around him and whimpered at the feel of his rock-hard form against my softer one. His hand snaked up, threading his fingers through my hair to control my mouth, and his tongue slid between my lips, tasting, and tempting mine to dance with his darkness. It swept against mine, daring me to cave into the hunger we both felt.

His teeth bit into my lip, causing me to gasp loudly, and I moaned into his kiss while my body melted into his heated embrace. Torrin's strength supported me, and for a moment, I didn't feel the weight of the loss or the pain of the grief trying to consume me. Torrin released my hair, which made me fear losing the bliss his kiss was promising me. I captured his hands and crushed my mouth against his lips again.

"Don't stop," I pleaded. Dark laughter echoed through my head as weightlessness filled me, and we were back in the bed with him silently watching me, waiting for the theatrics.

I peered into wintery eyes that searched mine, and I fought through what was fact and created from within his mind. Torrin sat up, looking at me as I peeled off the gown I wore, gazing down at the stitches that held my skin together. Dismissing it, I swung my attention back to him, sucking my swollen lip between my teeth before leaning over to kiss him slowly.

He allowed it, watching me straddle his hips while forcing him onto his back. His hands lifted, careful of the wounds covering my body still in stages of healing, while he gripped my hips tightly. Lowering my mouth, I slowly kissed his hungry lips, letting my body rock against his. I was sticky with sweat, covered in it from the fever I'd had from the poisonous bites.

I reached between us, searching for his cock, freeing it while he slid his fingers against the wetness between my thighs. The moment I leaned up to force him into my body, fully intending to let him take away the guilt from the losses consuming me and sitting heavily within me, he pushed me aside and sat up, staring down at me.

"You're not using me to break your vow just to punish yourself," he stated coldly.

"That wasn't what I was doing," I argued, watching him shut down. "I want to forget the pain."

"Fucking someone doesn't make it go away. You don't get to fuck me, so you can punish yourself for failing your team. You don't get to *use* me and make me your scapegoat for that anger you're looking to direct at someone. I'm not interested, Alexandria. You need to bathe. You fucking stink."

I exhaled slowly as he moved away from the bed. My head swam with the reality of what I'd just almost done. I deserved his rebuke because it was exactly what I'd wanted to do. If I could hurt myself, I'd feel better. It made little sense to most, but it was what I did to ease my pain. Craving pain and redirecting guilt at someone else worked for me. It was shitty, but sometimes the pain was too much to endure, like now.

Torrin went to the door while I covered my body. He spoke in the ancient language, which I realized more and more they all spoke around here. Whether it was to keep us from knowing what they said or throwing off travelers, it seemed the language they preferred. I listened while Torrin spoke to a woman at the door, her sultry tone slithering around every nerve within me, while his softened toward her.

"She's awake. Bring in water for her bath. She stinks so bad I can't stand it, so soap would be most welcomed," he continued.

"I imagine she smells like death and is offending your senses with her presence, my brave Lord. If you'd like, you could join me while she rids her body of the offending stench. You would be more than welcome in my bed, Torrin. I miss what you do to my body, and I hunger for their light with so many of them around."

"I may help you out later tonight, Kat," he said huskily. "For now, let's get the bitch bathed, so she is ready to travel in the morning. The king is rather tired of waiting for her arrival. I'm over babysitting her and dealing with her mouth, among other things."

"Does he intend to share her with you as you've done with me many times before?" she asked, a pout entering her tone.

"She's too thin and too much work to even try to bed, Katherine. She's simply a mission, and once I reach the palace, I can be rid of the bitch." Torrin exhaled slowly, pushing her hair behind her ear. "Get the staff to bring in water and have a light meal sent up."

I turned away before he faced me once more. My stomach flipped before flopping, and angry tears pricked my eyes. I was such an idiot. As much as we were working to seduce them, they were returning it tenfold. He moved toward a large leather pack and pulled out a silk gown, placing it onto the desk before a knock sounded at the door.

My mind wandered back to everything we'd done and how he'd acted through those things. He'd been turned on, or so I'd thought. This was Torrin, the legendary warrior who led his king's armies into war and had never lost a single battle. He was a notorious rake, known for enjoying women and leaving them the next morning.

"Your bath will be here shortly. I've set out clothes and a drying cloth for you. Tomorrow we will reach the palace. I don't want to chance another attack, so we will travel fast enough to reach it before nightfall. There's more tonic on the table. It seemed to ease your pain and keep the fever down. Use it; it's laced with moonflower dust, but not enough to make you lose your willpower. You won't have to ask me to get you off again."

"I don't think that will be a problem anymore." I breathed in sharply, pulling the sheet with me while moving to the edge of the bed.

I ignored the look that passed through his eyes, dropping my head into my upturned palms while I considered how stupid I'd been of late. I'd let my guard down because, admittedly, I'd wanted him. He was deliciously wicked, and yet those men always turned out to be huge pricks. I knew that, but unlike Amo, Tabitha, and the others, I hated meaningless sex with strangers in taverns.

"The pain of their loss will pass," he stated from behind me.

"I'm aware. I don't need a pep talk from you, Torrin. Thanks, but no thanks," I stated as the door opened and several young women entered, batting their lashes at the larger-than-life male while barely noticing me.

Once the water was full to the rim, I stood and dropped the sheet before sinking into the large round tub. Grabbing the soap, I made quick work of scrubbing my flesh raw to get the stink off before washing my hair. My eyes stared off into the dancing flames, and I replayed the last moments of the girls' lives, forcing myself to memorize it visually.

I stepped from the tub, wrapping my body in the drying cloth without turning to look at the brooding, dominating male, who watched my every move. He probably thought my anger was from being rejected when, in fact, it was at allowing him to slip between the walls that encased my emotions. I was usually pretty good at hiding my feelings or protecting myself from getting attached to anyone. I dressed but chose not to return to the bed, lying on the floor in front of the fire instead.

The door opened, and I listened as he issued orders. I struggled to get better control of my emotions as tears slid free from the tight hold I'd had on them.

I felt emotionally and physically drained from being feasted on by the wraiths. While it wasn't Torrin's fault, at least not entirely, he still shouldered some blame because he'd drugged us and tossed us into wagons. He'd left us exposed and then rushed us into a decrepit old house that was one strong wind away from being firewood, which it had become.

Torrin wasn't faultless, but we'd probably have been attacked by something else on our way here. I'd planned on getting captured before reaching the border so they would bring us into the kingdom. I'd never expected to be captured by the head of the army or a legendary warrior.

"Get onto the bed, woman," Torrin growled, and I closed my eyes, ignoring him as the fire heated my face.

He lifted me without warning, and the sheet dropped

from my body. I tensed, inhaling to release the anger that rushed through me with his touch. Torrin set me down gently, his eyes skimming over my body before he stepped back, turning on his heel to move to the bag he'd gotten the clothes from earlier.

Returning, he sat on the bed, staring at my impassive face before twisting the lid from the jar he held. Dipping his fingers into the salve, he leaned over to rub some over my side where the stitches were itching. I breathed past the lump in my throat, ignoring him while he tended to my wounds. He was gentle, slowly working the salve into my skin, which made it slowly numb from the pain and itching of the flesh that healed.

"I can do that myself," I muttered under my breath, feeling his fingers pause before he pushed them into the wound on my arm, causing me to cry out.

"Be a good girl and shut up," he growled, holding my stare before his lips tipped into a cocky smile. His finger pushed back into the wound, and I shuddered from the delicious bite of pain while he watched. "You like to be hurt. Don't you?"

"Leave me alone." I fortified my emotions, turning away from him.

Torrin shoved me down onto my stomach on the mattress. His elbow pushed into my spine before his mouth slowly hovered over my back. His body held mine down, somehow managing not to cause pain where I'd been injured. Lips brushed over my spine, sending heat rushing through me. Fingers slipped between my thighs, and his dark, husky laughter rumbled through me.

"Is this what you want from me?" he growled

hoarsely, pushing his fingers against my sex that clenched for more. "You need to hurt, so it's easier. It won't make it any fucking easier. You lost them, and they're gone. Hurting yourself won't help you or numb the guilt. You're a fucking leader; act like it," he snarled, telling me what he told me when my seven sisters were lost. Then he pushed his fingers into my body hard, spreading them wide before slowly withdrawing them. "Sleep, because we leave at dawn."

He lifted from the bed, grabbing his cloak before exiting the room. I closed my eyes, caving to the weakness of sleep that demanded I succumb to it, and eventually, I did. Nightmares met me when I entered my dreams, wraiths feasting on my body while I watched helplessly as the girls died. Tossing and turning, I gave up on sleep, dressed, and left the room.

Outside on the porch, I watched the stars that shot across the skies as the full moon approached. The closer it got, the prettier the darkness became. It also made my body ache with the coming call to breed. Swallowing the groan, I sat on a chair and looked at the stars, enjoying the cover of darkness that hid the silent tears burning my eyes.

A scream sounded from the woods, forcing my attention to where it had originated. Noting the eeriness of the darkness, I searched the surrounding forest. Exhaling, I grabbed one of the rusty swords from beside the chair and started from the porch. When I entered the woods, the scream sounded again, and I sucked my lip between my teeth, inching forward.

Rounding past the thicker trees and shrubs, I stopped cold at the sight that met my eyes. Torrin had the woman tied between two trees. Her body was covered in angry red welts from the branch he held in his hand, slapping it against her exposed back while she pleaded for more.

I fought down the unease that slid through me, watching as he whipped it over her back and ass. He moved around her, grabbing her throat before lowering his head against her shoulder, looking directly at me.

The blindfolded woman whimpered as his fingers danced over her spread sex, dripping with need. My air wouldn't escape my throat as I studied the way he pushed them into her body. My heart beat loudly, unable to tear my eyes from him, slowly bringing her toward orgasm.

I stood there, shell-shocked, while he spread her legs further apart, allowing me to see more. Withdrawing his fingers, he pulled something glass from his pocket, pushing it into her body hard and fast. His eyes never left my face as my lips parted, and heat flushed through my body. He wasn't gentle, using the thick, glass, penis-shaped object on her, forcing it deeper while she begged him to fuck her.

She shouted, screaming for more, and I stepped back, unable to look away as he watched me through fiery eyes. His eyes held mine, the object moving steadily into her body while his smile turned cold, his eyes dragging down my body as if it were me he was imagining defiling. My body heated, and his nostrils flared as though he could sense that I wanted her to be me. I ripped my eyes from him, noting the black lines that spread over her face as she whimpered.

My heartbeat pounded loudly, louder than her screams ripping through the forest. Her body crested the peak, and his name exploded from her lips, jolting me from the trance of watching him fucking her with the object.

"Fuck me harder, Tor! Yes!" her squeal echoed through me, forcing me to snap to attention. Turning on my heel, I rushed away from them, allowing them privacy to finish whatever strange fetish was unfolding without an audience.

Entering the tavern, I ignored the eyes that moved over me from the staff that was just waking up. Inside the bedroom, I pushed a heavy chair in front of the door and climbed into bed, staring at the flames that danced in the large, open-faced fireplace.

My mind replayed what I'd witnessed, and my body tightened with need. Ignoring the pang of unease, I pushed it away as my eyes flicked to the large, rounded moon, knowing that within two days, I'd be writhing in pain instead of lust—because fuck him.

I'd watched him with another woman. I hated him for doing it with her; even if he hadn't been fucking her, it was the same thing. He'd known I was there, and instead of stopping, he'd held my stare and made me want to take her place, which was insane! I was in dire need of a reality check. I'd thought he wanted me, but apparently, he wanted whatever was easy to get. That wasn't me.

I hated him.

I hated her more because I'd wanted to be her.

The man drove me insane, and obviously, he wanted to seduce me to keep me in check. I wasn't stupid. I'd let my guard down, which was absolutely stupid to have done around a rogue with a reputation for leaving women weeping and obsessing after him once he'd finished with them. How could I have done something *so* stupid when it was obvious he wouldn't want someone like me?

Men like him didn't crave skinny, tiny women like me. I knew that, and yet I'd thought maybe he was different. I wasn't this girl who lost her shit over a male. I was a leader who led forces into battle, yet at the first tidbit of attention, I'd caved like some tavern bitch who took any form of affection they could get. I'd always hated those women because I'd thought they deserved better. But I wasn't any better than they were. I was so starved for the touch of a male that I'd become just like them. How could I allow that to happen?

Easy.

I was close to the moon phase, which lowered my expectations of what I needed and wanted. At least that was my excuse. Obviously, I'd made a mistake. I wouldn't make it again.

I awoke to something sending off warning bells in my head. Prying my heavy eyes open, I stared into the wintery eyes of the male who I'd barred entrance into the room. He sat in the very chair I'd used to secure the door, smiling coldly at me.

"Did you enjoy watching me with her?" he asked, and I snorted, turning over to dismiss him coldly.

Torrin ripped the blanket from the bed, and before I could turn over, he slammed his body down on top of me. His hands captured mine, pinning them above my head as I bucked my ass up to unseat him from my back. His cock pushed against my ass, alerting me to the fact that I was in a very precarious position. Teeth skimmed over my shoulder, and then his hand landed against my exposed ass cheek. The sound cracked through the room loudly, and I whimpered against the red-hot pain his hand had created.

"That's for making me wish it was you tied up, being fucked by me."

"Get off of me," I growled, hating that even knowing he'd just been with her, my body still responded to his touch.

"You told me you sucking my cock changed nothing, woman."

"Because it didn't!" I snapped, fighting the angry tears pricking my eyes.

"Then why are you so fucking angry that I was with her?" he asked, rubbing my ass. His hand slid around my body, finding the wound in my side before he pushed against it, growling. I gasped, crying out as he chuckled huskily against my ear. "You enjoy pain, and you enjoyed watching me use the glass cock on her, didn't you?"

"No." I swallowed, hating that both had turned me on.

"Liar," Torrin laughed darkly, spinning me onto my back in a swift move. His hand pushed against my throat, and he watched my eyes darkening with desire. "I turned you on, admit it. You wanted to be her, and I wanted her to be you."

"You're sick," I whispered, staring into his hooded gaze.

"Am I? Because I'm pretty sure you get off on being hurt. You enjoy pain with your pleasure, Alexandria. I bet if I reached down between your silken thighs, I'd find you soaked with need. Should I test that theory?" he asked, lowering his mouth toward mine. I turned away from his lips and then gasped as he nipped the skin on my chin. "Pretend you're better than me if it helps you sleep at night. Get up, get dressed, and get over yourself, woman. You're a twisted, dirty little bitch, who can't admit what she likes. The only difference between us is I've learned to accept who I am and what I like, and you're too fucking self-absorbed and stubborn to see who and what you really want."

I pushed Torrin away, moving to the edge of the bed to stand. When I was up and moving, he captured me, slamming me face-first into the cushion of the chair, pushing his fingers into my body. I clenched around him, moaning loudly as he worked two fingers into my pussy. Everything within me threatened to combust. My stomach coiled with need, and my hips pushed against him, taking him even deeper. He didn't stop, not even when the orgasm built in my stomach.

Torrin released me without warning, and I slid to the floor, turning to look up at him while he slowly sucked his fingers clean.

"Thought so," he chuckled darkly, moving toward the bag. "If you're not downstairs in five minutes, I'll take it as an invitation to fuck you. Move, now," he snapped coldly, his eyes watching me with anger burning in them.

Chapter Fifteen

The ride was torture, which I was certain Torrin knew and enjoyed. I hadn't spoken to him much and didn't plan to either. He'd noticed my unwillingness to speak and hadn't liked that I refused to answer his questions. I'd reminded him several times where he could stick his anger, which had only made his ire more palpable.

I'd spent a little time with the girls, everyone listening while I explained what had happened. Since it was a sacrifice, their last act to protect the rest of us from joining them in death, we would shed no tears. No funeral rites would play out for the fallen.

It would be our act of honoring their sacrifice, silently carrying them with us as we continued to fight in their honor. We'd go on so that their gift to us wouldn't be in vain, or at least that was what the Order would command us to do.

I'd hugged Amo and Tabitha, holding in the

overwhelming need to break down and just *feel* something other than anger for once. As assassins, we didn't cry often. Hell, I couldn't remember the last time I'd cried before meeting the overbearing, dominating prick behind me.

I was the leader, the one who held everything in and never lost control. I stood stronger to allow the others to lean on me in their times of need. I was the rock they sat upon, letting the water drown me so they could remain above it.

That was my role to play, and I'd agreed to do it. I had to lead by example. I couldn't ask my team not to cry and then do it myself. I was the strength when the others were weakened and even when they weren't. It didn't matter that I had emotions. The Order had trained me to ignore them, to ignore my needs, to ensure theirs were met.

"You want me to take you into the woods and work out that frustration before we reach the king's court?" Torrin asked, tightening his hold on my waist.

He'd somehow managed to secure horses, replacing the ones the wraiths had eaten, while I'd been down with fever. Of course, they weren't of the strength or stamina of the ones lost to the wraiths, but they did get us through the few attacks that threatened us, so I wasn't complaining.

"I think if you want to go into the woods, you better call back your tavern girl. I'm not interested in doing shit with you anymore, Torrin. The sooner I tell your king where to shove his shit, the sooner we part ways, and we can be done with one another forever."

"You think Aragon is going to let you go?" he asked, refusing to release his hold on me.

"I think he'll see where I stand soon enough. I won't help him find the library. I won't assist him in doing anything he wants of me, and he *will* release my brother. You and your king have no right to hold any one of us."

"Yeah, you should start with that when you meet the king," he snorted before nudging his horse to move faster.

The entire night was a blur, but arriving at the Kingdom of Night was exhilarating. They hid the whole place beneath the cover of darkness, lit by stones that had once belonged to the Moon Goddess herself. Violet light covered the trails and illuminated the village. It was something I'd never imagined laying eyes upon in my life. The king had made it known that the gates were closed to the Moon Clan, and without an invitation, none would pass through the barrier he'd built to keep us out.

Torrin was silent behind me. It was probably best he didn't speak because nothing would have slipped through my lips. I wasn't sure why it had pissed me off as much as it had since I was the one who kept reminding him we weren't friends. So then why had it bothered me so much? Hadn't I told him that sucking his dick had changed nothing between us? Yes, and I'd said it several times to reinforce the claim. I dismissed the prickling of hurt that echoed through me and focused on the allure of the kingdom.

There were no words to describe the beauty of the Kingdom of Night, glowing with life below. The palace was enormous, much larger than I'd ever dreamed it could be. Weeping willow trees that shouldn't live without the sunlight covered the road into the kingdom. They adorned each of their massive tree limbs with glowing blue drops of luminescent paint.

People moved around the street, covered in dark capes, with their faces hidden while we neared the large silver gate that opened as we approached. My eyes bulged at the amount of silver used to build the wall surrounding the entire village situated below the dark palace. Everyone in the world hungered for silver. Its rare potency could ward against wraiths and other creatures that fed upon the living. How the king had found a mine to harness this much was beyond me.

The deeper into town we went, the more the light of the stones glowed. Only then did I realize why it shone with a life source of its own. They had used moonstones from fallen moon-touched people were used as lamps; the rocks collected and piled into glass pillars lit the eternal night with their glowing essence. Torrin tensed behind me as a guttural growl slipped from my lips.

"This is what your king does with *our* remains? He places us on display, ignoring our sacrifice, to light his streets?" I hissed, fighting the pricking behind my eyes as thousands of lamps came into view.

The other women echoed my sentiments with grunts. We silently took in the miles of moonstones that stretched in a circular pattern around the palace. Torrin wisely remained silent, even though I could sense the anger he felt at my words. To him and his kind, the Moon Clan were nothing more than slaves to the moon. We eradicated the threat so they could live lavish lifestyles in their protective city while the rest of the world outside fought to survive. They lived because we sacrificed our entire life to ensure their survival.

"They're not just any moon-touched warriors, Alexandria. They're our moon-touched citizens, who sacrificed their lives so that others here wouldn't have to. Do you think people outside of this kingdom care about those within it? When the Kingdom of Light fell, they flooded here, and one by one, they succumbed to their end. They were the Kingdom of Light and the first to be touched by the moon. The Sun Clan's princess was lost to the ocean, and their king and queen dead in their tomb. Their heir joined with the moon-touched to fight the darkness and abandoned their people. Now the only kingdom to stand is this one, and even though the prince was merely a child when he took his throne, he still welcomed all into his kingdom. The only thing he asked of them was that upon their deaths, they give to the pillars that prevented the evil from gaining access to his kingdom to slaughter his people."

"Indeed," I stated, ending the argument to escape the conversation.

Torrin moved us through the city, stopping the horses before the wide entrance of the palace. Several warriors, who nodded to Torrin in a show of respect, guarded it. Torrin handed me down to a soldier and dismounted to stand beside me silently as the others swarmed around us.

I spun in a circle with the girls, taking in the kingdom's beauty. "We're here," he growled, moving away from me as light glowed above.

I lifted my face to the moon, tasting the rays that warmed my face. Gasping sounded from the girls, and I turned to see the cause, only to slow blink at the palace.

What was lit from violet lights was now illuminated by the moon. It was an ethereal scene of moonlight touching the palace's lofty towers, shooting light into it to glow fluorescently bright. Everywhere I looked, the royal residence glinted with an iridescent radiance from the moon, kissing the sides and the glass of the palace.

Torrin watched my face, smirking boyishly as my eyes grew round with awe. I opened my mouth to speak, yet no words left my lips. I couldn't even start to explain the intense emotion that pulsed through me as my chest tightened. Tears pricked my eyes while the moon bathed the lofty towers in a glowing light. All around it, the glass with the moonstones ignited, pulsing with their essence being rekindled, fueled by the moonlight that shone throughout the kingdom in honor of those who had given their lives for its safety.

"Welcome to the Kingdom of Night, Alexandria." Torrin smiled roguishly, taking in what I saw through fresh eyes, with a sparkle of amusement burning in his stare.

"It's the most beautiful thing I have ever seen," I admitted in wonder.

"It was the most beautiful thing I'd ever seen, but not anymore," he stated thickly, and I blushed, flicking my eyes to his.

"Flattery will get you nowhere, sir," I warned. Also, he was a slut, but I kept that to myself. Women and men moved closer to us, and I paused as one tried to get past a guard to get a closer look at us. The moon hadn't only lit up the palace; it had also caused my hair to change coloring, exposing the rainbow within my eyes and hair.

"You must excuse their curious stares. We rarely see people so beautiful, or who glow within the light," he grumbled, and people rushed away from the frown creasing his brow.

"You have a way with people, Torrin. If I weren't sure of the taste of your kiss, I'd swear you're a nightwalker, what, with the black veins and eyes." His eyes studied my face before a wolfish smile replaced his frown. My sweet smile turned saccharine, and I exhaled, turning to the girls.

"Careful, I hear nightwalkers lust after the light and drink it from only the most beautiful maiden possible," he whispered. "You're exquisite too, Lexia. If I were one of them, you'd be the maiden I came for first. I'd drain you, drinking your sweet moonlit dew until it filled me with your light, and left me satisfied that you'd succumbed to the darkness within me as well."

"If you don't offer him your *dew*, you can bet your tight ass that I will." Amo swallowed hard, twirling a strand of her glowing, white hair while licking her full bottom lip teasingly. Unlike my hair, hers only turned white with the light of the moon.

I sucked my lip between my teeth and inhaled deeply through my nose. "If you want Torrin, you can have him because I don't," I stated, staring at the wicked glint burning in his icy stare. "It seems his attention isn't held for more than a moment, and I find myself unimpressed with him now."

Amo frowned as her focus moved between us slowly before she gave Tabitha a look that said something was up. I shrugged the moment her eyes settled back on me, telling her with mine to leave it alone.

"Follow me," Torrin announced, glaring pointedly at me. "Do try to behave like a lady, Alexandria."

Chapter Sixteen

Once we'd entered the palace, Torrin and his men asked us to wait in the largest room I'd ever stood inside. It had a massive arched entrance that mirrored the outside of the palace. More glowing moonstones filled the glass against the walls, lighting it up brightly. On the ceilings were enormous chandeliers that sparkled with crystals.

"I sorta want to touch everything, but I'm afraid if my fingers even skim over something, it would shatter into a million pieces. Then the king would lop off my head for doing it," Amo whispered excitedly, even though her voice echoed through the room. Amo's owl perched on her shoulder let out a loud hoot, forcing heads to turn in our direction. "Can you believe we are actually inside the Palace of Night?"

"Don't touch anything," I muttered beneath my breath. "I'd prefer to be outside of it since we're not guests here. We're prisoners, remember that."

All around us, women in huge gowns glared at us

while speaking behind their gloved hands. Most wore jewels, and some even wore moonstones from their ears or throat, turning my stomach. I doubted those were from the stones of the people willing to sacrifice their light to protect the kingdom dwellers. These were people who'd never had to work to survive. They'd been allowed into the kingdom's sanctuary, where men like Torrin did everything to keep them safe inside their little bubble. These assholes probably hadn't ever lived in fear for a second of their pampered lives.

"These men look—*weak*," Tabitha stated, which caused several of the men to turn at her words, staring down their noses at us just like the women in the ball gowns. "They're so skinny I could pick my teeth with their bones. Can I?" she asked, and I snickered until it came out as a laugh.

"No, you cannot eat the men here."

These men were dressed in flowing white shirts that did little to hide the scrawniness beneath them. They wore their hair back in bands, showing off sharp cheekbones, pulled back with pale skin that almost appeared transparent. They were nothing like Torrin or his warriors. In fact, I'd have been shocked if some weren't actually women who preferred to dress like men. Either way, they were entirely too scrawny to be desired. Not that I would judge them for that, but being so sickly skinny was fair game. My girls would eat them for breakfast and spit out their bones. Well, minus Tabitha, who wanted to pick her teeth with them.

"Are there no real men here? I need to feed the beast," Tabitha whined, her brows pushing together on her forehead.

"Moon-touched filth is not welcome here," a woman stated, her high nasally voice grating on my nerves, causing my eye to twitch.

"Well, then we'll just leave once you return our blades and our horses," Amo hissed, her sharp canines glinting in the room's light as she crossed her arms and popped her hip. I loved Amo and her fierce, sharp, and quick wit that had her willing to fight everything and everyone. She was my spirit animal, even though she wasn't an animal per se. Scout squawked, and the women stepped back further yet.

"Such ill manners," the woman whined.

"Fight me, bitch," Amo challenged, watching them step back again as her face sharpened with her elfin features. "Go suck something off. We're not here for you or your entertainment. Fuck off, pampered doll."

I silently took in the woman who spoke, noting her pale hair and bright green eyes that slanted exotically. She was beautiful, and the dress she wore exposed ample cleavage and wide-spreading hips. The gown was mint green, accentuating her eyes while making her light complexion seem darker than it actually was. On her throat was a strand of moonstones fashioned into hearts.

"You would do well to hold your viper tongue before Torrin removes it for me," she seethed, her friends swarming around her for support.

"I do believe that you accosted us, and not the other way around," I stated, stepping forward, folding my hands before me, and daring her to argue.

Her eyes studied me, dismissing me as unimportant before narrowing to angry slits at Amo. The woman pushed her chest out, and I lifted a single brow at the move. If she thought her overflowing bosom was going to impress us, she seriously lacked brain cells.

"What's that? You need out? I know, she trapped you in there, and it's so unfair that you're just bursting to get out and scream freedom. Right?" Amo snickered, reaching up to pat the woman's tits, which made Tabitha bark in laughter as the woman sputtered with rage, turning bright red.

The sound of footsteps echoed in the hall while I kept the woman in my sight to ensure she didn't make a move that would end with us in shackles. Torrin came into view, and her face softened as she was rushing toward him, jumping before she reached him to throw herself at him.

He caught her while I watched the scene unfolding. Her lips slammed against his while my stomach turned. Torrin didn't kiss her back, but his eyes sparkled with heat while she slid down his body.

"I have missed you, My Love," she announced loud and overdramatically.

"And I you, Karina," he rumbled huskily, causing me to roll my eyes. "I need to see to the king's guests."

"They're horrid creatures, baby," she whined, her eyes flashing to mine before slowly moving back to his. "They've offended me. You should have them whipped before the court for such a brazen slight against your lover and noblewoman."

I made a loud gagging noise, which was probably childish, but come on. What the hell was with the pathetic display?

"Is that so?" he asked, turning winter-colored eyes on me, which filled with a fire that crackled over my skin.

"Tor, they're horrid. Do something!" she sobbed, fisting her hands into his shirt.

"Yeah, *Tor*, do something," I laughed coldly with a shit-eating grin on my face, daring him to do something to me in front of the court. I crossed my arms over my chest, glaring pointedly at him while he unpeeled the woman from his chest.

Torrin grabbed my arm once he'd removed the court hussy from his shirt, pulling me with him toward the large archway that led out of the hall where we stood. He didn't stop until we were halfway down the long hallway, and I hadn't noticed that none of the others were brought with me. My heart slammed against my ribcage, fluttering wildly as he spun, shoving me against the wall, hard and punishing.

"You're not in your world anymore, little girl. You're in mine. I'd be very careful who you piss off here. You're not here under protection from either the king or me. You're a necessary evil to the goal he seeks to achieve. Don't make me have to fucking hurt you to get you to understand the severity of pissing off the wrong person."

I didn't speak or react. Torrin's hand slid up to my throat, applying pressure while he studied my reaction. His heady stare dipped to my mouth, smiling cruelly when he took in the way my lips trembled. He sensed how pissed off I was, yet he ignored it. Releasing me, he watched as I stepped away from the wall to continue glaring at him.

"I'd tread carefully here if I were you, Little Bird.

Not only has it been a very long time since anyone here has seen your kind, but they don't like your kind either. You're nothing to us, Alexandria. Less than nothing to me," he stated, starting away from me. "Follow," he snapped angrily.

"I thought we would see the king before you locked us away in cells," I asked thickly, running to keep up with him. His words had knifed through my heart, and the coldness within his eyes sent chills racing down my spine.

"You thought wrong," he growled without turning toward me.

Torrin turned down another hallway that had several doors with guards in front of them. I took in their weapons. Mentally, I noted each one had armor embedded with onyx, the opposite of what they needed to ward against nightwalkers. They were weapons used to kill the moon-touched, which we just happened to be.

"Open the door, Hensley," Torrin grouched, and a guard opened the door before stepping out of the way.

I followed Torrin into the room, pausing to give the guard a withering stare before entering behind him. The inside was decked out in finery, featuring a four-poster bed, with silk curtains hung in wispy waves down from the silver frame that adorned the top. A table sat with whiskey already in goblets on the smooth marble top. In the room's corner was a bath, fed water by a fountain that poured from the wall.

My bag hung on the partition that divided the bedroom from the bathing room. I crossed my arms, glaring at Torrin while he lifted one goblet, drinking it down, staring at me over the rim. He was cold. Whether it was because I'd openly dismissed him or because he'd finished his task of getting me here, I didn't know. I also didn't care.

"The king decided to throw a party in your honor. You're to attend it tomorrow night. If I were you, I'd be on your best behavior until then. You may not roam the castle without someone at your side. If you feel the urge to explore, you can summon me, and I'll show you around. Maybe we can even stop at the dungeon to test out some equipment."

I exhaled softly, moving toward the bed while giving him my back. "You're wearing Karina's lipstick. It's not your color," I frowned, pinching the bedding to feel the softness between my fingers.

A hand snaked into my hair, twisting me around until his mouth hovered over my lip. His eyes searched mine, ignoring the deadened look I gave him. I wasn't about to touch his mouth with Karina's rogue red lipstick on it.

"My room is close to yours. If you feel the need to scratch that *itch* you are ignoring, have Hensley find me. Until then, you should probably work on your fucking attitude."

"Screw you," I snarled, shoving him away. He didn't budge, and before I could guess his move, he ripped the dress from my body, causing me to cry out. Torrin picked me up and slammed me down on the bed. I huffed, spreading my legs to clamp them around his torso, but he smiled coldly, giving me pause. His gaze slid over my erect nipples, dipping further down before he growled.

My hands pushed against him, but he captured them, watching me struggle beneath him as he had in the street where he'd captured me. I lifted my head without warning, slamming it into his. He snarled, turning my body over before his elbow pressed against my spine threateningly, sending pain against it, forcing me to still.

"You want to play rough?" Torrin ground down harder before the sound of something ripping echoed through the room. He yanked my hands behind me and wrapped a piece of the curtain, tying them there. I bucked against him, but he ignored it.

Yanking my hair back, he put another length of material in my mouth and tied it around the back of my head, preventing my screams from being heard. Slipping from the bed, he ripped down more of the curtain to tie around my ankles. He yanked one toward the bedpost at the foot of the bed, his fingers quickly securing it as I tried to use my other foot to kick him. His laughter echoed through the room as he caught the flailing limb, attaching it to the post at the head of the bed. He pushed me over, forcing my head to slam into the silk bedding as my core became fully stretched and exposed to his greedy stare where I lay sideways, face-down on the mattress.

Once he'd finished, Torrin walked across the room, opening a door. I bristled in anger and fear, thrusting my hips to loosen the cloth, holding my legs apart. The sound of feet padding back across the room met my ears, and then something hard slapped down on my ass.

I howled through the cloth, the sound muffled. Again something hard and firm slammed into my ass, and I fought angry tears at being humiliated. His fingers slid through the arousal coating my sex, taunting me. He leaned over, kissing the sore flesh of my ass cheek while pushing his fingers into my body. I groaned, rolling my eyes back into my head at the pleasure he induced. I felt something cold against my opening and froze, and then it pushed into my core as he withdrew his fingers.

I shuddered at the feeling of being full, stretched further than I'd been in four years. Torrin worked the rigid object in as his mouth lowered to blow heated breath against the cold tool he used on me. His tongue licked around it, and I gasped through the cloth. He withdrew the item, replacing it with his tongue as I struggled not to come undone at the sensation he created.

Moments before I would have exploded, Torrin moved his mouth away. The firm, flat item slapped against my ass again, and I groaned loudly through the cloth, muffling my noises. His hand rubbed the offended skin, and then the cold object was back against my core, pushing into it as he growled, watching me rocking against it, willingly spreading my legs further apart. Torrin laughed wickedly, withdrawing the rounded tool to replace it with his fingers.

"You're so fucking wet for me, woman," he groaned, nipping the flesh he'd kissed. "If you weren't so fucking hell-bent on holding on to that vow until the last moment, I'd be fucking you until you felt me against your womb. You want that too, don't you, Alexandria?" he murmured, scissoring his fingers while my body clenched and tightened. "Your body needs release, and so do you," he whispered thickly, withdrawing his fingers to move from the bed. "I bet you wouldn't be such a bitch if you were coming for me. I bet you could fit that proverbial stick and my cock up your tight ass at the same time, couldn't you?" he asked, pushing his thumb against the place in which he was speaking. I tensed, and he chuckled darkly. "Virgin here, huh? You won't be for long."

Torrin walked around the bed, smirking at me while I glared at him. Defiance burned in my stare while he bent down, running his fingers over my cheek.

"You're gorgeous," he murmured, sitting in front of me. Torrin took me in with dark desire, igniting in his heady stare. "You feel the freedom you have right now?" he asked, and I shook my head. "You've never had to let go, have you? You've always had control. Right now, you have none. I took it away from you. All you can do is lie there and take what happens and accept it. It frees you from being in control. You look so hot spread out for me. Your sex is soaked from this," he stated, holding up the hilt of his blade, coated in my arousal all the way down to the guard of the sword, which he gripped in one hand. "Should I leave this here for you? Or should I take it and imagine you fucking it while pretending to be unaffected?"

I swallowed, observing him while I played his words out in my mind. This wasn't freedom. He tied me to the bed and fucked me with the handle of his sword! He was insane if he thought this offered any freedom at all. In fact, it was the exact opposite of freedom. I wiggled, and Torrin's eyes grew hooded, his smile tipping up the corners of his generous mouth. He liked it when I struggled, figuring out how helpless I was, realizing that I was truly trapped and at his mercy.

Torrin tilted my chest to the side and slid his hand beneath me to grab my breast, rolling the erect nipple between his fingers as I held his stare. He reclined on the bed in front of me, playing with it as a shit-eating grin spread across his mouth. His eyes studied me while I stared at him with wide, horrified eyes.

"Bloody hell, woman. Let go for a fucking moment and just feel what I've offered you," he urged, noting my eyes only grew wider. Grunting at my response, Torrin stood to pull a knife from his pocket, which sent all my blood rushing to my brain. "Now, tomorrow, there's a ball. You'll be provided with an outfit and will be expected to attend while being on your best behavior. Your girls are in the rooms next to you, separated, of course. You are assassins, after all, and we are not new to dealing with your kind. The moon-touched clan has sent many assassins into our lands. You're not the first female assassin I've played with, but you may yet be the first to leave alive."

Reaching over, Torrin pulled a lock of my hair up between his fingers, holding my panic-filled glare. Smirking, he cut it from my head, watching it return to dull platinum before graying. He dropped it to the floor, tilting his head, edging out of my sight. I jerked my head to the side before moving it the other direction.

Something touched against my opening, and my eyes bugged out of my head before I closed them. Gasping, I tensed against the cold metal touching my clit, and I sucked in air, whimpering. It slowly slid against my core, and I shuddered as pleasure rushed through me. Wicked laughter filled the room before he dropped the knife, licking his tongue through the arousal with a deep growl.

"You are wicked, Little Bird," he grunted, still

lapping against my opening. "You're soaked, so don't even try to pretend you're not into it."

Torrin moved around the bed, staring at me as he slid his tongue over the blade. My eyes locked on it as he tilted his head. Kneeling on the floor in front of me, he leaned closer, kissing the cloth placed over my mouth. Torrin reached behind my head, removing the fabric. I wanted to throttle him, but his words registered, and my eyes narrowed. How many assassins had entered this land before us? Why weren't we warned?

He reached up, pushing his thumb over my lips, then lowered his mouth before his fingers curled through my hair. He yanked my head back until his eyes were holding mine.

"Tomorrow night, you better behave. If you don't, you'll regret it, woman. I promise you that."

Standing, Torrin moved around the bed until the swish of a knife cutting through fabric sounded. I sat up, waited for him to remove the binding on my arms. He smirked down at me with heat scorching my flesh where his gaze slid over me. Moving behind me, he untied my hands and leaned over, kissing my thundering pulse.

"Tell me you didn't feel that freedom," he growled.

"You're insane!" I snapped, rounding on him as he backed away. His eyes smiled, sparkling with amusement at the way my chest rose and fell.

"And you're turned the fuck on, Little Bird. I should have left your mouth available and used it," Torrin laughed wickedly, gripping his cock while watching the anger burning in my eyes. "Keep lying to yourself that you're craving some basic cock. You're not turned on by it, which is why you can't get off. You need someone like me to take away your control. You've been so fucking close for me, and yet I've respected your vow. That ends tomorrow night. Sleep well, Alexandria. I suggest you get some rest. You're going to need it."

Chapter Seventeen

Screaming woke me from a dead sleep. I lifted my head, searching the room as the obnoxious noises seemed to come from inside it. Sitting up, I moved to the table, lighting the candle before turning toward the wall. Pushing the hair away from my face, I glared at it. Walking to the door, I opened it and then darted back as the guard outside lunged.

"Cool your shit," I snapped, glaring at Hensley. "Someone is being murdered in the room beside this one, in case you didn't hear it unfolding."

"The only thing being murdered in that room is pussy," he chuckled, dragging his heated gaze down my scantily covered body.

"Tell them to shut the hell up then," I groaned, rubbing my eyes.

"No can do. You want to tell them, you go right ahead, little lady."

I bristled, turning toward the noise as yet another round of high-pitched screaming began. Sucking my lip, I worried it between my teeth while scrunching up my face. Drawing in a breath to steady my nerves, I moved toward their door, pounding on it.

The screaming lowered, and male voices laughed from inside. Scuffling sounded before the doorknob twisted and the door was thrown open. Torrin stood before me, shirtless and wearing lounge pants that hung low on his hips, exposing his abdomen's entirely too sexy V-line. I swallowed hard, moving my gaze to several naked women and a nude male within the room.

My stomach flipped and dropped to my feet at the scene. Karina had her ass in the air while she kissed her way down the other male's chest. They were all preoccupied and uncaring that I watched as another woman slid down the male's enlarged cock. Torrin looked back, taking in the scene before turning his eyes back to me and narrowing them.

I stepped back and slammed the door closed. Turning on my heel, I marched back to my room as the guard snickered. Laughter exploded from the room currently hosting the orgy. Grabbing my bedding, I pulled it off the bed before moving to the other side of the room, far from the adjoining wall. I slid my back down the wall as the moaning started up and then more feminine squealing.

Pushing the bedding beneath my body to protect me from the cold stone floor, I held a pillow over my head, trying to sleep. A masculine voice bellowed my name, and I glared at the opposite wall, realizing Torrin had placed me in a room right next to his. Torrin's laughter followed the male screaming out my name, and then a woman screamed his name as hot tears pricked my eyes.

I turned, knocking on the wall behind me. Feet scraped across the floor, and an answering knock sounded. Tapping three times, I waited until it answered six times. Smiling, I placed my hand on the wall, knowing Amo was behind it. We had to get out of here. Torrin was confusing me on purpose and enjoying doing so.

I'd almost begged him to fuck me today. I'd felt the moon nearing its fullest state, and that meant that I was in trouble of losing control. Tomorrow, the moon would be full, and I knew it would call me. The moon hadn't called me in four months, which meant my body wouldn't be in control, and it didn't care about modesty or the fact that Torrin was a huge man-slut.

We couldn't be here when the moon reached its precipice tomorrow, but we didn't have our weapons or a means for escape. Torrin had brought us into his territory, and while that had been the plan, we had to figure out where the map was and get our shit back.

They had Landon, which meant I had to figure out where they were holding him, and the moment I had that information, I could escape this place and the infuriating male who was playing with me. I got it; Torrin was a warrior, and we all knew how to use what we had.

Torrin had sex appeal, and he was notoriously wicked-good in bed. He enjoyed dominating women, and while it was a tremendous turn on, I couldn't act on it. For one thing, I'd be very fertile the moment the moon phase started. Torrin's men had taken all our tonics, which meant anyone called by the moon would be in danger of breeding. There was also the matter that I didn't want to be yet another woman he womanized.

A knock sounded on the wall beside my head, and I answered it, listening as Amo tapped out a question.

Are we escaping?

I frowned, tapping my coded reply. *Hell yes, we're leaving.*

Another few taps, and another answer. We talked in code for over an hour before I rested my head onto the pillow, staring at the opposite wall. Frowning, I listened to the sounds of flesh meeting flesh and high-pitched screams of pleasure, mingling with the guttural groans that echoed through my head.

By the time I gave up on sleep and bathed, dressing for the day, it was morning. I opened my door, glaring at the guard. It wasn't Hensley. The new guard turned, staring at me with midnight eyes.

"I need to visit the stables," I stated, watching his eyes turn to slits before the door beside us opened, and a group of women slid from it, giggling as they started down the hallway.

"You're not allowed outside of the room," he snorted loudly.

"Take me to the stables," I repeated, glowering at him.

"You deaf? I said you're not allowed out of your room, you stupid bitch," he shouted, and I growled, balling my fists at my side as I prepared to attack him.

"I'll take you," Torrin interjected, leaning against the doorway with his arms folded over his chest in a lazy pose.

"No thanks," I seethed. "This Neanderthal can point

me in the right direction, and I'll go by myself."

"You're not permitted to be outside of your room without me beside you. You can leave Chivalry neglected, scared, and depressed that his pretty mistress has ignored him since she arrived, or I can escort you. Choose," Torrin grunted, studying my face.

"Fine, take me to my horse."

"Let me put on something more presentable," he said with a saccharine smile that irked me. He wore his lounge pants that looked way too enticing with how low on his hips they hung. The bulge in his pants was visible, forcing a blush to paint my cheeks as I looked away.

I waited at the door, but he didn't move. Smothering the need to scream, he lifted a brow and nodded toward his bedroom.

"Come on, woman. You can assist me," he grunted, and I swallowed down the need to tell him to get fucked, but then he probably would. He'd probably take it as an invitation.

I moved toward him, entering the bedroom without waiting for him. Inside, the room was in disarray and smelled of sex. Bottles of whiskey sat half-drunk, while penis-shaped items littered the floor. A whip sat on the bed, and other random items I assumed he had used last night lay there as well. I lifted my stare to the ceiling, bristling with unease and anger while he rummaged through his chest, withdrawing clothing.

"You sleep well?" he asked, and I scoffed.

I turned away from him, dismissing him outright with his outlandish question. He didn't need my reply because he knew the answer already. His wall was bathed in maps, which drew my interest. I crept closer, noting the lines drawn around certain places, with large *X*s that marked prisons and holding cells. On the furthest corner of the map was a blacked-out mark, one that forced me to move closer to see the words written upon it. It was too accessible, though, which caused my mind to turn it over a few times, slowly shaking my head.

I lifted my hand, and I ran my fingers over the fallen kingdom's symbol, belonging to the Sun Clan that was lost long ago. The Kingdom of the Sun had once been a powerful kingdom, according to our history books. It was the land that had held the light until it had fallen, leaving the world bathed in eternal darkness.

"The Sun Clan," Torrin stated behind me, causing me to jump and turn toward him.

He caged me in against the wall, letting his stare settle on my pulse that jackhammered at the base of my throat. My chest rose and fell in the corset left out for me to wear, pushing my breasts up to appear fuller than they were. He smiled coldly, dipping his eyes lower to take in the silver top and the sheer skirt that covered the leggings beneath it.

"I see you found your things," he rumbled huskily.

I didn't reply, choosing to remain silent. Torrin grunted, backing away from me as I slipped beneath his arm and moved toward the door. He swept his gaze over the room and scrubbed his hand over his face. At the door, he issued an order to have his room cleaned before he returned.

"You are choosing silence over conversation?" he

asked as I followed him down the hall.

"I have nothing to say to you," I grunted, ignoring the chilling look he tossed back at me.

"Tonight, the moon will be full," he announced.

"I'm very aware of the moon phase," I admitted, stopping as he spun, pushing open a door. He held his hand out, indicating I should go first.

I peered into the darkened stairwell, frowning while taking in the steep spiraling stairs that led down into darkness. Pursing my lips, I studied Torrin's body language before slowly entering and starting down them.

"Afraid I am taking you to the dungeon?"

"If you're asking if I trust you, the answer is no."

"For not caring who I fuck, you're acting like a jealous bitch," he muttered, and I turned, glaring up at him.

"Who you fuck isn't my concern. I don't care about you. I don't care what you do or with whom you do it. You're nothing. You're just some male slut who enjoys seducing women. Once the chase is over, so is your affection. You're not my type, Torrin. Stick with your floozy court and tavern girls. You're shallow like them, which I'm sure provides you with a lot to talk about when you've finished fucking. They're used to being used and discarded at a male's discretion."

I turned, starting down the stairs, only for Torrin to grab my hair and yank it back. He slammed my body against the wall, and his hand grabbed my throat, applying pressure while he studied me. Lifting my hands, I dug my nails into his wrist, trying to remove the hold against my windpipe. Lights burst behind my eyes as stars danced within them. Midnight-black eyes watched me as the lines spread over his face, moving down his throat.

My body trembled as a sinfully wicked smile played on his lips. He lowered his mouth, claiming my lips as he released my throat, feeding me air while I moaned against him. He continued gripping my hair, holding it painfully in his grasp while he pushed his tongue into my mouth. I bit down, drawing blood as he gasped. Coppery tang painted my tongue as he pulled my head away from his.

"You think you're so much fucking better than us, don't you? Why? Because the moon cursed you with light so that creatures like me can suck it out of you? You were escorted into the Kingdom of Night by nightwalkers, and you didn't even fucking notice. Poor Alexandria and her neglected cunt, couldn't think past the male who offered her a tiny bit of affection. You're the pathetic one."

My head swam with his words, searching his face as I realized he was a fully functioning nightwalker. I'd assumed he held a demonic presence, but never a nightwalker since they weren't capable of thought or control of their minds when hunger hit. I'd heard the whispers of the nightwalkers being able to retain their memories, but most were mindless killing machines that merely lived to destroy the moon-touched people. My body shuddered as I pushed myself against the wall, staring at him.

"You're lying," I argued, knowing he wasn't.

Torrin lowered his head, and when it rose, his eyes were filled with black that consumed the whites of his eyes. Now that his guard was down, I began to really explore his features, noticing that his ears were pointed, like those of the original families that had once lived in the land thousands of years ago. His teeth were sharp, the long canines exposed in the smile he gave me while my mouth opened and closed in denial. Torrin's arms were covered in delicate black lines that hummed and pulsed beneath his skin. His hair was silver and longer than it normally appeared to be.

"Tell me I'm lying," he whispered huskily. "Do you think your people will allow you back within their protection after hearing that their fearless assassin sucked off a nightwalker? Or that she allowed him to play with her inside her mind?" he asked, and the blood drained from my face.

No. They'd assassinate us. The Moon Clan would hunt us down as deserters, capture us, and put us down to keep their secrets safe. My heart pounded in my chest as I searched Torrin's face, praying to the Goddess of the Moon that he was playing some sort of sick joke.

His head tipped to the side, and the smile that spread over his lips wasn't friendly. He moved closer, and I slammed myself against the wall, watching the anger pulsing in his stare. His hands grabbed me, holding me in place while he pushed against my body, showing me how hard he was.

"Your fear excites me, Alexandria. If I were you, I'd at least try to conceal it."

Chapter Eighteen

Torrin took me to the stable and left me there momentarily while he spoke to the stable hand. I stroked Chivalry's mane, rubbing down his side as I told him we'd lost people and who they were. He bayed and rubbed his head against my shoulder, tossing his head back the moment Torrin reappeared. My eyes moved to his frosted glare.

Torrin was a nightwalker who'd looked normal until he chose not to. They were evolving. He'd been able to change at will. That meant nothing we knew about nightwalkers was right. They could be within the gates of the clan stronghold, and we'd never see the difference.

He'd passed every test we'd been trained to administer. Torrin had no problem ignoring the call to take my light, and he'd seemed normal. Okay, so he appeared normal for those within the Kingdom of Night, altering some signs I would have recognized.

Torrin had taken me within his dreamscape, which

required a lot of mind control and precision to do correctly. I'd been inside his mind, forcing my way into it, and nothing had been off about him. Usually, when one pushed into a nightwalker's mind, there was nothing, no brain activity besides the urgency to consume light. So how had he evolved into one displaying none of the symptoms?

"Done?" he asked, staring into my angry eyes, noting my frosty response.

"Yes," I whispered, uncertain how to act, knowing what he was.

I had spent my entire life training to murder his kind. He was the monster we hunted, striking them down without fear. Killing mindless enemies was simple when they didn't contain intelligent life.

Torrin was a man, a virile, living, breathing man with needs. He held conversations and indulged as any other man would. Cautiously, I followed him until we reached the stairs. I watched his body while we climbed them, noting no stiffness or deadening movement that led to the change of the mindless monster he should be.

At the top of the stairs, Torrin opened the door and led me down the hallway. My eyes flicked to the guards, noting their eyes studied me before bitter smiles spread over their mouths. Sharp fangs became exposed while they took me in, silently.

I tried to slip past Torrin to enter my room alone, but he didn't allow it. Instead, he pushed the door open and followed me inside, much to the guard's amusement. I backed away from him, staring around the room for something to use, but came up empty. Someone had left a dress on the bed, with a pair of soft shoes, presumably for the party tonight.

"Drink. It will calm the rate of your heartbeat," Torrin ordered, settling into a chair while he watched me staring him down.

"I learned that lesson when you allowed me to drink drugged whiskey," I stated, noting the way his mouth curved into a knowing smile.

"You're afraid of me," he grunted angrily, sitting forward to steeple his hands in front of him. "Do you fear I will drain you, Alexandria?"

"Shouldn't I? You're a nightwalker, Torrin."

"You can call me Tor. Women I plan to fuck get to call me such." His eyes studied my face as I shook my head.

"Don't take this the wrong way, but you're a whore, *Tor*. I wouldn't fuck you now, even if I hadn't learned the truth of what you are. Does the king know what you are? Is everyone here, nightwalkers?" I word-vomited my questions one after another without taking a breath.

"Yes, the king is aware, and no, they are not all nightwalkers," he stated, lifting the whiskey to fill two silver chalices. "If I hadn't told you or shown you what I was, you'd never have known. I have not harmed you, not out of anger. I didn't force you to do anything you didn't want to do with me. I protected you, and I ensured you made it here in one piece."

"You do understand that kidnapping isn't the same as escorting someone. Right?" He smirked, shaking his head while those pretty blue eyes noted my every movement.

I compartmentalized his words, pushing them through my mind while I crept closer to him. Sitting in the furthest chair, I stared at Torrin with curiosity. He'd fucked me. Not physically, but he'd ensured I could never go home. Our people wouldn't welcome me. It was treason to consort with the enemy, and he was so much the freaking enemy.

There would be no returning to our people. My team and I were now outcasts who had no home, no people, and nowhere to go that would accept us. My eyes flicked to his face, sliding down his body before they rolled back up to hold his gaze.

"Did you die to become a nightwalker?" I asked, uncertain if I should ask him questions.

"No," he said, sipping his whiskey while he watched me above the rim.

"How then?"

"You think it's a sickness, which isn't true. You and your people were awarded the light of the moon while we were bathed in eternal darkness. Do you think we weren't blessed as well?"

"Being a nightwalker is a curse, Torrin. You feed on the living. You *murder* us."

"And you fucking murder us!" he snapped, losing the thread he'd held on his composure. I jumped back, and he ran his hand over his mouth, glaring at me. "You hunt our people down, slaughtering them because, to you, they're wrong, they're an abomination. They don't glow in the fucking dark, and therefore they're lesser beings."

"Nightwalkers don't have coherent thought! They suck the fucking marrow out of us! What would you have us do to protect ourselves?"

"Do you think I have no coherent thought? Have I sucked the marrow out of you? Hell, Alexandria. I tasted your delicious pussy, but you're still alive, aren't you?"

"That was in a dreamscape."

"Was it?" he asked, and the room changed around us. I stared at the familiar bedroom, with the silk sheets and the desk where he'd pushed me down.

My heart stopped beating and restarted with a thud that thumped painfully. Moving my attention back to Torrin, I found him smiling roguishly, his eyes noting that I was putting everything together.

"You didn't break your vow," he stated on an exhale, pushing the whiskey forward. "Drink before your heart gives out."

"If it wasn't a dreamscape, and it was real…"

"I made you think you found release. The mind is a wondrous thing, Alexandria. Your mind allowed you to buy what I sold to it. You were in bed with me while I fed you images of what we were doing together. Easily manipulated once you assumed it was possible."

"Why not just tell me?" I asked, watching his face.

"Tell you what, Alexandria? That I was a nightwalker sent out to retrieve you? Tell you that nothing you did would have prevented you from being brought here? Our people are at war and have been since the plague of darkness divided the kingdoms, and the Order of the

Moon declared us monsters, knowing we weren't. If I had told you the truth, you'd have fought me the entire way here, more than you already were."

I shivered, peering out the window as the moon started its ascent into the sky. My body tensed, pulsing with the start of the call. Torrin watched me, his eyes slowly growing hooded as a knowing look burned within them.

"You should drink, change into the dress, and enjoy the night. Your moon will call you soon, and then I'm sure it will limit your time at the party. The king expects you to attend with your team. Be a good girl and don't cause a scene tonight. I'd hate to have to kill you for upsetting him."

I exhaled slowly, nodding even though I was sure I didn't know why I was nodding. Torrin stood, then moved to kneel between my thighs. His hands lifted, gripping them while I shivered at his touch. His smile turned up at the corners, and before I could judge his intentions, he leaned forward, capturing my mouth in a soft, slow kiss that sent my emotions thundering through me.

"It's treason to kiss my kind, Little Bird. What is it your people do as punishment for treason?"

"Exile or death," I admitted through trembling lips. "For moon-touched warriors, it is death, as we are the keepers of the knowledge of their deeds. We carry out the Moon Clan's missions and, therefore, would be sentenced to death to keep their secrets from our people."

"Pity," he chuckled. "You're so pretty. I'd hate to see you put down because you didn't adhere to their laws. Before you met me, you were such a good soldier, Alexandria. You did everything they ordered of you, slaughtered thousands of our kind in the name of laws that your people created because they thought they were more evolved than us. Do you know I have people inside your temples, sleeping and living with them? How do you think I got to you, Little Bird?" I swallowed as he rose, cupping my cheek while I stared up at him. "I'm the monster, right? We built a wall to keep your kind out, yet you still found a way through it. Do you know how wraiths are created?"

"They're raised by the darkness."

"No, Alexandria. In the beginning, we were all one people until the plague of darkness came, dividing us into opposing clans. The Moon Clan believed they were at war with the Kingdom of Night based on their interpretation of the call of the moon. As the darkness descended, some people from the Kingdom of Night became the banshees and creepers you saw during our journey. Most people remained unchanged within the kingdom walls, but the darkness that descended transformed many of us into nightwalkers. Your people, the moon-touched, are also changing into nightwalkers when touched by the darkness. Because they shunned the people of the night in order to live in the light, their transformation is much more difficult, and many do not survive. Your people killed those who lived after being touched by the darkness to hide their lie about the nightwalkers' origins. Those that escaped either went mad, becoming a creeper or banshee or they came to the Kingdom of Night seeking refuge, as did Hensley, your guard from last night. When a moon-touched kills a nightwalker, the moon brings them back as a wraith, seeking justice toward those that killed it. So, in essence, you're killing your people, turning them into wraiths, and a wraith's only purpose is to consume those that stole their lives—the Moon Clan. If you will recall, the wraiths were not attacking *my* people other than to get to you and your girls."

I stared at Torrin, unable to process what he'd said. It was too much. I needed to return to the temple to find answers, but I didn't think I'd be allowed back within it. Torrin had probably already ensured we couldn't return. I watched him reach for the glass, handing it to me.

"Drink, it's going to be a long night, and you're going to need the alcohol to get through it."

Chapter Nineteen

Inside the bedroom, I sat hugging my knees in the large tub. I was numb, confused with everything that had been dropped on me in such a short time. I kept waiting to wake up and learn that I'd had a nightmare. I released my legs and stood, moving to where a cloth had been left to dry myself. Wrapping it around my body, I sank into the nearest chair, shivering as my mind replayed how Torrin had looked bathed in darkness.

Everything he was, called to me, which meant I deserved to be removed from the clan. Hell, *I'd* kick myself out for the feelings he created within me. I couldn't ignore it, which meant tonight was about to be a colossal mistake that would end up with my head on a chopping block, *literally.* Sleeping with a nightwalker wasn't discussed as an executable offense because we'd thought them all mindless killing machines.

Nightwalkers were nothing like the Moon Clan had taught us.

I'd had some serious foreplay with one and held conversations with him.

I still had to figure out how to explain the situation to my team without everyone freaking out. The girls would have a fit, knowing they'd inadvertently slept with a nightwalker, and I knew they had because if Torrin was one, then the chances were high that his men were too.

Standing, I moved to the dress lying on the bed, staring at the sheer material. The entire bodice was a see-through lace halter top without sleeves. The dress's skirt parted up the thighs, exposing them through the thin fabric that felt softer than the silk covering the bed. The waistline was cinched and tight to show off my slender hips.

Dropping the cloth, I slipped into the dress and moved toward the large mirror that sat beside the pool. Frowning, I looked at the dress from several angles, deflating at my slight figure. Giving up on what it looked like, I returned to the bed to grab the sheer panties, pulled them on, and then slipped into the soft shoes.

After digging through my bag, I found my hairbrush and ran it through my hair. I left it down to flow along my back, which the material failed to cover. Torrin had taken all tonics and elixirs from my things, which meant I had to maintain control tonight. I couldn't chance losing it and become pregnant.

I had nothing to offer a child or to give them, including a home in which to return to where I could raise them safely. I had no security or promise of tomorrow. Torrin had taken it all from me, whether by choice or design, I had no idea. I wasn't naïve. The chances he'd done it on purpose were very high. I was no one to him, just an assassin who slaughtered those he had included in his race.

To him, I was the monster.

Murderer.

Why would he care if his choices ruined my entire life?

Realistically, it didn't change my course. I had set out to find my brother and discover the clues to where the library was hidden. Once I read from the Book of Life, the plague of darkness would be eliminated, or so we hoped. Torrin messing up my entire life didn't change that.

I moved toward the door, opening it to find several guards waiting. Stepping out into the hallway, I closed the door and peered between them. Their eyes were filled with dark obsidian and absent of color, which identified them all as nightwalkers. Swallowing past my unease, I smiled tightly.

"I am ready," I stated, offering the guards a nod while they studied me like a bug they wished to squish beneath their heavy boots.

One stepped forward, his nose in my personal space, his lips peeling back to reveal sharp canines. I didn't blink. I didn't cower or move because on any given day, I'd have taken his head without breaking a sweat. This guard was scrawny; his unworked muscle tone exposed his lack of training and age.

I did the only thing I could do. I smirked, turning my head to brush my lips against his, which sent him tensing as the light within me jolted the darkness within him. Fuck around and play stupid games, and you get a stupid prize. His eyes slanted to angry slits the moment he realized I'd done the action on purpose.

"I am ready," I repeated, knowing they were all wary of me now.

Housing as much light as I currently did had perks. I was holding enough to level the entire palace to rubble. I followed them to the door beside mine, knowing it was Amo's room. The guard knocked on the door, and Amo stepped out, her green eyes sliding through the guards, widening with unease. Her shocked expression swung to me, and I watched her throat bobbing with worry before she stepped up beside me, holding my soft gaze.

It was the same thing at every door in which we stopped to retrieve another moon-touched girl. Eventually, after the asshole guards made a show out of trying to scare each one, we started toward the sound of laughter and music.

We entered a large ballroom with stairs that led down onto the dance floor and into an actual room. At the stairs, the guards indicated for us to wait. My heart rocketed into overdrive as I took in the dark eyes of those below us.

Every single person turned, staring up with eyes the color of freshly polished onyx. I felt the girls tensing behind me. I looked over my shoulder to Amo, who was staring out over the assembly with an expression of sheer horror.

Darkness consumed light, and we were the only light present. The crowd gawked openly, hungrily, up at us while we waited. The guard stepped out from in front of me, and my gaze slid down the long red carpet and straight to the throne where a male sat with his leg kicked over the arm, lazily watching us. Torrin stood beside him, his eyes narrowing on me while I again turned, looking to Amo, who was behind me with the others, ensuring they were okay.

"You remember the time we crashed the clan leader's party? Let's do that one again," I stated, watching their eyes sparkle as a smile crept over my lips.

"It's perfect," Amo chuckled.

"I'm down," Tabitha agreed, and the others laughed nervously, fully aware of what I intended them to do.

Well, they'd be executing the plan while I kept the head of the guard busy in other ways. The moon was about to take me over, and then I'd be out of commission for at least twenty-four hours. I watched Amo peering up where the ceiling was opening for the moon to shine down into the room.

"The moon is going to call me," I admitted, shoving past the unease that came with what would happen tonight.

"Those who aren't called can stay and play," Amo agreed, barely above a whisper.

"Quiet, or you'll regret it," the youngest guard snarled.

I smirked at him, tilting my head before facing forward. The moonlight bathed the path in iridescent light, forcing the others back from the carpet that led to the king. My heart was thundering painfully in my chest while I scanned the crowd. My hackles were up, and everything within me said to turn and run or fight.

Torrin's eyes slid down my body, and I exhaled the unease. I wouldn't show fear in the face of impossible odds. I wouldn't allow the girls to see me tremble before the mass of people who craved our fear. I'd show them all that, even in the face of death, we weren't weak.

"Move," the guard stated, and I frowned, slowly descending the stairs with sure-footed steps until I was inches from the light.

The moment I stepped into the moonlight, the crowd gasped as my skin changed, appearing as if there were thousands of tiny stars shining light within me. My hair turned a glowing white, with rainbow-colored tips starting at my ears and sliding down my back to brush against my ass. My arms pulsed, exposing the thin, shimmering lines of light that burned from inside me.

I didn't stop or slow until I reached the king's throne, where I bowed low at my waist, letting my hair shield my face. My team followed my lead, bowing to a king that wasn't ours. It was a show of respect because regardless of how we felt; he was the King of the Night Kingdom.

He left us there for several minutes, which was fine with me. I could feel my body clenching from being bathed in the moonlight. I could feel the power summoning me to cave in to my baser needs, preparing me for mating with the man of my choosing. I closed my eyes while the room remained silent. The moon shone from the ceiling where it had separated, allowing it to reveal the moon's healing light.

King Aragon was bound to notice a few key things when I rose. One of these was the symbol that would shine upon my forehead, showing that I was from the Sun Clan's royal line, mixed with the moon-touched symbols. He would also notice the delicate lines framing my face, painting the length of my nose with the fallen court's royal emblem. Then there were the tiny sparks of light that shine from within me, which he may have already noted as if my bloodline carried the sun within it.

"Rise," Aragon said in an amused tone.

When I did, his eyes widened, and he quickly dropped his leg, sitting up straighter. My eyes flicked to Torrin, finding him frowning as he took in the markings. No, I wasn't a Sun Clan princess, but I was of the bloodline connecting me to the poor babe sent down the channel and out to sea by her father to escape being mated to the King of the Kingdom of the Night.

King Aragon's intended mate hadn't died as presumed. Instead, she'd been discovered and raised within the temple. She'd died long ago, but before she had, she'd lived a happy life and bore her mate many children. I was one of the few female descendants born to our line, making it dangerous to be around this king who felt entitled to collect our line's women as his own.

"You didn't notice this?" Aragon asked Torrin, standing to move closer to me.

Torrin's eyes held mine, and something swam in their icy pools. I flicked my eyes away from him, rolling them up to look at the moon, bathing me in its light. I felt my eyes illuminating, shining with the glow of the golden sun that forced them to mirror the color of freshly polished emeralds, no longer the color of the once cloudless skies. They combined with soft gold, changing them for the full moon to expose the truth within my blood.

I turned back to the king, flinching from his hand that lifted to my cheek. Torrin had moved closer, his chest rising and falling while he searched my face, transfixed on the bloodline markings.

"You're from the Sun Clan," Aragon stated breathlessly, his fingers trembling while he touched my face.

"I am," I admitted, uncomfortable with his hands on me.

Suddenly, they were on me everywhere. In my hair, touching my face, exploring my arms, everywhere. All while Torrin stared at me without speaking or intervening. His eyes changed between black and ice blue as if he were looking at me through both his sights.

"How is this possible?" Aragon demanded, moving closer to touch my exposed sides.

"The Moon Clan found the basket carrying the sun princess. They raised her within the temple and wed her to their prince. They had many children, and I am but one of their children's offspring."

"She died," Torrin stated, finally speaking.

"No, they made your kingdom believe she died. Ironically, the Moon Clan assumed that the Kingdom of Night would accept the darkness or be immune to it. At first, they protected her in order to bargain with you, but you never came. You never looked for the princess, so they presumed you had no interest in brokering a deal with the devils that created the plague of darkness. My grandmother lived a long, happy life with her husband."

"There are more of you," Aragon stated, clapping his hands with excitement.

"I am the last surviving female of our line," I admitted.

His mouth dropped open, no longer smiling. Torrin's eyes slanted into an angry glare while he sized me up. He seemed unable to look away from me, and I wasn't sure it was a good thing. My body was reacting to the moon, demanding I create life.

"We're being rude to our other guests," Aragon announced, watching me with a heated look. "You'll be in my room tonight, Alexandria."

"Excuse me?" I asked, turning to look at Torrin.

"The moon is calling you, and I am King. You're mine tonight. The court expects it, and so it shall be," he stated with a sinful smile curving his mouth. "I suggest you enjoy the party while you can."

I flicked my stare to Torrin, who didn't offer any help. I nodded, then exhaled. Stepping back, I glared at them both before I turned, walking to the other side of the hall, pretending to be unaffected by the king's declaration.

I wasn't certain how to turn down a king. He'd left no room for argument, either. I was apparently sleeping with Aragon tonight, and it had nothing to do with slumbering. My attention shot to Torrin, who had Karina on his arm, whispering into his ear while he stared at me. Whatever she said, he didn't react, unable to remove his eyes from me.

Karina was still hanging on his arm, her lips moving

by his ear as he started forward. My heart hammered, and a gasp slipped from my lips as he strode toward me with purpose. My body clenched tightly, growing heated while his icy stare held mine prisoner.

"We're dancing," he announced, dragging me out on the dance floor while Karina glared at us from the side of the open area, forgotten and discarded.

Torrin stopped in the middle of the floor, uncaring that no one else was dancing. The moment he wrapped his arms around me, he jerked my body against his, hard. His nose brushed against my ear, and I moaned, unable to ignore the contact while under the influence of the moon. A shudder of need shot through me, and my hands tightened onto him. His dark, husky laughter sent warmth pooling at my apex.

"You kept secrets from me, Little Bird," he growled.

"You didn't ask, and you seemed to have already researched me before deciding I was your target," I replied, pushing my body against his. "I don't want to be the king's tonight," I admitted, resting my head on Torrin's solid chest.

"It's an honor to be chosen as a bedmate to the king," he stated, dipping his eyes to my mouth.

"For others, maybe. Not me."

"Who would you choose?" he asked softly.

"My hand, as you've thrown away the tonics I had brought with me. I intended to accept the pain and lessen the need of my body by myself." I inhaled sharply through my nose and blinked.

"You think I'd allow that?" Torrin mused, turning

me around the floor surprisingly smooth for a warrior.

"I don't think it would be your choice. You enjoy women, and you've fucked several since I met you. Seemingly more than one last night alone. Then there's me if you include what you and I have already done together."

"I have fucked no one since meeting you, Little Bird. Did I offer relief to a woman in the woods so that her hunger didn't take control when there was an entire tavern full of moon-touched women, wounded and within her reach? Yes. Did I wish she was you the entire time? Yes. The king held an orgy for my return, and yet I fucked no one. I didn't even come because they pale compared to the intensity and desire I felt from your touch. I know it may be hard to wrap your sheltered little brain around, Lexia, but some people can be around others while allowing themselves freedom from the restraints this world placed on them. You should probably permit me to escort you to the king's chambers. It's about to get a little too wild in here for you."

"What is that supposed to mean?" I demanded, and a woman cried out before I'd even finished speaking. My head spun, watching as three men pleasured a woman at once. "Wow, I didn't see that coming," I admitted.

All around us, couples were shedding their clothes. I turned toward Torrin, who smirked, watching the heat painting my cheeks. He slid his hand around the back of my neck, yanking me close against him before his mouth crushed mine, causing tension to build in my abdomen.

"I need to get out of here," I whispered, unable to get Torrin close enough to my skin.

"Do you now? I think you should watch them play and take notes."

"Torrin, please," I pleaded. "My response to the moon isn't like the others. It's magnified and violent when ignored. I can't be around them because I lose all self-control. Get me out of here, now."

Torrin searched my face, finding the panic in my glowing green eyes. He grabbed my hand, nodding to the guards, who moved toward the other girls in my team, stopping in front of them while creating a barrier between the frolicking crowd of nightwalkers. My eyes held Amo's, nodding subtly to tell her I was okay and to go on with the plan we'd started.

Torrin moved us through the dark hallway, heading up a spiraling staircase. When we reached the top, he nodded at the guards, who stood in front of an extensive set of doors. They moved forward and opened them so we could enter the bedroom.

I barely made it inside before I groaned, leaning over to rest my hands on my knees to ignore the pain echoing through me. Torrin silently watched me, moving toward the large desk that I'd seen in his dreamscape. Shoving past the unease, I watched him filling two glasses of amber-colored whiskey into the goblets. Exhaling, I started toward him until he turned and smirked at me.

"Strip, slowly," he commanded.

"You intend to start before the king arrives?" I asked, watching his eyes dance with mischief.

He abandoned the whiskey and table, stalking toward me to cup my cheeks between his hands. He smiled, staring into my eyes while I studied his.

"You're mine tonight, Alexandria," he whispered, watching the worry fill my eyes. "I need to taste you and feel you clenching down around me. I crave to taste your pussy and to hear your screams as you succumb to the pleasure that I give you."

"What about King Aragon?" I asked, barely able to contain the moan that built in my chest.

"Aragon only claimed you because he knew I wanted you. You're in my bedroom, Little One. Not his. You were never meant for him. You're mine, all mine," he stated firmly.

"Torrin." I inhaled, fortifying my resolve. His lips pressed against mine, and I kissed him like there was no tomorrow because, for us, there wouldn't be. "I'm yours for tonight."

Chapter Twenty

I had expected Torrin to move quickly once given my permission, but he wasn't fast enough at giving me what I needed or craved from him. Instead, he was slow and meticulous. He didn't pick me up and devour me; he simply moved back to the large table and nodded toward the goblet.

"Drink. You're going to need it tonight."

"You planning to make it hurt?" I asked through trembling lips, and the look in his eyes made my breath hitch in my lungs and come out as a breathy moan.

"Among other things I plan to do to you," he laughed soundlessly. "Strip, I need to see you." It wasn't a request. It was an order, his voice commanding and hoarse.

My hands trembled as I reached up, grasping for the clasp at the back of my neck, but they shook too much to accomplish the task. Torrin smirked lazily, with liquid ice pooling in his stare. He didn't offer help. He just watched me nervously fight with the delicate clasp at the back of my neck that wouldn't come undone.

"Do you need help?" he finally asked, and I nodded. "Use your words, Little Bird."

Blushing, I worried my lip while contemplating admitting defeat. I let my lip pop free, casually moving toward him as I swayed my hips, and he dipped his icy stare down my body. Torrin's scent was an aphrodisiac to my senses. It encouraged me to act brazenly.

"Will you undress me, Torrin?" I asked huskily. My voice escaped from my throat like a seductress tempting her prey into a snare.

He turned my body around, slowly moving my hair from my back before unclasping the dress, which pooled at my feet. I didn't move as his lips brushed against the back of my neck while his hand snaked up to apply just enough pressure against the front of it to hold me in place. A shudder of need rushed through me as he trailed his lips to my ear, fanning my hypersensitive flesh with his heated breath.

The back of his other hand slid down my spine, his knuckles brushing against it until he cupped my ass cheek and growled hungrily. Torrin turned both our bodies, forcing me to lean against the table. I tried to reach for him, but he captured my hands and placed them against the table.

"Do not move them," he ordered through a voice filled with gravel.

Torrin's lips brushed against my spine, carefully

working his way down the hip that he bit into softly, stealing a moan from my lips. He chuckled, grabbing my panties to pull them down, forcing the air to still in my lungs. Torrin nipped my butt, laughing as I yelped. He stood abruptly, pushing my knees apart as I stepped out of the panties.

"Are you wet?" he asked, and when I didn't answer, he shoved my head down against the table and slapped his open palm against my ass. "Are you wet?"

"Yes," I said breathlessly, lifting for more.

"Is your body in pain?" he queried, and I shook my head. "If you're not going to use your words, I will not fuck you. I'll tie your sexy ass up and watch you writhe in pain and need all night long. Now, are you in pain? Do you need me to fuck you right now, or do we have time for a drink?"

"I need a drink," I said while fighting past the need tightening in my throat. "The pain doesn't come until the moon reaches its zenith in the sky. At that time, my body will turn against me, and I'll be mindless with need."

"Then I suggest you drink before it reaches its highest peak."

I nodded, not moving as he hovered behind me. I would give him full dominance in this room for one night because I didn't want to regret not trying it before running from him. Torrin stepped away, and I held myself in place, feeling his eyes taking in my body while I waited for his permission to move.

"Drink," he stated, and I turned, giving him a saucy smile as I sat on the table in front of the chalice.

His eyes dipped to where my legs parted, allowing him to see that the Sun Clan's markings painted my abdomen. He chuckled audibly, lifting his eyes until they met mine. He downed his drink, moving closer to settle between my thighs.

"You're tempting me on purpose, Little Bird," he noted, lifting his hands to squeeze the weight of my small breasts, testing them in his palms. His thumbs trailed over the hardened peaks, and he smiled, holding my stare. "I want to give you pleasure through pain and listen to you sing for me. More than that, though, I want to pour the whiskey over your pussy and drink it from you."

I trembled, leaning closer to kiss him, but he didn't allow it. His eyes heated, and he nodded at the cup, reaching for the bottle to refill his and top mine off. I smiled, downing the whiskey, setting aside the cup while he watched. Torrin refilled it, and I frowned, wondering if he was trying to get me intoxicated.

"The last lover you took, was he gentle with you?"

"Incredibly so," I admitted.

"Did you enjoy it?" He watched my face, smirking as the answer lit in my eyes.

"I don't think we need to talk about him." I let out a breathy moan as Torrin pinched my thigh, creating pain while he studied me. When I still didn't answer, he pushed me down and slapped my pussy, causing me to moan while my legs parted for him.

"Did you enjoy it, or was it boring?"

"Boring," I admitted, knowing I probably should

have lied.

His fingers slid through the arousal coating my sex, and he moved closer. His fingers danced over my thighs before he leisurely pushed my legs further apart. Torrin eyed the chalice, watching me with heated eyes as he glided his hands around my waist, jerking me closer to his body. I could feel his erection pulsing against my sex.

I lifted my hands to remove his shirt, but he grabbed it, jerking it over his head, revealing rippling muscles and tattoos that filled with glowing light from within him. My hands grazed over them, watching as he tensed, capturing my hands to place them on the table beside my legs.

"Hold still," he ordered, lifting the bottle to my lips.

I opened my mouth to drink, but he pulled the bottle away, exhaling as his eyes filled with warning. He tilted the bottle and poured the whiskey down my body, starting at my lips before moving to my breasts to let the cold liquid flow down their peaks. I moaned at the sensation of cool whiskey poured over my heated flesh. Torrin pushed me back, dripping the amber liquid over my pussy, then lifted his eyes, studying me. He rubbed the rim of the bottle against my clit until I was crying out at the slow torture.

I whimpered, dropping my legs apart while Torrin set the bottle down. His hand moved around my neck, pulling my head against his to claim my lips in an earth-shattering kiss that stole the breath from my lungs. His tongue danced against mine as a growl escaped his chest, pushing into my airway as he pulled away. His tongue snaked out as he kissed his way down my throat, trailing over my nipple before he bit it playfully, causing a cry of need and surprise to slip free. He moved to the other, seductively flicking his tongue over my nipple, and then started down my belly.

Lying back, I lifted my feet to place them onto the table, offering him access to my core. It flexed hungrily, demanding he devour it. He held my stare, running his tongue down my abdomen, and then he was there, flicking my clit with his tongue. His fiery breath fanned my clenching need, and he growled, sending the vibrations rushing over my pussy that was drenched with anticipation and whiskey.

"Place your hands above your head, flat on the table, and don't move," he ordered, hovering, yet not doing or giving me what I needed.

I didn't question the order, placing them flat against the table as he'd commanded. He moved his arms around my thighs, encircling and capturing my legs while he lowered his mouth. His tongue slid out, lapping from one length of my slit to the other. I cried out, knowing that I wouldn't last long. I'd neglected my sex, and he was very aware of the short fuse I held over my need. His mouth seared me with heat while his tongue pushed into my core.

My entire body clenched around it, holding it there as my hips moved. Torrin didn't care that I was riding his face, pressing against him with the need to reach for the orgasm pulsing through me. I was almost suffocating him with the need to get him deeper into my body as his hand moved over my apex, pinching my clit hard.

I exploded, screaming, and then everything in me tightened before releasing at once. Pain mixed with pleasure while my thighs clenched his head, holding him there as I broke apart, shattering into a million pieces. Light exploded behind my eyelids, and my body arched, using his mouth to stay within the orgasm that tumbled through me violently.

When it abated, he chuckled, lifting his body to undo the buttons of his pants. His cock jutted free, and my eyes widened, taking in the sheer size and girth of the monstrous thing. He suddenly seemed much bigger than when I'd taken him into my mouth. He noticed the look of panic, causing his lips to twitch.

Torrin naked was a work of art. His tattoos were exquisitely placed and linked with power that pulsed deeply from within him. The glowing ink changed sometime between being bathed in whiskey and now. There was a violet hue to it, and I needed to taste it. I craved to see what his darkness tasted like and learn it carnally.

I didn't move from where he'd placed me. My hands were still flat above my head as my breathing grew labored. I didn't need to see that the moon was about to crest the sky. I felt it to my soul. The moment Torrin was in front of me again, panic flared to life. My chest rose and fell with it while he watched. His fingers pushed into my body, lazily scissoring while he witnessed desire bathing my face. Rocking against them, I took them deeper into my body as my cries of pleasure filled the room.

"You're tight and tiny. It's going to be a violent entrance, no matter how much I prepare your body. There are things I can use to make it easier, but I don't think we have that long before the moon hits its zenith, and I can't wait that long to be in you, Moonflower."

"I can handle you." I swallowed, uncertain that I spoke the truth.

"You sure about that?" he asked, pushing three fingers into my body.

I cried out, arching my back while continuing to hold my hands against the table, but it was getting harder to keep them there. Torrin slid his hand beneath my back, lifting me without warning. My arms moved around his neck, and he smiled, withdrawing his fingers before he pushed them into his mouth, holding my stare while he made the sound of a starved beast. He took us to the bed, placing me onto the mattress while he sat back, stroking his cock, staring down at me through hooded eyes.

"Turn onto your stomach and lift your legs," he murmured.

I turned, presenting him with my backside, spreading my legs apart. I arched my spine, waiting for him to push against my entrance. His hand came down hard on my ass cheek, and I moaned loudly. Rocking my hips, I silently pleaded for more. He didn't give it to me, choosing to rub the offended skin. The other cheek scalded as he slapped against it, chuckling, and a needy sound escaped my lungs, and I parted my thighs further, showing him my approval.

"You're drenched to be fucked, aren't you?"

"Yes," I admitted huskily. "I need you."

Both hands landed against my ass, and I yelped as pain and pleasure fought for supremacy over my body. Torrin's hands didn't offer relief, choosing to grip my hips while he placed me where he wanted me. I felt him against my opening, rubbing his shaft against the sleek wetness of the arousal he'd created. He silently lined up with my entrance, and I felt his cock pushing into me.

I trembled around him. My sex muscles clenched down around him while the narrow walls burned from how large he was. He stretched me, and my body rebelled against it, burning with fire while he rumbled huskily, watching me slowly rock against him.

He was torturing me, giving me a single inch to allow me to grow accustomed to his size. I pushed back all at once, gasping in pain and pleasure while I took him to his balls. My body clenched and protested as my muscles complained at being stretched so full. He took up every single ounce of space in my body. My face slammed into the bed, the cries escaping without stopping.

"Fucking hell, Little Bird. Stop clamping down on me," he uttered hoarsely.

"Move, please," I whimpered, rocking against him while the friction built.

Torrin wasn't just large; he was extremely blessed. My body greedily clamped down around his, demanding he gives me what I wanted.

"Fuck, you're so tight and needy. Your pretty ass looks perfect painted red for me," Torrin growled, slowly withdrawing to the tip, only to slam into my core harder.

His hands caged my body in, and his stomach slid over my back while he let loose of his control. There were too many sensations, too soon, from having nothing over the past four years to this. He learned the rhythm fast, forcing the orgasm to grow until it threatened to release, but he didn't allow it.

One of his hands slid around my throat, anchoring to it. Torrin pulled me back and then pushed apart my legs with his other hand. My pussy clenched around him, sucking him off while he chuckled at the feel of me milking him. I was stretched painfully around his cock while his hand tightened on my throat, and it turned me on.

There was pain, but it was pleasurable.

There was pleasure, but also pain.

It was a thin line he'd perfected because he had me dancing on edge.

One hand snaked through my hair, yanking it back as my scalp screamed in pain. His cock pulsed as it thrust in and out of my body. I had no control, and I didn't care. He was inside of me, outside of me, and all I cared about was the orgasm growing within me.

"Don't you fucking come," he hissed, but it was inevitable.

"Torrin," I whimpered, feeling every thrust of his body into the very marrow of my bones.

"Fuck, you feel so fucking so good, woman," he snapped, never releasing the hold he held on my hair and throat, and I wasn't sure I wanted him to.

It was a dominant position, stealing all of my control that silenced the worry in my mind. In his hold, I wasn't the leader of the assassins. Lives didn't depend on me. In this position, I felt free to let go and just feel what he offered me. I was just a woman with a man, finding the release my body craved.

I shattered without warning. My entire body tensed,

and I screamed from the turbulence that rocketed through me as his thrusts turned primal. Torrin shoved me down onto the bed, gripping my hips painfully as he let loose of his control.

I didn't care. I was in the throes of endless orgasms that tumbled from one to the other. Torrin fucked me throughout them all, growling and hissing while my body greedily clenched onto his. He slammed into me over and over, grinding against my backside with every single one. My hips faltered, and his fingers trailed through my hair, wrenching it back as he pulled me up against him. I dropped my head onto his chest while his hands slipped to my hips and lifted, seating him deeper into my body. He fucked me hard and without mercy, and I *loved* it. I didn't fucking want vanilla. I wanted this.

Torrin was unhinged with need, and mine met his like we were two massive storms colliding and combining into one. This was hate fucking now, and fuck if I didn't love it. It made me feel dirty and used, and I craved it. He unseated me, tossing me to the bed before stalking over to me.

Yanking my legs apart, he leaned down, caging my body beneath his much larger one. Torrin's hands pushed onto the bed on either side of my head. His cock slid against my wet entrance, and I opened my mouth to tell him what I craved when he thrust forward, stalling the words as a scream took precedence.

I slipped my hands around his back as he fucked me hard and fast, watching my eyes while he gave me what we both craved. I smiled, staring into his hooded gaze before my nails drug across his back, and he howled. He sat up to grab them, slamming them down beneath his hands while he thrust painfully into my body.

"Yes, yes, yes! Fuck yes," I shouted as I lifted my hips, slamming my body against his with every thrust, meeting his need with my own while he watched me.

Torrin slammed into me harder, faster, and made sure I felt every single inch of him. Leaning his head down, he bit into my lip as I groaned, rocking my hips to meet his cock. He released my hands, gliding them behind my head to pull me up with him. He yanked my hair back, exposing my throat, which he dragged his lips over my skin, kissing the thundering pulse while I took control of the position.

I rode him, uncaring if he held control or I did. He could have it because the next orgasm was already rising to shoot through my body. It started in my toes, slipped up my thighs, wrapped around my clit, and exited through my mouth as a breathless cry. My eyes opened, and I screamed his name to the heavens, shuddering so violently that he had to hold me through it.

Torrin growled, and I felt him filling me, releasing his need within me. He continued to hold me through the violence of his release, causing my body to milk his, holding him within me.

We fell over onto the bed, both of us panting in labored breathing that filled our lungs. Torrin hadn't exited my body, and already he was growing hard for more.

A satisfied smile curved my lips while I lifted my leg over his hip, rocking against him while he gazed into my eyes. I could do this for a few hours, but my body was already deliciously sore. His eyes dropped to where we were joined, and something dark and wicked passed through them. He watched me using him, grinding against his steel length while another orgasm was building.

"You're beautiful, Little Bird," he uttered as if it pained him to say it.

"Shut up and fucking give me what I want," I growled, pushing him down while I took control. He smiled, moving to sit up, but I shoved him down hard.

My eyes held his, daring him to take control. He smiled wickedly and rolled us, pushing deep into my body in one fluid motion.

"You're not the fucking alpha in this bed, woman," he laughed darkly, lifting black eyes to hold mine. "Let's see how dirty you really are, shall we?" He placed his hand around my throat while his other slid to my clit, twisting it until I was bouncing on the bed with the orgasm that shot through me without warning. He released my clit, running his fingertip over it softly. "I don't remember saying you could come. Do you?" he asked sarcastically. He pushed my legs up to my shoulders, going hard and angry against my body.

I screamed, exploding around him from the multitude of sensations he created within me. Torrin wasn't good at sex; he was a master, showing me what it could be like with the right man. He removed the idea of what I'd wanted, replacing it with this raw, brutal, dirty sex that left me boneless beneath him.

"This is going to be a long night, but I will not pretend that I won't be enjoying every fucking moment of it. Now, try not to come, because each time you do so, without my consent, I'll fuck you harder. Do you understand me?"

"Yes!" I cried, exploding yet again. He chuckled, staring into my eyes before his widened with the realization that I wanted it as hard as he could go. I wanted to taste the pain his pleasure offered. "I'm waiting," I challenged, observing the heat pooling in his frost-colored depths as they thawed with need.

It was going to be a very long night, and he wasn't the only one planning to enjoy every moment of it.

Chapter Twenty-One

I woke to hands groping me and my body being lifted onto another. Peering down through heavy lids, I watched the insatiable male beneath me before he entered my sore, exhausted body. Moaning, I rocked my hips slowly to accommodate his girth.

Last night, things had gotten violent, and the hate slid into a frenzied passion. It was wild, mind-blowing sex that hadn't ended until we could physically do no more. Bruises covered my skin, and I'd enjoyed every single one of them. I had peppered Torrin in scratches and bite marks, which he hadn't seemed too bothered by either.

This wasn't the same kind of sex this morning, though. It was slow and methodical. My hips swayed unhurriedly while I rode him, watching frost-colored eyes that slowly dropped to my breasts. Torrin cupped them painfully, and I groaned while the tension in my body built. It unfurled, and he sat up without warning, grabbing me behind the neck as his mouth crushed against mine.

Holding me in a half-sitting position, Torrin moved methodically, forcing me toward the precipice. Before my body could fully unravel, he shoved me down onto the bed. One hand rested beside my head to hold up his weight, while the other cupped my chin. Holding my mouth in place, he devoured me at the same leisurely pace at which his cock moved. It was erotic and sexy as he claimed my mewling sounds, working me to the edge of the cliff before he lifted, staring into my eyes with a burning desire.

"Come for me, woman," he ordered, slowly increasing his pace until I had no choice but to do as he demanded.

I exploded around him, clenching him tightly with my core. He continued moving slowly, holding me prisoner within my orgasm. Smirking at me, Torrin rested his forehead against mine as he tensed, growling his release, pumping into my body to a rhythm that sang to me.

He rolled from the bed, smiling like a cat who had finally tasted cream for the first time. I watched him as I sluggishly moved to the edge of the bed to stretch my limbs. I ached everywhere. It was a delicious feeling that left me satisfied, which was more than I'd ever felt before.

Moving to the large table, I stood behind Torrin. Slowly wrapping my fingers around the thick bottle of whiskey, I watched him from beneath my lashes. He turned, and I smiled, watching his eyes while he took in the bruises he'd marked upon my body.

"You're a dirty little thing, woman. You were incredible last night and worth the wait." I sucked my lip between my teeth as he leaned forward, intending to kiss me.

I brought the bottle up as hard as I could against his head, sending him to the floor unconscious. Smiling to myself, I stared down at his body. It was a canvas of art, exquisitely sculpted to lure a woman in and make her crave him. It really sucked that he was on the wrong side, considering my body had never responded to anyone else as it did with him.

Pulling his limp form to the bed, I hefted him up onto it. Grabbing the rope I'd asked him to tie me up with last night, during one of our many rounds of sex, I bound him to it, spread out in all his naked glory. The man was entirely too fucking hot for his own good.

He was all firm muscle and not a single ounce of fat on him. Forcing my eyes away from his body, I gagged him. Glancing between his legs at the large, soft cock that even limp, was impressive and proud, I made a sound of regret in my throat. My hand slid down his body, smiling at the legendary warrior now tied to each corner of his bed.

I looked back while taking in the incredible curves and sleek edges of his body, and my gaze rose to lock with icy eyes that promised retribution. Leaning over, I nipped his nipple while he shook with anger. He threatened me through the cloth over his mouth, and I considered using a knife on him to see if it made him as hot and bothered as it had made me.

"Come on. You had to know I'd escape you, Tor. I'm an assassin, not a pet you can keep on a chain. You had something I wanted, and now I know where it is. I would never help Aragon reach the library, not knowing he unleashed this darkness because he lost his child bride. My grandmother was fully mated to my grandfather, and the moon is never wrong when it chooses our mates."

Torrin glared at me, his eyes slitting to angry, narrowed pools of icy water. I slid my body over his cock, reaching behind my ass to cradle his balls, squeezing them gently, feeling him grow hard beneath me.

"Honestly, you are the best dick I've ever had in my entire life. I've never felt freer than I did with your hand around my throat and buried in my hair. Thank you for showing me what that was like." I leaned over, kissing his cheek before I climbed off of him and moved to the dress I'd worn last night, still discarded on the floor.

His muffled growl filled the room, causing me to smirk. Pulling the dress over my aching body, I secured it around my neck. Wintery eyes frosted my heated flesh, and I sucked my lip between my teeth, frowning at the look burning in his angry scowl.

"Maybe in another life, this could have lasted longer," I stated, hating that I wanted to ride him more. I wanted to feel his dominance and experience his version of pleasure endlessly. "Damn, you fucked me good. I already crave you, and I can't even blame it on the moon anymore. I just want you and what you offer me," I admitted, turning toward the door as a knock sounded.

I retrieved the bottle and moved toward it in bare feet. Slipping behind it, I waited for the guard to enter. The moment it opened, I smiled at the sound of the guard discovering Torrin in a delectably compromising position. He moved toward Torrin, intending to free him as I stepped up, slamming the bottle down over the back of his head. I eyed the bottle, turning toward the door as a sword sliced through the air, narrowly missing me.

I jumped back when it shot toward me again, missing me with each swing. The guard swung his sword again, missing me and embedding his blade into the table. He yanked on it, but I lunged, slamming the bottle down on his head. Exhaling, I shut the door and surveyed the mess.

It took several minutes to shred the bedding to secure each of the guards onto the bed above Torrin's body. I place the first guard on top of Torrin, facing him, resting the guard's face on Torrin's shoulder. I put the other guard on top of the first, spooning the first guard's backside. My eyes rolled up to meet Torrin's, and I grinned while he glared murderously at me. Once the newcomers were gagged and bound together, ensuring no escape, I dusted off my hands and flinched, taking in the sandwich of men piled onto one another.

Turning toward the door, I started forward, retrieving the trusty unbreakable bottle and the smaller warrior's blade. The door opened, and I barely escaped it from slamming into my face.

"Okay, you've been in here with her for far too long. You promised to share your newfound friend once you subdued her—well, *that's* kinky, even by my standards," Aragon announced, turning toward me. My foot closed the door, and a blade met his chin. "Did not see that coming."

"On your knees, Your Majesty," I grunted, flicking the blade subtly when he failed to do as I had instructed soon enough. "Don't make me into a King Slayer,

Aragon. I am simply trying to get out of this place as soon as possible without shedding blood. Be a dear and get the fuck on your knees for me."

"I have to admit; this is a first. Normally, women are on their knees for me."

I clucked my tongue at his statement, watching him sink to his knees. Silently, I held the blade in place while I walked around him, staring at the marking on his spine that his hair failed to conceal. My eyebrow lifted before sliding my gaze to Torrin, who had narrowed his gaze on Aragon. Lifting the bottle, I brought it down over his head, rendering him unconscious.

I placed the blade and bottle on the ground, grabbing the king's limp form to add him to the pile. Unfortunately, I couldn't lift his weighted body high enough to place him on the second guard. Instead, I settled him beside Torrin, whose muffled words promised payback and death. The king's mouth was pushed against Torrin's cheek, and his eyes widened as the unconscious king began pumping his hips, unaware he was doing so.

I chuckled, standing back to watch Aragon grinding his cock against Torrin's leg. My chest shook with laughter before my eyes rolled up to hold Torrin's threatening stare. His face turned red with rage, and I clicked my tongue against my teeth, fighting the peals of laughter that threatened to escape at the horror and murder burning in the warlord's angry stare.

"That's awkward. I won't tell anyone if you won't," I offered and turned to the door as the girls walked through it cautiously.

"Mmm, I almost want to know what is happening

there," Amo chuckled, her arms filled with robes. "Laundry delivery," she chirped in a cheery voice, dressed in a white cloak with her arms filled with midnight-colored ones.

"You know, I just had some of the craziest sex in my life," Tabitha sighed dreamily. "They may be scrawny, but damn, they are packing some serious trouser swords around this place."

"Weapons?" I asked, ignoring their curious looks while they took in Torrin's current predicament. Luckily, he was mostly covered up by the guards. A violent shudder of jealousy slithered through me out of nowhere, catching me off guard. "Eyes on me, ladies," I snapped, flinching at the sound of my voice, which caused heat to burn in Tor's stare. "We're on the clock. Weapons, cloaks, and map?" I watched as they placed everything on the table.

My gaze flicked to Torrin, who was watching me over the king's unconscious head. Stepping toward the bed, I lifted on my toes to draw closed the sheer curtains surrounding it. It wouldn't prevent him from seeing us, but it offered a thin barrier. Once done, I moved back to where one of the girls had dropped my bag.

"Dresses on, ladies. We're more than likely going to need them. We have about forty minutes before the guard changes at the door, and when they discover no one standing sentry, they'll investigate. We can't be here when that happens."

I removed my dress, doubling as a gliding suit from my bag, putting panties on before sliding my legs into black thigh-high stockings. I could feel their eyes on me. I didn't need to see their expressions to know they were taking in my body's bruised state. I clicked the weapon sheaths into place, holding Torrin's angry glare through the sheer curtains with a soft curl of my lips.

My top was comprised of leather straps that crisscrossed over my chest, compressing my breasts until they pushed up against the top. My neck was covered with leather, securing the halter top to my body. I turned so Amo could fasten the back, and I met Torrin's heated gaze as it slid over my outfit and thigh-high stockings that left barely a single inch of skin bare.

Once Amo had finished, I grabbed the weapons, slipping them into their respective places. I placed several daggers in their hidden pockets on my hips, thighs, and forearms, along with two blades in sheaths inside the boots that Tabitha tossed me.

"The map?" I asked.

"About that—we didn't find the map in any of the rooms we were in while we worked over the guards." Tabitha frowned, her eyes holding mine with an apology. "You were right, though; the ones in his other room were decoys, so we left them there."

"Where would they keep a map that held their strongholds and their prisons?" I asked, turning to study the room, with power rushing through my blood. "In the room, no one would dare to breach?" I smirked, slowly moving around while my eyes scanned the masculinity I hadn't had time to enjoy last night. Torrin's room was tidy, unlike the one beside mine where he'd watched the orgy.

I felt Torrin's eyes following me, knowing he'd forced his head to the other side. Moving around his room, I explored it carefully. On the furthest table were rolled-up scrolls, and my eyes slid over them, noting they had used one more than the others. Plucking it from the pile, I picked it up, unrolling it while the smile grew over my lips.

"Inside the bedroom of a legendary warrior. Where else, ladies?" I slid my eyes to the male in question, who watched me with an iciness that cooled my heated blood.

I went back to my girls, pushing the map into the satchel draped around my shoulder. Sliding my pack onto my back, I grabbed the cloak and head wrap, slipping it around my face until only my eyes were visible. It was shocking that most of the common people in the kingdom wore these. The people outside the palace wore black, while inside the palace, they wore white head wraps, specifically those who served the king.

"Ready?" I asked, taking in my team to ensure their cloaks and head wraps fully covered them. My attention slid to the male who had rocked my world and shown me what it was like to be seriously fucked sore. He held my gaze momentarily until I flicked my attention back to the women, nodding.

At their nods, we exited the bedroom without another glance. It took us several moments to reach the hallway where Torrin had taken me to see Chivalry. The guards at the door watched us approaching, smiling as they took in our eyes.

"There's no exit here, ladies," one stated, smiling softly. "You must use the main doors to leave."

My hand shot out at the same moment Amo's did, each of us catching a guard in a chokehold. We wrapped our bodies around them, pinching their throats with our arms to knock them out. The rest of my team blocked the view of anyone who might happen upon us. Once the guards were down, we pulled them inside the door and left them on the stairs, securely gagged and bound to the railing.

"Once we reach the horses, they'll need our help to change," I stated, watching as understanding enter their gazes while we moved down the winding staircase.

I entered the stable and paused dead in my tracks. Slowly with anger rising within me, I moved to where the stable hand was laughing, tossing a moonstone into the air before catching it. Fury sizzled through me as I stopped directly in front of him.

"What happened?" I demanded, staring at his yellowing teeth and a crooked smile.

"Those two wouldn't shut up, so I slit their worthless throats," he laughed cruelly. "Sliced them up real nice too. I thought they'd make some good eating, but then they went and exploded into worthless stones. Good riddance, I say."

My blades moved with my body, sliding from their positions on my forearms. I sliced through his stomach, spinning rapidly, striking him in his sides. I moved to face him, sending one blade through his chin and out the top of his head. I pushed the other through his eye, narrowly missing the other blade within his skull. I shoved him back, dragging his body toward the stones so that Torrin would figure out why I'd murdered the bastard. Kneeling, I piled the stones onto his chest, uncaring that I smeared them with the cruel male's blood.

"Boys, I need you to change and get dressed. We're leaving," I ordered, standing while turning as the women stepped closer to the horses, pushing power into their bodies as they trembled before becoming men. "Here, get dressed. They're expecting us to be on horseback, so we're not going to be." I smiled sadly at Chivalry, watching his form shimmering while his silver eyes held mine. "There's my man," I stated, watching him transform into a naked human male. He looked at the pile of moonstones that had once been his friend, nodding to me solemnly. He made an inhuman sound and reached for me, hugging me tightly. "Get dressed. We need to get out of here."

"Missed you," he grunted, his words barely understood over the noises he created deep in his throat.

"I missed you too." I swallowed, patting him on the back awkwardly.

Amo handed cloaks out, and the women helped the equinarians dress since the transformation always took them a while to adjust. Equinarians were a rare and unique breed of horse that could transform into men, for a short time, by using the magic of their moon-clan partner, paired up and bonded at birth. Once they were all dressed and their nudity concealed by the midnight-colored cloaks, we moved from the stables and into the crowd littering the streets.

It took us twenty minutes of trekking through the people of the town before we separated from them. On the dark, empty street, we hugged the wall while heading to where the guard had taken Amo on our first night here to have some privacy with her. It was a maze of hidden tunnels that had once been used to hide the people during the war against the Sun Clan, my people. It was ironic that we were now using it to escape the Kingdom of Night.

Once safely inside the tunnels, we rushed through them toward a smaller one that led out into the woods. It wasn't something that Torrin or his men would assume we'd know about, which would aid in our escape. They were expecting us to leave on horseback out of the kingdom and would lock down the gates to prevent that from happening.

A horn blew loudly, causing us to pause, slowing to a crawl while we listened. My heart leaped into my throat, and my palms began to sweat. Everyone held their breath while we waited to hear the orders and what was happening. Shouts echoed above and around us, coming through the holes of the tunnels. I nodded for everyone to move. We were being hunted by Torrin, a notorious tracker rumored to have never lost his prey. That was a record I intended to break.

"They're here! Find them and bring that little bitch back to me. No one hurts her but me," his voice sounded above us.

I closed my eyes before turning down another tunnel that stunk of mold, decay, and wet earth. We moved blindly in the dark while creatures scurried around us, screeching or hissing as the sound of claws over stones filled the tunnel. The tunnel opening, lit by moonlight, came into view, and I paused, turning to ensure everyone was still with me.

The moment we broke free of the underground shaft, the equinarians shed their cloaks and changed back into horses without a word. There was no usual banter or jokes about them being hung like a horse because we had just escaped the king and his warriors, which meant we were within the enemy's territory and heading deeper into it still.

I kneeled, unfurling the map to study it, noting the direction we would head before rolling it up and pushing it back into my bag. Adjusting the cloak, I tightened the face-covering while Chivalry nudged me with his nose.

Mounting the horse, I turned to take in the eyes of my team, smiling as the screech of an owl sounded above us. I watched a single arrow flying by Scout before he turned, narrowly missing the attack. Scout didn't fly directly toward Amo, choosing to lead those chasing us in the opposite direction.

"I don't think I need to say this, but just in case anyone hasn't figured it out, I will. Torrin and his nightwalkers are hunting us, and they won't try to take us alive. They want to get us by any means necessary. I drew blood for those they needlessly killed when we were promised they wouldn't harm our horses. We avenge those pointlessly slaughtered by cruelty, and they were. Therefore, I took the stable boy's life as payment for his trespasses against our team. Torrin will more than likely kill me as retribution, but I will not go down without a fight. We've lost many, and we're fighting alone now. We've lost the right to call ourselves of the Moon Clan for our unknowingly entertaining nightwalkers. That is on me, and if any of you wish to leave, I will not hold it against you. We have no home in which to return, but we can finish our mission. I intend to find Landon and the others who are missing, and then I plan to find the location of the library."

"I am with you," Amo said softly, her hand touching my shoulder.

Tabitha snorted, "I am with you as well. You know that without asking. I am your friend and your sister. Not because the Moon Clan asked me to be, but because you've never left me behind, not even wounded. You've risked your life countless times for ours, and you're my family. We're together until the end because that is what and who we are. We are warriors, but more than that, we're sisters. We have grown together, fought together, and bled together. I am with you, Alexandria Cira Helios. Until the end," she said with tears shining in her eyes. "Besides, I've never liked rules, anyway."

"Yeah, cantankerous, old bastards created them, and now we're free of that shit. Let's get this party started, shall we?" Amo grunted while the others agreed.

A horn blared in the distance, and we turned in its direction before riding the horses through the dark forest. We started toward the prison on the map, marked with the moon's symbol. We hoped to put enough distance between us and nightwalkers that would allow us to lose them or arrive at the prison in enough time to break out Landon before they arrived.

Torrin wouldn't go easy on me, that much I knew. He would be the death of me; that was a given. His king would demand it, and I had no intention of losing my head while a shit ton of nightwalkers watched it rolling from the gallows.

Chapter Twenty-Two

We didn't rest, but then we didn't dare stop because Torrin and his men were less than a few hours behind us. Amo's owl, Scout, had brought us evidence that they were on our trail and tracking us. We carried out our plan right down to the smallest detail, and it didn't change because of who was chasing us. I could feel Chivalry tiring. Having not been properly exercised, he fatigued easily.

The sound of horse hooves echoed behind us, and I slowed, staring back while the rest of my team continued. On a hill that looked down on where we were, rode a large force. I could make out Torrin in the lead, thundering down it toward us. I spun Chivalry in the direction of the open meadow, forcing him to continue even though he was exhausted.

"Fuck!" Amo shouted, sliding her horse to a stop in front of what I assumed was a shallow decline. Her wide, green eyes turned toward me, and her mouth opened and closed as she dismounted, staring down. *Fuck* indeed.

I dismounted mere feet from Amo, rushing toward the edge. I paused at the drop, peering down a sheer cliffside that was a few hundred feet deep, if not more. My heart leaped into my throat as my stomach bottomed out. My eyes swung back to the angry male, rapidly closing the distance between us.

"Change now! Everyone, get ready to jump," I ordered. Pulling out my blades, I moved to stand in a defensive pose while they did what I commanded. "Make sure your wings can deploy and that your chute is on."

"It's insane!" Tabitha argued, and I nodded.

"So is being captured when they're this angry. I don't want to lose my head on the gallows while a bunch of nightwalkers watches it roll, do you?" I countered, uncertain why it needed to be said in the first place.

Torrin's eyes held murder in their depths, and I wasn't sticking around to see if he intended to deliver on that threat. My body tensed, and I whispered a prayer heavenward to the moon, praying for a miracle here.

"Valid point," Tabitha agreed.

"Go!" I stated, feeling the equinarians change into their male forms.

"Bottoms up, bitches!" Amo shouted, jumping moments after her horse had in his human form. I refused to call him Pony Up Boy, as she'd named him.

The others trickled over the edge, but they weren't moving fast enough. Torrin dismounted, shouting for his men to fan out into formation. His men drew their swords while his eyes promised to kill me slowly, giving no mercy. I stepped back, lowering my body as my arms spread out wide, my swords pointed forward, facing them all down. They stalked forward, a cold-intent filling their every move.

I backpedaled, holding them back so they couldn't rush forward without one getting harmed by my blades. I'd at least take out one or two before they reached me. I hoped. Torrin hesitated, his eyes slipping over my shoulder to where the girls were plummeting over the edge with their equinarians, leaping into the air.

"Now I understand how you slipped past us and out of the kingdom undetected. Had I known your horses were equinarians, they would have been treated differently." His smile was deadly, and all teeth as he advanced closer. "You're not getting away from me so easily, *assassin*," Torrin spat out, his anger palpable while crackling in the air between us.

"Oh, but I am." I swallowed, uncertain if I spoke the truth.

My team and their partners were still jumping, needing time between each free fall. They had to force their arms open, engaging the wingspan within the suit. They also had to dive to catch their shifter and secure him with their legs before deploying their chutes.

Torrin shouted an order, and their swords aimed at those still on the cliff's edge, waiting to jump. I stepped forward, glaring at Torrin, who smiled wickedly. His wintery eyes slid to Chivalry, and he narrowed them to slits while taking in the naked male who waited silently behind me.

"Get on your knees, and I will give you mercy,

Alexandria," he growled.

"I'm not into mercy. I like it hard and punishingly twisted, Tor. I thought you figured that out one of the dozens of times you took me last night," I returned, hearing Tabitha's strangled laugh as she hooted, jumping over the edge. "I'm offended that you've forgotten me already."

"On your fucking knees, now," he snarled, and I stepped back, hearing the earth giving away against my heel as rocks slid down the cliff.

"Chivy go, Mistress," Chivalry muttered in a half-human, half-baying tone.

I stood straight, counting in my head as Torrin rushed forward. I leaped blindly backward, his fingers brushing against my leather bodice, catching air. The sensation of free-falling took control, and I smiled, staring up as his head came over the edge of the cliff. My middle finger lifted while the smile grew on my lips.

His snarled growl of rage sent a shiver of need rushing through me. It was the same one he'd made while driving into me as hard as he possibly could. I spun in the air, staring down at the falling bodies as wings slowly unfurled, and they started their descent to catch their shifter.

I slammed into Chivalry, catching him with my legs. Lifting my arms behind me, I used my upper body strength to hold them open to slow our descent. My eyes slid to Kaitlyn, who dropped her shifter as her arms gave out, and a piercing shriek cut through the night. The blood drained from my face while I watched her flapping her arms aimlessly as panic took control.

"Amo!" I shouted, watching her eyes lift to mine. "Catch!" I screamed, and Chivalry dropped, knowing exactly what to do as he flew toward Amo.

The moment I was free of his added weight, I dove toward Kaitlyn. My body slammed into her hard, and I gasped at the pain that rushed through me. Her hands turned, climbing me.

"Stop, or you'll kill us both! Breathe, Kaitlyn," I demanded with my voice in control, holding none of the panic I felt while she stared up at me. "Wrap your arms around my waist, and I'm going to wrap my legs around you. Now," I ordered, staring at the distance between us and the ground that was fast approaching. No sooner had she secured her arms, and I secured my legs, I pulled my shoot, and we jerked back, heading toward the ground hard. "We're coming in fast and hard, so brace yourself," I warned.

A moment before we hit the ground, I reached up and cut the shoot. We slammed down hard with Kaitlyn's added weight. Our bodies bounced, and I cried out, smacking my head into the ground. A blinding light filled my eyes, and I looked down, staring at the pile of stones beneath me. Tears pricked my eyes, but I'd mourn her later when it was safe to do so. My eyes rose to the others, watching them come down in uniform positions.

Standing to take stock of the damage, I turned, staring at the other side of the water where my team had landed. Exhaling in relief, I rested my hands on my knees until I noticed dark silhouettes appearing beneath the water's surface. The others were pulling their chutes in, unaware of what was coming.

"Incoming!" I shouted, watching as they spun

toward me, dropping their gazes. "Cut the shoots and move!" I demanded, watching in horror as banshees and water creatures exited the river together, striding toward the women still trapped in their chutes.

My heart got stuck in my throat, and I knew that there were too many to fight. I was going to lose everyone if I didn't act quickly. My body sang with power, and I stripped out of the outfit, baring skin before I let it loose. My light exploded as if my life had expired, and I didn't stop pushing it toward my team. I blinded both moon-touched and creature alike in pure, unfiltered sunlight.

The sky shifted, and the sun took precedence over the dark sky, albeit weakly. The monsters turned, staring at the light coming from me before they changed course. Amo and Tabitha screamed, both moving into the water blindly behind the creatures to reach me before the monsters could. I slid my daggers from my sleeves into my palms as I awaited their arrival. Exhaling a shaky breath, I watched unwaveringly as the creatures moved toward me.

My eyes rolled up the cliffside, noting Torrin watched while his men stared up at the sun that had filled the sky with daylight. The first creature reached me, and I swung wide, flipping my body to render a killing blow as my sword swung down onto it. More slid from the water, and I backed up, calculating my moves before a banshee let a scream rip from her mouth. I rushed her, jumping at the last moment to seat myself on her back as my blades stuck in her shoulders. Using them and my weight, I flipped over her shoulders, sending her body sailing with the power of mine.

One creature touched my back, and I flew backward,

sending my leg in the air, catching its legs, and I came up as it went down. I whipped my blade out, removing the head from its body before I swung at the next one.

One after another, I slaughtered the creatures as sweat beaded on my brow and neck, slicing and fighting while the girls worked their way through the now empty water. A banshee wailed, and I turned, shoving a blade into her mouth to stop her scream from splitting my head in half. Another echoed her, and I slammed my blade into her throat, twisting it.

I turned toward the sound of feet scurrying over rocks and gasped as a monster ran forward, piercing my chest with its steel-like claws. I lowered my eyes to my breast, then looked up, sending my blade into the creature's eyes. Twisting the blade, I turned, dispatching the beast over my shoulder in a defensive move.

The sounds of blades meeting flesh filled the day as it slowly turned back to night. I withdrew my blade, dropping it from my shaking hand. Pulling my shirt open, I stared at the seeping wound with black lines already spreading as the creature's poison filled my bloodstream.

The sound of splashing filled the night, and I turned, seeing more creatures pushing through the surface of the water. Retracting my blades, I moved toward them, coughing violently. I spit out blood, staring down at the ground barely long enough to notice the crimson painting the earth as the sun began to set, and the world returned to darkness.

"Formation!" I shouted, coughing while I took a stance, facing the wilted and water-logged creatures.

I drew my blades wide and waited until the line

was formed. The moment we stood together as a unit, a creature sprinted forward, and I scissored my blades across its neck, removing its head. Lifting my blades again, I spun, slicing through another, peeling it like an apple. One after another, they fell, my strength waning as the poison rushed through me, driven by the adrenaline pulsing in my veins.

My knees gave out as a monster ran toward me, but a blade slammed down onto it, and Amo moved in front of me. Her eyes widened in horror. Tabitha stepped beside her, and I dropped backward, landing on the ground, coughing up blood and poison that exploded from my lungs.

When they were done fighting, my team surrounded me. Amo searched my body and discovered the festering wound with panic-stricken eyes. I didn't need to tell her what was happening because the pain was there, burning her vision.

"Get me on Chivalry. I am not dying on the ground," I murmured.

"You can't die. You can't leave us, Lexia. We need you," Amo sobbed, standing to move away from me.

"Amo, get me on my horse and move out," I demanded, and she turned.

"We're not leaving you!"

"Well, you can't take me with you unless I'm on my fucking horse."

She laughed soundlessly, peering up at the cliff. "Torrin has the tonic."

"And we don't," I whispered, turning to cough

violently.

"You can't die. You promised me you wouldn't die! Everyone leaves me. You can't do that too! Do you hear me? You're the leader. We follow you!"

"I'm not the leader anymore. You are. I trained you well, Amo. You're ready even if you don't think you are."

Amo shook her head, anger and denial filling her eyes. She snarled, screaming in frustration as she and Tabitha moved to pick me up. Once on my feet, I exhaled, coughing and sputtering as black blood leaked from my lips. They tied me to Chivalry, and he neighed, whining as he brought his head back to nudge me. Consciousness slipped from me the moment he moved forward, with Amo leading his reins.

Chapter Twenty-Three

I awoke to someone slapping my cheek. My eyes focused, and I saw Amo hovered over me, her wide green eyes filling with relief. Apparently, I wasn't dead yet. She gripped my chin, prying my stiff jaw open, forcing water down my throat. I coughed violently, watching her.

"Why the hell did you stop?" I demanded, but it was barely even a whisper.

"Because you're my fucking family," she hissed, her eyes holding mine. "We also have no idea where we're going."

I nodded, reaching for the map. Amo's hand touched mine, and she shook her head slowly. I studied her eyes as she lifted a small vial between her fingers.

"A large bird delivered this a couple of minutes ago. There was a note with it," she explained, producing it with a look of unease.

I blinked, dropping my eyes to the note she held

in one hand and the bottle that sat between her fingers. Sitting up, I held my hand out for the message. Unrolling it, I laughed at what Torrin decreed.

"He says I don't get to die unless it is by his hand. Arrogant prick. Do you think that means he likes me?" I asked seriously.

Amo stared at me, holding in her laughter until it burst from her, half-sobs, half-laughter. Her green eyes held mine, and her hand with the tonic moved forward.

"It could be poison," she warned.

"Hmm, maybe. It would be a really shitty thing to give someone dying of poison more poison, wouldn't it?" I asked, using my teeth to remove the stopper. I downed it while she watched, sitting back on her haunches with worry in her gaze.

"I think he likes you, but then he's a male. Maybe his endless hunting for us is his form of flirting?" she asked, and I sat back, smiling as the tonic entered my system. "Maybe even foreplay?" I laughed, coughing until I almost threw up the antidote.

"Chivalry?" I asked, and he neighed, nudging my head.

"He won't let us feed or water his stubborn ass. He hasn't left your side since we stopped." Amo's eyes slid to the horse that neighed in complaint.

"Go eat and drink, Chivy. We need to move soon," I ordered, moving my head before his tail slapped where it had been lying. "How far behind are Torrin and his men?" I asked, and Amo looked away. "Amo, how far?"

"Maybe an hour, maybe less now," she admitted,

handing me dried meat and water. "Eat, and then we will move. You need your strength. You should also check the map; see how far we are from the place they're holding Landon."

"The place we *hope* they're holding him? There are over sixteen prisons with the symbol of the moon. We're merely nearing the first one." Granted, it sucked, but the possibility of Landon being at the first one was slim.

I chewed the tasteless meat, gnawing at it while the others moved in around me. My stomach roiled, and I gagged, leaning over to vomit. Amo handed me a water skin, and I washed my mouth out as Tabitha kneeled, offering me a mint that I accepted to ease the nausea.

"Send Scout out to see if he can find Torrin and his men, Amo. I need a moment," I admitted, knowing that I had to give my body time to accept the tonic, which was working to nullify the poison. "Five minutes for it to kick in, and another if I have to throw up more poison," I explained, watching as Tabitha held up fingers to the others, who were tending the horses.

Torrin had saved me, but I was certain there was a more sinister reason for him doing so. One, he needed someone to help him find the library because if the rumors and lore were right, you needed darkness and light to open the doors.

Only light could read from the Book of Life, while darkness read from the Book of Death. He needed me alive, and after having exposed my powers to save my team, he knew I was more than just one of the women from the Sun Clan. I was the heir to the fallen kingdom, one led by a long line of women.

Furrowing my brow, I blinked past the splotches that lined my sight. Heat surged through me, making me sway as I sat up. My body felt strange, fueled with adrenaline, which meant it hadn't just been a tonic. There'd been some serious healing herbs and something else mixed with it. I unrolled the map, placing it on the ground before peering up at the multitude of stars and then back down at the map.

"We're less than two hours from the first prison," I admitted.

"It's going to be protected," Tabitha stated.

"It's going to have guards, but they will be cocky since they're within their territory. They don't think anyone is stupid or suicidal enough to try to take it from them." I nodded at Amo's words.

"We'll go in silently and stealthily. Remember when we were told to figure out how to take control of the temple without being seen?" I asked and watched the huddled heads nodding as smiles tipped their mouths. "We do that, and then we go in through the front door. By the time we gain entrance, the army chasing us will have caught up. If that happens, you're going to run. I can get myself out of Torrin's grasp a lot easier than it will be to get everyone out again."

"Alexandria, not a fucking chance," Tabitha argued. "We will die without you. Amo got us lost, moving in a straight line."

"There were trees!" she argued as I laughed.

"You never were great with navigation. Remember the time you ended us up in the town filled with—"

"Wraiths!" someone shouted, and my blood turned to ice.

I peered at the girls, turning my head to watch the few wraiths trudging slowly through the path they'd diverted onto to give me the tonic. Gasping, I waited for the bone-chilling ice to come, yet it didn't. I stared at the others, noting none of the other girls had responded to the chill or the freezing fear the wraiths usually sent through us.

I stood, slowly moving toward them with shaking hands. I stepped directly into their path and waited for them to attack as my blades slid free and I palmed them. The wraiths shouldered past me, moaning, and didn't even acknowledge me or our presence. My eyes widened, and I turned, staring at Amo and Tabitha, who stared back like I'd grown another head.

Turning, I watched the wraiths continue down the path while worry and apprehension slithered through me. What the hell had just happened? Walking back to the girls, I fought down the uneasiness rocking through me.

"Maybe the bites made us immune?" I asked, and they shook their heads. "Let's go before they change their mind and decide we're dinner."

After an hour of moving through the thick terrain, we left the horses in the woods. Placing the heavy cloaks over our heads and with our face-coverings in place, we observed the target site before heading out. I examined the prison layout, marking the entrances and few guards I could see before sliding through the wide-open entry gate. Two guards stood, sleepily guarding it.

"For Glory of the Moon Goddess," I whispered.

"No," Amo groaned. "For those of us left behind to light the way. For us, and whatever is to come. For family, and because it isn't our end," she smirked. "I'm too young to die without it ending on some really good dick, anyway."

"For those that we lost on our way here. For the sisters who sleep within the embrace of the moon and continue to protect us from afar," Tabitha injected.

"Because being captured isn't an option and being the pet to an obtuse man isn't in my future." I chuckled soundlessly. "Okay, so we suck at the whole charge shit, but we're better together. I'm glad it wasn't my end because Amo would have gotten you assholes so fucking lost without me."

"Amen," Tabitha whispered.

"There were trees! It wasn't a straightforward map, either. It's literally based on the stars, and stars burn out!" Amo growled, giving each of us a pointed look.

"Yeah, they actually do," I stated, smiling at her as she sniffled.

"I'm glad you didn't die, bitch."

"Me too. Let's go find Landon. I need a nap and something stronger than water to drink," I stated, as Amo sent Scout into the air, and we started through the thick foliage.

Chapter Twenty-Four

My heart thundered, beating painfully against my ribs while approaching the front gate. Blood rushed through my veins, filling them with the high octane that had been within the tonic. I could feel my body responding to it and wasn't so sure it wasn't an aphrodisiac or something close to one. At our approach, the guards turned, checking out the delicate forms on display.

"About time they sent us some entertainment," one guard muttered to the other.

"Hopefully, they're not as hideous as the last batch," his companion complained.

Amo unwrapped her headdress, smiling at the look of lust that entered their gazes while they took in her delicate, ethereal perfection. She was lust in the rawest form, perfectly curved while being fierce and all toned muscles. Her robe dropped to the ground, and she swayed her hips while moving toward them.

Her baton came up as they lurched forward in a rush to claim her. One pulled back at the last moment, but not before she spun, clapping both over the head with her short club.

After they went down, we retrieved the guards, placing them against the immense columns that would conceal their drooping bodies. Tabitha bound their hands while I ripped part of my robe to gag them. Once Amo was redressed, and we secured the men, we entered the gates, quietly closing them behind us.

"You know where to go to take down your assigned guard. No bloodshed. Keep it clean unless you have no other choice but to defend yourself. We've already drawn blood; let's not add to it," I ordered as we separated to take down the guards in our way.

"Listen," Amo whispered, stopping me. "You're still wounded, Lexia. If you find Landon and he's—changed, you must be careful."

I exhaled slowly, jerking my head in reply since words failed me at the idea of finding Landon turned or mindless with the need to kill. I had known he was sick because he'd been rambling things off that made little sense. I'd argued his coming out to find the library's location with the clan members, but it had fallen on deaf ears.

The Sacred Library could hide from anyone it thought or found unworthy. My brother had spouted on and on about what I thought was nonsense, which no longer sounded so crazy. He'd spoken of the nightwalkers as coherent beings, and now I knew they were. He'd told me the legends pertaining to our family, which I'd laughed in his face about, but I wasn't confident he'd been off about those either.

It was of paramount importance now that I find Landon and ask him what he knew of our bloodline. What if the legends were true, and the reason why I hadn't been born male was because the true mate of the King of Night was within me? Aragon was a man-whore. He wasn't a warrior worth mating. According to the legends, only a true mating of dark and light could remove the plague of darkness.

My hand moved to my belly as I slowly pushed further into the darkness of the massive prison. All around me, silence prevailed, and my skin pebbled with the feeling of being watched as a foreboding sensation slithered over me, sending my hackles up in warning.

Easing open the first door, I found the guard missing. Moving in deeper yet, I slipped into the shadows, palming my blades while strolling into what looked like bare walls covered in smears of something written on them. Unfortunately, the lettering changed to appear like smear marks.

It looked almost as if someone had dragged bloody fingers over the wall, trailing them further into the darkness. Entering the next room, I shivered. The little light from the torches wafted with the breeze, and my eyes slowly took in the layers of cells that stretched up the walls.

The entire place was a network of cells, accessed by little weight-driven elevators attached to a pulley system. Gazing up, I frowned at just how many cells were within the place. It would take hours to explore them all. We didn't have that much time since there was an armed warlord on my heels, nipping at them.

Struggling past the nervousness that filled me within the looming silence, I peeked into the first cell, finding it empty. It was the same story for the next and the next. I moved across the aisle and came face to face with moon-touched warriors, caged.

"Landon Helios? Is he with you?" I asked in a hushed tone.

A man hissed, tilting his head before he lunged at the bars. I jerked back, steeling myself against the darkness that burned in his silver eyes, spreading over his face. Moon sickness, which meant the king, was collecting them, but why? The man's face smashed against the bars again, forcing me further back as his arms reached for me.

I pushed down the worry that all the cells were filled with people suffering from moon sickness and soon to be a pile of rocks. Closing my eyes, I exhaled slowly, listening to the mindless beings moaning inside the cells.

Turning to stare down the length of the cell-lined corridor, I slid to the side, checking each one until a dark form huddled in the corner of one caught my eye. My heart sank as he turned into the torch's soothing light, cocking his head to the side before he stood.

"Landon," I whispered as tears burned my eyes.

He moved forward, exposing his silver hair before his hands wrapped around the bars, and he breathed out a worried exhale. I moved closer, touching his hands before my lips lowered, peppering his hands with kisses.

"You're alive," I gasped softly. "I knew you would be."

"You shouldn't be here, Alexa." His voice was weak and dry, as if dehydrated. "They pulled the guards an hour ago," he stated, forcing the blood to leave my face.

If they'd pulled the guards, then Torrin was already here. He'd known where we were heading and must have known a shortcut. That explained the lack of guards and how easy it had been to gain access to the cells.

"It's okay. I'm here to get you out of here," I argued, putting my arms through the bars to pull Landon closer. Neither one of us was leaving; that much was a given.

"You can't, Alexa. I am sick. We're all sick," he grunted, pushing me away. "Leave."

"I'm not leaving you, Landon! It's okay if you're sick. We will get you better together. We can find the library and figure out how to cure this sickness. Some nightwalkers can speak, and those that could didn't try to murder us. You weren't crazy, and I can't apologize enough for telling you that you were."

"Go, now," Landon snapped harshly.

"I'm *not* leaving without you!" I snarled back, watching the lines of blackness running through his face. "We're family, Landon. You're the only blood relation I have left. You know that everyone else is dead. It's just you and me now. We stick together, remember? You promised me, and we promised our parents."

"Until the king catches you too," he snapped as the blackness began spreading through the veins on his cheek. "You're not supposed to be here! You're the promised one," he groaned, placing his back against the bars to look away from me, dropping his head back. "You're the only female born in the last two hundred and fifty years. Don't you see? You were born to fulfill a prophecy. You're the key to raising the sun, and you can't do that if he catches you, Alexa."

"I don't care about the prophecy. I care about *you*! I care about getting you out of here. I can't leave you!"

"But you will, sister. You will leave now and find the library to save the other Moon Clan people from meeting my fate. The Order of the Moon depends on you being successful in discovering the location of the library. You're pure and untainted by darkness. It will let you in to read from the Book of Life. It's your destiny to read from the pages and right the wrongs of our ancestors. You're the light in the darkness, don't you see it? Why do you think your light is so much brighter than the others? Why do you think grandmother had to die for you to be born?" he asked, turning to look at me with obsidian eyes. "Because her soul was reincarnated through you, as is her light. You house the light of the Royal House of Sun, Alexandria Cira Helios. You're the king's promised mate in a new body, reborn to be the light to his darkness. If he catches you, and you create life, the moon loses its hold over the lands. He will kill you to protect the darkness. He's the most powerful creature in the world because the darkness feeds its power to him."

"That's insane, Landon. I've met the King of Night. He's a lazy, pompous weakling who probably hasn't ever held a steel blade in his hands! He spends his days and nights with women, choosing pleasure over anything else! He couldn't be my mate. The fates of legend wouldn't be so cruel."

"The king isn't weak. If he was weak, he couldn't house the darkness and control the creatures who feed upon us. You have not met him if you think him weak, sister. He often comes to see us, checking on our progress through the change. I've felt his power when he heals us from the sickness as it becomes too much. You're wasting time, Alexa. You need to go before he comes," Landon begged.

The others in the cells around us screamed, howling until it became deafening. My heart dropped as the cold steel of a sword touched against my chin.

"The king has come," Landon whispered, staring behind me with a look of worry mixing with wonder in his darkening depths.

"That's not the king," I groaned, smelling Torrin's scent heavily in the surrounding air.

"Oh, but I am, my sweet mate. I am the King of Night, and you are now mine."

My heart stopped beating as Torrin lifted the blade, baring my throat as he moved out of the dark shadows that swayed around him. I hadn't even heard him over the sound of the people within the cells going crazy. I was grabbed and held against the bars by Landon as Torrin stepped closer, lowering his blade as he searched my face.

"I should have known from the first taste of you that you were created for me," Torrin growled, lifting his hand to trail his knuckles against my cheek. "Hold her there for me, Landon."

"I told you to run," Landon whispered with regret filling his tone, his fingers biting into my arms.

"You're not the king," I whispered through trembling

lips as the sound of swords crashing together echoed through the prison.

"You, of all people, should have figured that one out. I am a warrior and don't belong hidden behind walls. Aragon is the face of the kingdom, but I am the king. You, Little Bird, were created for me and only me."

"You're the darkness," I seethed.

"No, my mother is the darkness. I am the night, and you're the light. The child growing within your womb is of both."

"I am not pregnant," I argued, watching his lips curving into a wicked smile.

"Listen," he whispered, placing his lips against my cheek. His breath heated my face as he slowly ran them over it, sucking my lip between his teeth before he released it, kissing my forehead.

A tiny heartbeat sounded, and I frowned, shaking my head. "I don't understand," I whispered thickly. "How is that even possible? It was last night, Torrin. This isn't possible so soon." He nodded, his eyes sparkling with amusement.

"I found Landon spouting nonsense about the Sun Clan bloodline behind my kingdom walls, but I didn't believe him. Of course, I had to see you and your team to know for sure, so meeting you in that village was by design. You see, my mother is responsible for losing my first mate. When she killed my father, she was cursed to become the darkness, commanding all the creatures that live within. Seeing this, the ruler of the Sun Court sent his daughter, my intended mate, away, fearing that I was as evil as my dear mother." Torrin smiled, and it was all teeth as he narrowed his gaze. "I was told she had perished. I never dreamed that she lived and had a family of her own. Not until you told the story last night, and the pieces fell into place."

Landon's hands tightened around me, and he whispered in my ear, "I'm so sorry, Alexa."

"I made a bargain with a seer two hundred and fifty years ago to bring my mate back. I had given up the hunt, convinced my mother had taken my mate from me once again. When I found you, I had hoped that I was getting a female of the sun bloodline who could read from the Book of Life. I never imagined that you were my mate, placed into the pretty, little spitfire package that fought me. Not until I saw your markings last night, and then I knew you were mine and that I would never let you go." Torrin lifted his hand, cradling my cheek. "Now you house our child, also by design. I needed to bring life into this world to help break the curse I unknowingly placed on the land, craving the mate I lost. I can't say I'm upset about it being you. Not after last night, Alexandria. The world, as you knew it, is gone forever. Now your new life begins with me."

"What the hell does that mean?" I asked, and Torrin's eyes turn to obsidian as he brushed his lips against mine.

"You'll see soon enough, won't you?"

The End, For Now

About the Author

Amelia Hutchins is the number one national bestselling author of the Monsters series, The Fae Chronicles, and the Legacy of the Nine Realms series. She is an admitted coffee addict who drinks magical potions of caffeine, turning them into spellbound, fantastical worlds. Amelia writes alpha-hole males and the alpha women who knock them on their arses, hard. She doesn't write romance. She writes fast-paced books that go hard against traditional standards. Sometimes a story isn't about the romance; it's about rising to a challenge, breaking through them like wrecking balls, and shaking up entire worlds to discover who they really are. If you'd like to check out more of her work or just hang out in an amazing tribe of people who enjoy rough men and sharp women, join her Author Amelia Hutchins Group on Facebook.

Stalker Links

Facebook group: https://www.facebook.com/groups/1240287822683404/

Facebook Author Page: https://www.facebook.com/authorameliahutchins/

Instagram: https://www.instagram.com/author.amelia.hutchins/